Meet Me at Oakham Mount

Melanie Schertz

Edited by Pat Weston

ISBN:1493685597
ISBN-13:9781493685592

DEDICATION

This story is dedicated to my grandmother, Ethel B Whitaker Moreland Young. She taught me how to find something positive in even the worst of times. She also taught me to never allow anyone to take away my dreams, especially when what I wanted was not considered to be "women's work".

CONTENTS

ACKNOWLEDGMENTS

I am grateful for the great works of Jane Austen, who gave us characters who continue to touch our hearts after 200 years. Here is to another 200 years of people loving Jane Austen's stories.

In the story, there is a fictional surgeon. The school he studied at was real, as was Dr Benjamin Bell. Benjamin Bell was believed to be the first scientific surgeon in Scotland, and was described as the father of the Edinburgh School of Surgery. His son Joseph, grandson Benjamin, and great grandson Joseph were also surgeons at the Royal College of Surgeons of Edinburgh. The great grandson, Joseph Bell, was known to Sir Arthur Conan Doyle, and it is believed Doyle's fictional character, Sherlock Holmes, was based on the younger Joseph Bell. Thanks to Wikipedia and other webpages for this information.

CHAPTER 1

Fitzwilliam Darcy was near ten when his father, Gerard Darcy, died in a carriage accident. His mother, Lady Anne Darcy, was deeply distraught for two years, and then she decided that she needed a husband to help her. As a young girl, Lady Anne had grown up at her father's estate of Matlock. Nearby was the estate of Carrington Manor, home of the Earl of Covington. The Earl's third son was Albert Carrington, a kind and caring young boy, who fell instantly in love with Lady Anne, the daughter of the Earl of Matlock. Young Master Albert always wished to marry Lady Anne, and he was determined to do well in his studies, so he could find a proper vocation to be able to support a wife and family.

Unfortunately, Lady Anne's father had other plans for his daughter. Lord Matlock was suffering from financial setbacks due to failed crops. So, when he was approached by the extremely wealthy Gerard

Darcy seeking Lady Anne's hand, Lord Matlock quickly accepted the suitor.

Albert Carrington went on to become a solicitor, and then a barrister. He was well respected and liked, and rose quickly in his field. About the time Lady Anne gave birth to her son, Carrington married the daughter of his mentor and partner. Two years after they married, his wife, Julia, died in childbirth. Carrington was deeply despaired of ever having happiness in his life.

When he learned of Lady Anne becoming a widow, Carrington's heart was torn with emotions. He still loved Lady Anne dearly, and knew that one day, he would ask her for her hand. He also knew that Lady Anne cared for her late husband, and they had adored their son. Young Fitzwilliam was the spitting image of his father, and he had the same love for their family's estate of Pemberley, as had his father.

The year after Gerard's death, Carrington's family suffered a tragic loss. A fire had broken out in the barns at Carrington Manor, bringing all of the men to fight the blaze. Unknown to them, there had been several barrels of wine stored in one of the barns. When the heat of the flames struck the flammable liquid, it caused a fireball to soar through the area, killing a dozen of the men who were battling to save the estate. Amongst those killed were Carrington's father and brothers. When news arrived in London, announcing the tragedy and the new heir to the title of Lord Covington, Carrington was devastated. He had never thought he would carry the title, nor had he been taught how to care for an estate. Everything he knew had been turned upside down.

After his year of mourning for his family, Carrington finally approached his beloved Lady Anne, asking for her hand in marriage. She accepted immediately, not only due to her love of Carrington, but as she wished for a father figure for her son. Not long after their marriage, Fitzwilliam was sent off to school. He was not comfortable in groups of people he did not know well, as he was extremely shy. School was difficult for him, as he found it a nearly impossible task to interact with the young lads there. Only due to his cousin's efforts did Fitzwilliam manage to survive his school years. Richard Fitzwilliam, second son of Lady Anne's brother, the current Earl of Matlock, was extremely protective of his younger cousin, treating him as a brother more than a cousin.

When Fitzwilliam turned five and ten, his mother announced he would be a brother soon. Two months later, a daughter was born to Lady Anne and Lord Albert. They named her Georgiana, and she quickly became the center of their lives. This pushed

Fitzwilliam further away from the family, as he had already found being the stepson of Lord Covington difficult. He had no desire to forget his own father, and the heritage that he was given as a Darcy. By accepting Lord Covington as a stepfather, Fitzwilliam felt he was dishonoring his father.

This caused a rift between Lady Anne's son and her new family. When he was on holiday from school, Fitzwilliam preferred to stay at Pemberley or Matlock rather than Carrington Manor. And Lord Covington knew of his stepson's dislike of his living at Pemberley. Fitzwilliam felt it was a betrayal to allow his mother's husband to live in the house where his father had devoted his life for his family.

Though Georgiana was the daughter of Lord Covington, she was also a member of Fitzwilliam Darcy's family. They shared the blood of their mother, and she also shared her big brother's shy nature. She adored her brother, wishing to be with him whenever possible.

After graduating from Cambridge, Darcy decided it was time to take complete control of his inheritance. His uncle, the Earl of Matlock, had been assisting the steward of Pemberley until Darcy was of age.

Darcy spent three years at the estate, working diligently and making improvements in the crop rotations and repairing the tenant homes. He also invested some of his money in business ventures, with a great deal of assistance from his university friend, Charles Bingley, who had a mind for business. Bingley's father had been in trade, though he had built an empire for his family. His greatest wish was for Charles to become a member of the landed gentry. This was another area which brought the friends closer, as Bingley was able to lean on his friend for advice in finding an estate to purchase.

As Darcy worked his estate, he would spend time with his mother and sister when they would come to visit Pemberley. It was difficult for Georgiana to understand why her brother did not live at Carrington Manor, and why he referred to her father as Lord Covington. The young girl wished her brother would live with them and that they were a family, as her cousins were at Matlock. But that was not to be.

~~ ** ~~

Sitting at his desk in his study, Darcy was sorting out the daily post. When he came to a letter with familiar splotches and poor penmanship, Darcy smiled. It was easy to find Bingley's letters, as the man did not take care when he wrote. If he had not known better, Darcy would have sworn that the letter was written by a child.

He began to read the letter, chuckling at his friend's description of events that had been happening. Near the end of the letter, Bingley spoke of finding an estate in Hertfordshire, near the village of Meryton. He found it to his liking, and it was close enough to Town for his sisters to enjoy the delights of society.

Bingley wished to have his friend's advice on the estate. He had taken a lease of the property and wanted to know whether Darcy could inspect the estate. Bingley was to take possession of the estate near the first of September.

Picking up his pen, Darcy dipped it into the inkwell and began to write.

Bingley,

It is wonderful that you have found a lease. From what you have said in your letter, it sounds like a decent enough estate.

September is when we have our harvest, and the annual Harvest festivities. I will not be able to leave Pemberley before the end of September.

At that time, I would be pleased to join you at this estate, this Netherfield Park. I will have until Christmas to enjoy myself, so I can take some time to go over the estate and the books with you at our leisure.

I will send word when I can set a date for my arrival. And pray, speak to your sister with regards to leaving me at peace.

Your friend, Darcy

He finished the letter and prepared it to be mailed off with the other posts. Just as he laid his pen down, there was a knock on his study door.

"Enter" he called out.

"Good day, Son." Lady Anne said as she entered the room. "And how are you today?"

"I am well, Mother. And from your appearance, I would lay odds that you are quite well also."

"I take that as a compliment, William. Yes, I am

very well. Albert and Georgiana are also well. Georgiana has missed you, and told me to say that you promised riding lessons on a horse you deemed perfect. It is my understanding that you were being quite picky about which horse would be the best for your sister."

"I was thinking that Aphrodite would be perfect for Georgie, as the horse is gentle, with spirit. She has been impressive for a two year old."

"And I have noticed a sweet nature about her as well. I believe Aphrodite is one of finest horses you have raised."

"Other than discussing horses, what else has brought you here this morning, Mother? You have that determined look in your eyes."

"Fitzwilliam Gerard Darcy, you are not supposed to know all my secrets." Lady Anne smiled. "But you are correct. My brother and I have spoken and it appears that the Viscount has been at it again."

"And how much has Anthony lost this time? Why is it Uncle never sets his foot down with his heir?"

"After Lady Matlock died, my brother has been more indulgent with his children. Fortunately, Richard is the wiser of the two. Anthony learned how to use his mother's death to his advantage when it came to his father."

"So how much has this latest bit set Matlock back?" Darcy asked.

"Twenty thousand pounds."

Darcy was furious. "So, my uncle feels that I will just bail them out again, for the fourth time in three years? I have already loaned them eight and twenty thousand."

"I understand, William, but your uncle knows nowhere else to turn. If you do not aid him, he will be forced to sell part of Matlock." Lady Anne said as she walked over to the nearby window, looking over the land of her son's estate. "He has even approached Albert of an arrangement for Anthony to wed Georgiana."

"That is ridiculous. Anthony is nearly twenty years older than Georgiana. And Georgie is but a child, not even two and ten. Please tell me that Albert told them to scamper off."

"Of course Albert refused them, for he cares deeply for his daughter and would not wish her tied into such an alliance for the sake of her dowry. We all know Anthony would burn through any dowry he was to claim from a marriage, just as he has every other coin he has ever been able to lay his hands on."

"Will Uncle be forced to sell part of Matlock to cover Anthony's debt? Is this a fact?"

Lady Anne nodded her head. "It breaks my heart to see my father's estate so poorly attended. Papa would be angry with Anthony's behavior."

"As much as I would wish to keep Uncle from having to sell part of the estate, I am afraid I cannot cover such a large debt. And, if I did, I am certain that my cousin would see it as his private reserve. He would continue in the manner in which he has become accustomed and expect me to constantly protect him. I cannot do this and keep my own estate protected."

"I understand, my son. I am only fulfilling the request your uncle made of me. And I agree with your assessment of your cousin. Anthony would take advantage of your aid, as he has obviously not learned any lesson from your assistance as yet."

~~ ** ~~

Darcy prepared to make his journey a fortnight later, planning to spend at least two months with Bingley at Netherfield Park. Bingley had already arrived at the estate, and was settling into the neighborhood, enjoying meeting his new neighbors. Bingley's sisters were of a different mind about their neighbors.

Louisa Hurst was the eldest of the Bingley siblings, and had married a man she was quite taken with, Mr Gilbert Hurst. He was an heir to his father's estate, a decent sized property which was located in the east side of Norfolk. When they married, the couple had been quite happy, though it did not last long. Due to Louisa's sister, the Hurst marriage had suffered greatly.

Caroline Bingley was the youngest child, and quite spoilt. All the years of her youth, their parents had allowed Caroline to behave inappropriately, indulging her every whim. Their fortune had come from trade, though the family was attempting to raise themselves from the stigma. Caroline believed she was worthy of the first circles of society, and she would settle for nothing less.

When Louisa married Mr Hurst, Caroline voiced her opinion of how lowly the Hurst family was in society. Her cruelty caused a wedge to develop between the couple, and Mr Hurst began overindulging in drink. After her first visit to the Hurst family estate, Mr Hurst's mother and father forbade Caroline to ever visit their home again.

Being the only son, Charles was given a gentleman's education. He also had been told of the expectations of the family for him to eventually find an estate, thereby establishing the family as landed gentry. Their parents died shortly after Charles had graduated from the university, leaving him to guide his sisters towards their futures.

It was at university where Charles met Fitzwilliam Darcy. The two were as different as night and day, yet became friends quickly. Where Bingley was friendly and outgoing, Darcy was shy and withdrawn. Where Darcy was brilliant at managing his estate and business, Bingley was like a newborn babe. But the two learned to rely on each other to fill in their own deficiencies.

The most difficult part of their friendship was Caroline Bingley. As soon as the young lady laid her sights on Darcy, no one else would do. He was wealthy, handsome, master of one of the grandest estates, as well as one of the most sought after bachelors. If she could catch him, she knew her life would be perfect. Unfortunately, Mr Darcy had other notions.

Fitzwilliam Darcy had become frustrated with the actions of the young ladies of the *ton*, wishing to find someone to love. It had been a frustration to him when his mother remarried, he felt she had not loved his father enough, or she would never have married Lord Covington. And Darcy had decided long ago that he would not settle for a marriage of convenience. If he could not find love, he would not marry.

Far from the ladies he was used to meeting, his preferences as to what his wife should be like were quite unusual. He wished for a lady with intelligence, wit, the ability to debate many topics and not just agree with his opinions, someone who was gentle and kind, and had a natural sense of humor. He felt it would be pleasant if she had some of the standard talents of the young ladies, such as singing or playing the pianoforte, art or stitchery. But those were secondary. And most importantly, she must hold a desire to better herself with extensive reading.

When weighing merits, Caroline Bingley felt she was perfect to be the next Mistress of Pemberley. In Darcy's opinion, he found her merits to be very far from meeting what he desired. The problem was making Miss Bingley realize the dislike he held for her so she would leave him alone.

~~~~~~~~ ** ~~~~~~~~
~~~~~~~~

CHAPTER 2

"Caroline, Charles told you to behave yourself while Mr Darcy is here. The gentleman has made it quite clear that he wants nothing to do with you, and if you continue to make a fool of yourself over him, you will incur his anger."

"Louisa, you are a fool. Of course Mr Darcy will appreciate my being here. He needs a wife, and will have to have an heir to inherit his estate. You know I am perfect to fill the position of Mrs Darcy. I am sophisticated, accomplished, beautiful, charming, and a proper hostess. And, best of all, I am the sister of his dearest friend. What more could he ask for?"

"Someone he can tolerate being in the same room with for more than an hour would most likely make life somewhat easier for the man." Mr Hurst said as he entered the room. "If you make a fool of yourself again, Caroline, your brother will follow through on his threat to send you to Scotland. He has already spoken with your mother's sister and made arrangements in case you do not listen to what he told you, especially when it comes to Darcy."

"I have always behaved myself with Mr Darcy. I will not be threatened by the likes of you, Mr Hurst."

Caroline sneered at her brother in law.

"As I have said, you had best behave or you are off to Scotland, and I will happily assist Charles in putting you into the carriage." Hurst said as he poured himself another glass of brandy.

~~ ** ~~

"Bingley, I must say, from what I have seen so far, I am pleased with the estate." Darcy said, as he accepted the glass of brandy from his friend and took a seat. "We should go for a ride about the grounds, so I can better see the farms and the tenant homes, amongst other aspects. When would you like to do so?"

"Would you be willing to wait for two days? Tomorrow night is an assembly in Meryton, which I plan to attend. You will meet Miss Jane Bennet. She is an angel."

"Not another one." Darcy said, watching his friend closely. After a moment or two, he could see that there was something different this time. "Tell me about your angel."

"Well, if I tell you that my sisters dislike her, does that improve your outlook on her?" Bingley laughed. "Miss Bennet is the eldest of five daughters. Their father, Thomas Bennet, owns the next estate over,

Longbourn. His family has been there for five previous generations, and the estate has flourished. Land wise, it is larger than Netherfield, though the house is smaller, which makes Caroline constantly belittle the Bennets as poor. She does not know the truth of the family, nor have I told her."

"And that is?"

Bingley took a sip from his glass. "Mr Bennet is successful. He has preferred to live comfortably, though reservedly. Mrs Bennet sets a fine table, and makes sure her daughters are well dressed and educated on being proper young ladies. Mr Bennet's income is near my own. But, because the Bennets do not spend frivolously or put on a show of their wealth, Caroline sees the family as country nobodies."

"I must admit, when I am at Pemberley, I have no desire to worry over dressing properly in the eyes of upper society, and I prefer comfort to ostentatious décor. You say that there are five daughters? No sons?"

"No, the only son was born after the third daughter, and he died of influenza when he was a small boy. The estate is entailed to Mr Bennet's nephew, who is in Scotland at his father's estate. The nephew is the second son, so Mr Bennet made him the heir to Longbourn. A cousin was supposed to inherit, but he died recently. As a matter of fact, the cousin was your aunt's parson."

"That strange little man who was always fawning over Lady Catherine when we visited her last year?" Darcy asked

"Mr Collins. He was with your cousin in the carriage accident." Bingley knew that, though Darcy was grieved at his cousin's death, he was relieved his aunt, Lady Catherine de Bourgh, would no longer hound him to marry her daughter.

"I remember him. I cannot say I was impressed with him." Darcy shook his head. "So, there is to be an assembly. Do I truly have to accompany you, or could I stay home and enjoy some quiet time, reading?"

"You know, as well as I do, that if you stay here, Caroline will insist on staying with you. It is your choice though." Bingley knew what his friend's reaction would be.

"What time is the assembly to start?"

~~ ** ~~

The Bingley party arrived just after the assembly had begun. Bingley was pleased to make the introductions of his friend to some of his new neighbors, all the while he was searching the crowd for Miss Jane Bennet. Finally, he spotted her from across the room. “Come, Darcy, there is Miss Bennet.”

Mrs Bennet was pleased to see Bingley coming towards her eldest daughter. She had always believed Jane to be the most beautiful and serene young lady, as sweet natured and kind as Mr Bingley appeared to be. “Ah, Mr Bingley, it is a pleasure to have you here at the assembly.”

“Mrs Bennet, wild horses could not keep me away. Miss Bennet, you look very pretty tonight. That shade of blue does your eyes justice.” Bingley bowed over Jane’s hand.

“Mr Bingley, you flatter me, Sir. And you seem to be in high spirits. Are you looking forward to the hunt on Friday?” Jane asked.

“Yes, I am. Sir William has proclaimed it will be a most promising day. Will your father be attending?” Bingley asked.

“He will be, as he enjoys a good hunt.” Jane smiled as she spoke.

“Forgive me, ladies, might I introduce you to my dearest friend? Mrs Bennet, Miss Bennet, this is Mr Fitzwilliam Darcy of Pemberley in Derbyshire. Darcy, this is Mrs Frances Bennet and her eldest daughter,

Miss Jane Bennet, both of Longbourn."

"Ladies, it is a pleasure to meet you. My friend has spoken of your family fondly." Darcy bowed as the ladies curtsied.

"Welcome to Hertfordshire, Mr Darcy. I pray you will enjoy your time here." Mrs Bennet stated.

"I am sure I will, Mrs Bennet. If you will excuse me, Bingley, I wish to make my way to the refreshment table for a glass of punch. Do either of you ladies desire a drink?"

"Thank you, Mr Darcy, but I am fine." Mrs Bennet replied.

Jane agreed with her mother, and Darcy walked off, leaving his friend in the ladies' company. As Darcy picked up a glass of punch, he heard a most whimsical laugh coming from a young lady nearby. Looking up, he saw the most beautiful young lady he had ever seen in his life. With hair the color of dark chocolate, curls hanging loosely about her neck, while the rest of her hair was pinned in a most becoming manner, and a smile that was infectious, Darcy could not resist smiling himself. She had a light and pleasing figure, with curves which made him blush that he had taken such notice. He estimated she was near twenty, and very good natured. But it was when she looked up and caught his eye that his heart nearly stopped. He could lose himself in the depths of those eyes. Light brown, with flakes of gold, which sparkled with life, those eyes looked as if they could see into his very soul.

The young lady smiled at him and he nodded his head towards her. She then returned her attention to the young lady with whom she had been speaking. How he wished he could walk up to her and introduce himself. Where was Bingley when he needed his assistance? Looking around, he found Bingley dancing with none other than Miss Bennet. Turning back towards the young lady, he found she had moved. She was now speaking with two much younger girls, who skipped away from her towards the refreshments. *They must be her sisters,* he thought as he watched the girls. Returning his gaze towards the young lady, she had yet again moved, further away from where he was standing. He continued to watch her, moving whenever needed to keep sight of her.

From the looks of things, the young lady was well known in the neighborhood and well liked. Everyone greeted her with the utmost kindness and genuine affection. Darcy suddenly heard Miss Bingley walk up beside him. "Mr Darcy, what do you think of this quaint gathering? I feel as if any moment now, someone will release a greased pig onto the floor for everyone to chase about."

"Do not be ridiculous, Miss Bingley. You may not be accustomed to country ways, but this is a very cultured gathering for country society. I am quite impressed by the people I have seen here."

"You cannot be serious." Miss Bingley stated. "The fashions are outdated, the people are vulgar in their manners. I am shocked you would approve of being acquainted with such people."

"It is not me who will be neighbors to these people, but, from what I have seen, I can find no true fault with anyone here." Darcy was irritated with Caroline Bingley's snobbery.

Turning his attention back towards the last location he had known the young lady to have been, Darcy was frustrated when he could not find her in the crowd. Giving a slight growl, Darcy moved away from Miss Bingley and continued his search. All the while, Darcy thought *"if only Bingley would stay off the dance floor for a few moments so he can introduce me to the young lady, then I would be able to speak with her rather than search everywhere for her."*

Finally, Bingley took a break from dancing. "Come, Darcy, I must have you dance. There are many pretty girls here, I am sure you can find someone to dance with. Oh, there is one of Miss Bennet's sisters.

She is quite pretty and I am sure she would enjoy a dance."

"Bingley, you were dancing with the only pretty girl in the room. While she may be nice, she is not handsome enough to tempt me." Darcy replied, his eyes still scouring the crowd.

Just then, someone bumped into him as they walked past. Surprised, Darcy glanced towards the person, who had come from behind him, only to see the young lady he was looking for. "Dear me, Darcy, I do believe Miss Elizabeth heard you."

Darcy's eyes rolled back in his head. *"What an idiot I am. I was frustrated in not seeing her and end up accidently insulting her. How can I speak to her now?"*

"Miss Elizabeth? You know the young lady who just passed by?" he asked.

"Why, of course I do. Miss Elizabeth is the young lady of which I was speaking. She is Miss Bennet's sister." Bingley replied.

"Good God, could it get worse?" he asked himself. "Bingley, would you do me the honor of introducing me to Miss Elizabeth so I may beg her forgiveness?"

"Of course, old friend. Come with me." Bingley

smiled as he led the way towards where Miss Bennet and Elizabeth stood, speaking of what had just happened.

"Miss Elizabeth, my friend has begged me to introduce you to him. If you will allow, Miss Elizabeth, this is Mr Fitzwilliam Darcy of Pemberley. Darcy, this is Miss Bennet's next eldest sister, Miss Elizabeth Bennet."

"Miss Elizabeth, I am pleased to meet you. I would ask your forgiveness for my comment of moments ago. I was frustrated and had not even turned to see to whom my friend was referring when I spoke. I wished him to leave me be and I foolishly opened my mouth when I should have remained silent."

"I accept your apology, Mr Darcy. Might I ask what has frustrated you tonight?" Elizabeth asked politely.

"Those eyes, they are even more entrancing up close." Darcy needed a moment before he could speak. "To be honest, Miss Elizabeth, I had been searching the room for a young lady to which I wished to have my friend introduce me. I had been watching her from across the room all evening and suddenly she was missing. When Mr Bingley finally arrived at my side, and I could not locate the young lady for him to introduce me, my frustration became such that I spoke so foolishly. Little did I know, the young lady

for whom I was searching was standing behind me, becoming the object of my foul behavior."

Elizabeth blushed. "You had been searching the room for me?"

"I was quite taken when I first spotted you. With Mr Bingley on the dance floor, I could not have him make the introduction, therefore, I could not approach you to speak with you." Darcy felt bold in his declaration. Standing beside him, Bingley was shocked at his friend's behavior.

"Well, Mr Darcy, as you have spoken so openly of what led to the statements, I do not know whether you are quite suave at speaking to ladies or if you are speaking from the heart."

Bingley nearly choked from laughter. "Miss Elizabeth, let me tell you, Mr Darcy has been my dear friend for nearly seven years. In all that time, I have never seen him speak to a lady outside his family and close friends, let alone speak so openly as he has to you. I am amazed at his behavior. It is also my privilege to tell you, my friend is one of the best men in all of England."

Darcy blushed with his friend's portrayal of him. "Miss Elizabeth, now that we have been introduced, might I finally have the honor of asking for the next dance?"

"After so much effort, Mr Darcy, how could I deny such a request?" Elizabeth chuckled.

Darcy offered his arm, and Elizabeth placed her hand gently upon it. He then led them to the line forming for the next set. Bingley quickly claimed another set with Miss Bennet and they stood next to Darcy and Elizabeth.

From the side, Caroline Bingley was fuming. Darcy never danced, with the only exceptions being members of his family or sisters of very close friends, and only then to keep from offending his friends. How was it he was now on the dance floor, with that country nobody?

Watching his partner from across the dance floor was pure delight, and Darcy enjoyed dancing for the first time in his life. As Elizabeth moved, a healthy glow formed in her cheeks, adding to her already beautiful face. Never in his life, had Darcy found such pleasure in dancing.

As the set came to an end, Darcy escorted Elizabeth to the nearby chairs. Bingley and Jane followed them, Jane taking a seat beside her sister. Bingley smiled at his friend as he spoke. "I have asked if I may have permission to call on Miss Bennet tomorrow, at Longbourn. She has been most kind in obliging me. Perhaps, Darcy, you might wish to join me."

"I believe that is an excellent idea, Bingley." Darcy turned towards the ladies. "That is, if you would not mind my presence, Miss Elizabeth."

A blush came over her cheeks as she looked at her sister first. "Mr Darcy, I believe you would be welcome to visit Longbourn with your friend."

"I thank you, Miss Elizabeth. I will look forward to the treat immensely." Seeing that the dance was ending, and carriages were being called for, Darcy was deeply disappointed in not having more time to spend with Elizabeth. "Shall we assist you in gathering your wraps?"

"Thank you, Mr Darcy, your efforts would be appreciated." Elizabeth and Jane stood and took hold of the arm each man offered to their particular favorite Bennet sister. Once the ladies had their wraps, and the gentlemen had their coats and hats, the men escorted the ladies to the foyer to await the arrival of their carriages. The Bennet carriage arrived first, and it was with great pleasure that Bingley handed in Miss Bennet, and Darcy followed suit with Miss Elizabeth. Both men watched as the carriage pulled away, lost in the delights of the evening.

Caroline Bingley sauntered up to Darcy and wrapped her hand around Darcy's arm. "Mr Darcy, I must tell you how disappointed I was not to have had the chance to dance with you myself. Seeing how light you are on your feet, I am quite envious of Miss Eliza for her ability to charm you into dancing."

Disgusted by her obvious attempt at belittling Elizabeth, as well as her wish to capture his attention, Darcy pried himself free of his friend's sister. "It was I who charmed Miss Elizabeth into dancing. And, as you know, I am not fond of dancing."

"Forgive me, Mr Darcy, I only wished to convey what pleasure it would have brought me to have had such an opportunity. I should warn you, Charles believes he has fallen in love with the eldest Miss Bennet, and I know that it will be the ruin of our family to be connected with them, as they are obviously so far beneath us."

"Miss Bingley, I would suggest you leave your brother's choices to him to make. He is a grown man. And to be honest, I see nothing wrong with the Bennet ladies. From what I understand, they have been raised as the gentlewomen they were born to be. You, on the other hand, are wealthy by your father's and grandfather's ties in trade. Bingley would actually be raising himself in society by marrying Miss Bennet."

Caroline was shocked. Standing in stunned silence, she watched as everyone, except her brother, entered the carriage. When Charles handed her in, she took the seat next to her sister and stared out the window the entire journey to Netherfield.

~~~~~~~~ ** ~~~~~~~~
~~~~~~~~

CHAPTER 3

Caroline fumed as she paced in her rooms. *I am to be the next Mrs Darcy, Mistress of Pemberley, not that country nobody. How could she have used her arts and allurements to turn Darcy's head? The best young ladies the* ton *had to offer, who did everything they could to land the illustrious Fitzwilliam Darcy, had been unsuccessful. And then Eliza Bennet comes along and leads the man to the dance floor. Darcy had not even danced with me, why would he make a fool of himself with that chit?*

I have to put a stop to this, immediately. I have to secure him, tonight, before it is too late. Caroline walked into her dressing chamber and selected the most transparent nightgown she owned, quickly donning it. She would slip into his bed, and be compromised. She had the keys to the entire house, so he could not lock her out.

Once she had dressed for the night, she went to her desk and began to write. As a young child, she had learned to copy the handwriting of most everyone. It had been a useful ability, and she had used it quite often. Pulling out a letter from one of the drawers, she opened it up to examine the handwriting. It was a strong hand, the script was precise and elegant.

She began to write a message to her brother. It would do no good if she were compromised if no one knew it. She had to plan for her brother to discover her in Darcy's room.

The note stated for Charles to meet Darcy at his rooms in half an hour. That would give her time to get into Darcy's rooms and into his bed, before her brother arrived.

She then rang for her maid. Agnes had been her maid for many years, and would do as she directed. She handed her maid the note, asking that she have a footman deliver the message to Bingley. Then she made her way from her rooms, sneaking through the servants' corridor until she reached Darcy's rooms. She slipped inside the darkened rooms, with the only light coming from the fire.

Quietly, she made her way to the side of the bed, only to discover the bed empty. Caroline did not care; she pulled back the bedding and made herself comfortable, thinking Darcy would return shortly. As the minutes ticked away, Caroline grew nervous. *How can Charles catch us in a compromising position if Mr Darcy is not here with me?*

~~ ** ~~

Darcy had been excited after spending time with Elizabeth Bennet. His mind was wrapped around the feel of her hand in his as they danced and when he handed her into her family's carriage. As he entered his rooms, his valet handed him an express which had arrived from his mother. Bingley had given him use of the Mistress' study to use while Darcy stayed at Netherfield, so he went to the study to read the express and respond.

The news that was so dire was that Lord Matlock had suffered a bout of apoplexy. He was still alive, though he was quite weak. Lady Anne insisted there was no need for her son to travel to Matlock, for she knew he needed the rest after the harvest had been completed. She promised to keep him updated on the news of her brother's condition.

Darcy wrote a letter to his mother, thanking her for informing him, as well as her advice that he should remain at Netherfield for the time being. Then he decided to tell his mother of his evening, and his meeting of Miss Elizabeth Bennet.

As he finished his letter and posted it to be sent express the following morning, Darcy made his way back to his rooms. He had dismissed his valet for the evening, so he was planning to have a glass of port and do some reading before sleeping. Walking down the hall, he heard Bingley call out his name.

"Darcy, I was just on my way to see you. I got your note, is everything fine?"

"Of what note are you speaking?" Darcy asked, a crease formed on his forehead.

"The one asking me to meet you here. The footman delivered it to me." Bingley was confused.

"Perhaps we should step into my rooms as we determine what is going on." Darcy said as he opened the door and stepped inside his bedchamber.

"Fitzwilliam, I have been waiting for you to return." Caroline coo'd from the bed. "I came, just as you asked me."

Bingley was behind his friend, becoming pale at the situation his sister had created. Stepping around Darcy, Bingley walked directly to the bed, pulling his sister, by the arm, from the bed. "Caroline, I know that Darcy did not ask you to meet him here, nor did he ask you to join him in bed. As I know Darcy was not in this room, prior to our entering together, I am well aware who has attempted to compromise whom."

"Charles, how can you speak so of your sister? Mr Darcy asked me to be with him. You know that we are perfect for each other and he told me he could wait no longer to be with me."

"Enough, Caroline! You will remain in your rooms for the rest of the night, and in the morning you will be making the trip to Scotland to live there. I have told you time and again, Darcy has no desire towards you and would rather marry the scullery maid than you."

"Bingley, how did your sister access my rooms? I keep the doors locked when I am in the same house as she." Darcy was concerned.

"Caroline, do you have a key to Darcy's rooms?" Bingley was growing angrier by the moment.

"How dare you accuse me of such behavior, Charles? What sort of brother are you to allow your friends to take advantage of me, promise me a future with them, and then you throw me out of your home while they refuse to honor their promises? I am ruined because you are not strong enough to stand up to Mr Darcy and make him marry me."

"You are ruined because you have made a fool of yourself. If you keep acting in this manner, I will think you should be laced in Bedlam instead of living with our aunt." Bingley was angrier than he had ever been in his life.

"You should be locked up in Bedlam, and I will speak with Louisa with my concerns." Caroline attempted to move away from her brother.

"I am here, Caroline." Louisa Hurst was standing in the doorway, still tying her robe shut. "You have awakened the entire household with your behavior, Sister. And now you will receive just what I expected from our brother. You are mistaken if you believe I will stand with you, against Charles, for I agree with him. Mr Darcy has been quite clear in his feelings towards you. He despises you, totally and completely, for you are everything in a lady he hates."

"Louisa, do you know if our sister has a key to enter these rooms? Darcy stated that he had locked the doors, but Caroline made entry."

Louisa turned towards her sister. "Did you lift the master keys from Mrs Romans? She searched high and low for the set, and fortunately had a spare set. If she had not, the entire house would have had to be rekeyed. She fretted for days, trying to find the keys and all this time, you selfishly had them so you could sneak into Mr Darcy's rooms? You are an idiot, Caroline, and thick skulled in not listening to the truth from anyone. Charles, I believe you might be correct in the belief in taking our sister to Bedlam, for it is the best place for someone like her."

Caroline lunged at her sister, attempting to wrap her fingers around her sister's throat. Fortunately, Bingley grabbed hold of Caroline and stopped her. In her fury, Caroline turned her anger from her sister to her brother, beating on his chest and finally reached out her fingers and clawed the back of his neck. Crying out in pain, Bingley lost hold of his sister and she ran from the room. Arriving at her own rooms, she locked the doors and refused to open to any of them, even for her maid.

Darcy called for the housekeeper to come quickly, as he assisted his friend to a nearby chair. Louisa went to fetch some water and a towel to clean the wounds Caroline had left on her brother's neck. When Mrs Romans came quickly and was shocked at the sight before her.

"Mrs Romans, bring your bag of medicines, and some bandaging. And have two footmen stand guard over Miss Bingley's rooms. Tell the men they are not to allow her to leave her rooms, under any circumstances."

Frightened, but extremely capable of handling the emergency, the housekeeper was quick into action. Dictating orders to her underlings, it was not long before the footmen were in place and Bingley's wounds were being tended.

"Louisa, I see no alternative at this point. We will have to send Caroline to Bedlam. In the morning, we will need to send to Town for our family physician. He will be able to make the arrangements."

"I have never seen her so out of control, Charles." Louisa said, a sob escaping her. "She is behaving more and more like Mamma. If she had not taken ill, I am sure that our father would have been required to make the same decision we now face. Poor Caroline, she has lost her mind."

One of the footmen entered the room, breathless in his haste. "Mr Bingley, we heard glass breaking in your sister's rooms, and when Fred and I went to check on Miss Bingley's welfare, she would not open the door. Finally, we decided to break the door in, fearing she had hurt herself. We found several windows had been shattered and, when we rushed to look out the window, thinking Miss Bingley had done herself harm, your sister ran from her hiding spot and out of the house. We cannot find her anywhere, though one of the horses is missing."

Darcy was instantly alarmed. Would Caroline Bingley, in her deranged train of thought, go to Longbourn and attack Miss Elizabeth? Had his dancing with the young lady been the final straw to push Miss Bingley over the edge? Her comments to Darcy as they waited for the carriage to arrive flowed through his mind. "Bingley, we should send word to Longbourn, warning the family to be watching for your sister. I know it is the last thing you wish to do, to let the world know your sister has lost her mind, but for the safety of the Bennet family, it must be done."

"Why would Caroline wish to harm the Bennets?" Bingley asked.

"When we were preparing to leave the assembly, Miss Bingley was not pleased with my having danced with Miss Elizabeth. In your sister's current state of mind, I would not trust her to not attack Miss Elizabeth, or even Miss Bennet, for that matter."

"Good God, Darcy, you must ride over to Longbourn at once and inform Mr Bennet. I cannot go, and cannot send a note. It must be done in person." Bingley was becoming more and more agitated.

Darcy sent a footman to have a horse saddled and brought to the front of the house. "You must rest, Charles. Mrs Hurst, please see that he is given something to aid him in resting comfortably, once Mrs Romans is finished bandaging his wounds."

"Of course, Mr Darcy. And would you please inform Mr Bennet that we will do whatever we can to find my sister before she can bring any harm to his family?"

With a nod of the head, Darcy stepped into his dressing room to obtain his great coat and hat. Once prepared, he left for Longbourn.

~~ ** ~~

When Darcy arrived at the front of Longbourn's house, he noticed the only candle lit room he could see was that of an upstairs window near the north corner of the house. The only other light in the house appeared to be from the fires burning to warm the occupants. He realized the chances were that the Bennet family was all asleep, with the exception of the person in the candle lit room. As much as he hated to wake them with such news, he knew it was vital he do so.

He had to knock several times before he heard footsteps leading to the door. Quietly, he was asked to enter, though he could not see the person holding the door open. All he could hear was the soft whisper of a young lady. It was when he smelled the scent of lavender he was certain that it was Elizabeth.

"Mr Darcy, has something drastic happened tonight, since you left the assembly?" Elizabeth asked.

"Yes, and I would not be disturbing your household if it were not vital to inform your family of the events."

They could hear a cough coming from the top of the stairs, as well as see the light of a candle descending towards them.

"Papa, Mr Darcy has come with urgent news." Elizabeth said, blushing as she realized the impropriety of standing alone with a young man, while she wore her night gown and robe.

"Mr Darcy, would you prefer to step down the hall, to my study, to speak?" Mr Bennet motioned for the young man to follow him. "Lizzy, I believe you should return to your room, my dear."

"Actually, Mr Bennet, if you do not mind, Miss Elizabeth is involved in the situation, though she is unaware of it." Darcy said, hoping to have Elizabeth in the study with her father as he informed them of the events. Having little knowledge of Mr Bennet, Darcy was nervous as to how the elder man would react to the news.

"Lizzy, do you wish to remain for the discussion?" Mr Bennet asked.

"Y-Yes, Papa. If the news pertains to me, I should hear what Mr Darcy has to say."

"Very well, my dear girl. Mr Darcy, follow us to my study, please."

Mr Bennet offered his guest a glass of brandy, but Darcy turned him down. He wished to have a clear head for this meeting. Taking the seat next to Elizabeth in front of the desk, he began.

"Mr Bennet, I ask for your discretion in what I am about to tell you. Tonight, we had a situation at Netherfield, which could come to cause your family difficulty. Miss Bingley has had a breakdown of sorts. She has been obsessed with marrying into the first circles of society for years. Because of this obsession, she has fixated upon marrying me since she first met me. I have made myself clear that we would never be more than acquainted due to her brother, though Miss Bingley has refused to believe anything anyone has told her.

Tonight, at the assembly, I did something I rarely ever do. I danced with a young lady who was not related to me or the sister of a friend. Two years ago, I danced one time with Miss Bingley, and vowed never to do so again. So, to say that she was upset when she witnessed my dancing with Miss Elizabeth, would be a phenomenal understatement."

"Why should she be any threat so severe that you would come at such a time of night to tell us?" Mr Bennet asked, obviously confused.

"cWhile I was in the study Mr Bingley has allowed me to use during my stay, Miss Bingley attempted to set up a situation in which to force me to marry her."

He stopped when he heard Elizabeth gasp.

"She attempted to have herself compromised?" Elizabeth asked.

"Unfortunately, yes. She had stolen the housekeeper's master set of keys and let herself into my room, slipping into my bed. Fortunately, I had received an express from my mother earlier this evening and was replying to it during this time frame. When I was returning to my rooms, Bingley met me in the hall, claiming to have received a message from me to meet me in my rooms. We entered the room to find Miss Bingley, and I must tell you, the lady has completely lost her mind. Mrs Hurst became angry with her sister for her foolishness, and the two sisters quarreled. When Bingley attempted to protect Mrs Hurst, Miss Bingley savagely clawed his neck. We thought we had her secure in her bedchambers after the attack on her brother, but she fooled the staff and escaped the house. A horse is missing from the stables."

"As I said, Miss Bingley was displeased with my having danced with Miss Elizabeth tonight. She made her feelings known when we were preparing to leave for Netherfield, which is why I feel she became so desperate tonight and did what she did. What worries me now is if she would retaliate against Miss Elizabeth, for she knows I was impressed with your daughter tonight."

Elizabeth was overwhelmed. *How had all of this come to be in one evening? I only just met Mr Darcy a few hours ago and am in danger due to his simply dancing with me. And what had they spoken about which would make Miss Bingley wish to harm me?*

Seeing his daughter's distress, Mr Bennet walked to the sideboard and poured a glass with some wine and a little water. He carried the glass to Elizabeth and told her to drink. Still in a state of shock, Elizabeth took a sip as her father held the glass to her lips. Mr Darcy became concerned, praying that Elizabeth would be well. He knew it was not a pleasant conversation, but he was certain that Elizabeth was strong enough to handle the news. The reason he included her was to protect her, and here she was, disturbed and frightened by what she was told.

"Forgive me, Miss Elizabeth, I wish I could have kept the news from you, but I fear for your safety. You are the one Miss Bingley sees as standing in her way. I will do everything in my power to protect you and your family from Miss Bingley."

"Why would one dance be such cause for anger? We only met this evening, just before the dance." Elizabeth asked, her eyes pleading with his.

"Miss Elizabeth, I am embarrassed to have to admit this, in front of your father, but the moment I saw you, there was something about you which opened my heart. Never before have I seen a young lady such as you. Beyond your beauty, your ability to converse with all who were at the assembly made it easy to see that you are not only easy in speaking with others, but they also treated you with respect and kindness."

"Then I saw the look in your eyes, and I felt as if you had pierced my soul with one glance. Never in my life have I wished for an introduction to any lady, yet I wished Bingley to come immediately to do just that. But he was busy dancing, so I could not meet you. Miss Bingley knew I had never behaved in such a manner before, and she grew jealous of my attention towards you."

"Mr Darcy, I am amazed at your being so forthcoming with your words with regards to my daughter." Mr Bennet said. "I find it amazing you would be so taken with someone of Lizzy's status in life. I would have thought her to be far beneath your notice."

Darcy bowed his head as he thought of how to say the words which were in his heart. "I will speak honestly with you, for I despise deception of any sort. Mr Bennet, your daughter is a gentlewoman, I am a gentleman, and though your family is not of the upper circles of society, I am pleased that you are not. I am not fond of London society, nor of the matchmaking mammas and their daughters who have attempted to capture my hand. Forgive me if this sounds conceited, but my family's wealth and connections make me quite eligible for every young lady of the *ton*. I despise being treated as a commodity rather than a person."

"I have always wished for a marriage of true worth, one with an abiding love and a shared future with a partner, not someone to adorn my arm only. So, if it is not too much to ask, on such an early introduction, I would wish to court Miss Elizabeth. In that way, she and I can come to know each other better."

"Courtship?" Elizabeth asked, her eyes were filling with tears. "This is all happening too fast, Mr Darcy. Yesterday at this time, I had never known you existed and now you ask for a courtship."

Mr Bennet could see that this was a young man who could treat Elizabeth with the respect she deserved. "I will agree to a courtship, though I insist it remain a secret from the rest of the neighborhood. You have a huge task before you, Mr Darcy. I will not announce a formal courtship until Elizabeth is comfortable with such an idea." Turning around, Mr

Bennet looked out the window. “Ah, Lizzy, the sun is preparing to rise. I am certain you will wish to take a walk to your favorite location.”

~~~~~~~~ ** ~~~~~~~~
~~~~~~~~

CHAPTER 4

"Mr Bennet, I do not think it wise for Miss Elizabeth to be walking out by herself. It would be the perfect chance for Miss Bingley to harm her. I would be happy to accompany her."

"That would be highly improper, Mr Darcy. I will not tolerate improper behavior, especially with regards to my Lizzy. She is my favorite child, and I will not see her harmed in *any* manner."

"Papa, Susan could accompany us. She will not be needed to attend my sisters until later." Elizabeth suggested. "I would like to know more about Mr Darcy before I agree to any sort of courtship, secret or openly public."

"I am grateful, Miss Elizabeth. Shall I wait outside for you?"

Elizabeth nodded slightly. "Susan will be in the kitchen, so I will fetch her and change my clothes. It would not be proper to be walking out in such a fashion."

Darcy suddenly realized Elizabeth was still in her night clothes. "Forgive me, Miss Elizabeth. In all that has happened, I forgot that I interrupted your sleep.

Perhaps we should postpone the walk until later, after you are able to rest."

"No, I will not be able to rest now. It would be better for us to have some time to talk and walk."

"Very well. I will be waiting for you outside." Darcy began to walk to the door of the study.

"Mr Darcy, you are welcome to remain here with me while my daughter changes her clothes. There is no need for you to stand outside in the cold." Mr Bennet stated.

"I thank you, Sir." Darcy said as he watched Elizabeth leave the room. "I must say, Mr Bennet, you have quite a library. You must be fond of books."

"Indeed. It is also a passion my Lizzy shares with me. She is quite intelligent, and we have enjoyed many a debate in this room. Unlike most ladies, my daughter will be reluctant in allowing you to win an argument just for the sake of winning your favor. She will share her opinion openly, and stand by her opinion unless proven wrong."

"I look forward to that. I tire of young ladies who wish to please me, so they agree with anything I say. They must have ideas of their own, but they never dare speak them." Darcy smiled.

~~ ** ~~

Elizabeth was amazed at all the emotions coursing through her. At the assembly, she had noticed the handsome stranger while she was speaking with her best friend, Charlotte Lucas. Charlotte commented on the way the man had watched her carefully, his eyes following her through the crowd when she moved about the room. But, as they had not been introduced to the man, neither Charlotte nor Elizabeth could properly speak to him. They had debated on asking Charlotte's father, Sir William Lucas, to make the introductions, but at the time, he was not in the room.

Through the entire evening, she had felt as if someone was burning holes in her from staring intensely. Each time, when she looked up, Elizabeth found the man's eyes locked on her.

When she went to speak to her mother with regards to her youngest sister, Lydia, and how the girl was behaving, she lost track of where the stranger was. Seeing him standing with Mr Bingley, Elizabeth thought to speak to their new neighbor, since he had been dancing most of the night and she had not had the chance to welcome him. As she approached, she could not believe her ears. The man who had been watching her so intensely throughout the night had just exclaimed that she was not handsome enough to tempt him to dance. The nerve of him, obviously he had been watching her to find fault in her.

Purposely, Elizabeth had bumped into him as she walked past him and walked to her sister. How furious she had felt at that moment, for him to be so callous and rude. But then, the man came with Mr Bingley, begging for an introduction. His words of apology were obviously heartfelt and true, it was clear to see in his eyes the embarrassment he was experiencing.

Accepting his offer for a dance was an honor and a pleasure. Though he claimed not to be much of a dancer, he was quite efficient in his steps. When his hand touched hers, she felt as if lightning had struck her.

When they stepped into the carriage, she was amazed at his kindness in handing her in. It was clear that she was being singled out. Arriving home, Elizabeth had found it difficult to sleep, which was why she was awake when Darcy arrived. She had been reading in her room, but she instantly knew something was wrong when she heard the horse riding up to the house.

Seeing Darcy standing in their foyer in the middle of the night, Elizabeth could not believe how attractive the man was. Though he was wearing his great coat, he only wore his shirt sleeves and short coat underneath, with no cravat. Elizabeth was amazed at how taken she was by his appearance.

Learning all Darcy had said was shocking. She had not imagined such a man as he could ever find the likes of her to be perfect for courtship, let alone for a future partner. She was certain that, once he knew her better, he would flee from the area and realize how foolish a marriage with her would be. Every other young man she had met had made it clear, they did not approve of a young lady being so well educated and opinionated. But she refused to change for them. If they did not like the way she was, that was their problem. Elizabeth had always teased Jane that she would never marry, and would end up being the nanny to her elder sister's ten children, teaching them to play the pianoforte poorly.

So Elizabeth would go on the walk with Mr Darcy this morning, and he would leave. *It is too bad; I believe I could have come to like him.* She thought as she dressed. At least it would be nice to have one morning where a young man wished to walk with her.

~~ ** ~~

Elizabeth returned to her father's study to find Mr Darcy still happily speaking with her father. Seeing she had returned to the room, Darcy's smile grew, showing his dimples. A small gasp escaped her as she saw the expression she was sure was foreign to most who knew the man.

"Ah, Lizzy, just in time. After your walk, I have asked Mr Darcy to join us for breakfast before he returns to Netherfield."

"Papa, I am sure that Mr Darcy is only being polite. He has been awake all night and will most certainly wish to return to Netherfield after walking with me." Elizabeth said.

"On the contrary, Miss Elizabeth, I feel as if I have gotten my second wind. I look forward to spending as much time with you as possible."

Blushing vividly, Elizabeth led the way to the back door, where they met Susan. Once outside, Darcy offered an arm to Elizabeth. "Where is your favorite path to take, Miss Elizabeth?"

"Come this way." Elizabeth motioned towards the path which led towards Netherfield. Seeing Darcy's raised eyebrow, Elizabeth smiled. "No, I am not leading you to Netherfield. There is a path that leads off to Oakham Mount. It is near the middle of the way between the two estates. Oakham Mount is my favorite place in the world to go and think, or read a book in peace. Jane is the only other member of my family who would venture so far, and even then, that it rare. From the top, you can see the neighborhood.

It is also a wonderful place to take in the sunrise."

"Ah, I see we are of like minds when it comes to watching sunrises. There is a ridge near my home in Derbyshire that is my favorite place to watch the sunrise. The view of the sun on the water of the pond, near the woods, is incredible."

"That does sound pleasant. So you are fond of nature?"

Darcy nodded. "I feel the most comfort at my estate. The land has been in my family for many generations, and it feels as if my father and grandfather are at my side, a part of the land itself. It is difficult to explain to most of the *ton* the draw the land has for me."

"From what I have heard of high society, it is a unique way of thinking. My mother tells me constantly that I am not being a proper young lady when I am constantly tramping about in the woods and trails, coming home with the hem of my gown filthy and sometimes torn from tree branches." Elizabeth looked down towards the ground.

"Tree branches? Am I to understand from your statement that you climb trees?" Darcy attempted to keep a straight face.

Elizabeth pulled her hand from his arm and

stopped walking. "It would be best to return to the house now. I am sure you will wish to be on your way, now that you know I am far from being a proper young lady."

"On the contrary, Miss Elizabeth, I was just considering the many trees I have climbed over the years, including one just last month. My valet was scandalized when he saw the condition of my clothing. Fortunately, I was wearing some of my work clothes, and not any of my dress clothing. If it had been my better clothes, I believe my valet would have been far too mortified to remain in my employ."

Finally, Elizabeth's eyes rose so she could look into his. "You are not disgusted by my actions?"

Darcy stepped to her side and took hold of her hand. "Miss Elizabeth, there is nothing about you which has caused me distress or disgust. You are just the sort of young lady I have longed to meet. Would you mind if we were to sit down?"

Elizabeth shook her head and followed him to a nearby overturned tree trunk. Darcy took out a handkerchief and placed it down to protect her gown. Laughing lightly, she sat down and Darcy sat next to her.

"Miss Elizabeth, I wish to tell you about myself, if you would allow it."

"Of course, Mr Darcy. I will listen."

Taking a deep breath, Darcy began. "My father died when I was but a child. My mother loves me, I have no doubts in her regard for me. But I have lived my life knowing that my mother did not love my father as deeply as I believed she should. After the mourning period was over, my mother married Lord Covington. They have a daughter together, my sister, Georgiana. She is near twelve years of age. Lord Covington's estate is further north of my estate, and he is not comfortable staying at Pemberley. That is my estate, Pemberley. Not long before they married, my mother sent me off to school. Though I know she loves me, there were times I felt as if she would have preferred I have been the son of Lord Covington.

While I was at school, Mother became Lady Covington, and Pemberley was left to the servants and staff to tend to until my graduation. Then I moved home to my estate. All the while, as Mother was making a new life with Covington, and my sister was born, I began to feel lonely. I saw my mother moving forward, not mourning the man who had made her a widow at such a young age. I wanted what I had never known before, I wanted a loving marriage with a young lady who will love me, wish to be a part of my life, will be a partner to me rather than a decoration on my arm. It would be my greatest wish to have my wife be able to discuss everything with me, aid me in decisions of the estate, be intelligent and able to give me her advice and opinions as well. Not just what they think I would wish to hear, but their true opinion on matters."

"I am afraid you would find me to be too opinionated for my own good. My mother tells me this constantly." Elizabeth stated, unable to look at Darcy.

Taking a finger, Darcy gently lifted her chin to look towards him. "Miss Elizabeth, from the sounds of it, your mother has a very low opinion of you. And she might be correct for most men of the *ton*, but, as I have told you, I am not like most men of the *ton*. What I see in you thrills me, I am impressed by the young lady you are. You are beautiful, intoxicatingly so. You are kind natured and caring of others, it is clear to see the way you are welcomed to most any conversation. I witnessed this happen last night at the assembly. No matter who you spoke to, it was clear they enjoyed your company and were pleased to see you."

"And you are highly intelligent. I can only imagine the debates you and I will have. Your father told me that you have a voracious appetite for books and are constantly learning. This tells me you will be able to assist in changes that the estate will need to make in the years to come, as advances in crop rotations come about, as well as modernizing the household in the future. You would also be a good influence on my sister, as she has only been exposed to ladies of the *ton*."

"I am sure that your family would disapprove of your marrying someone such as me. They would most likely find you to be deranged and require you to be placed in a sanitarium while they sent me off to the continent, most likely to France, to be rid of me permanently." Elizabeth tried to keep a smile on her face, though she was far from teasing him.

"My mother and I have already spoken of what I wish to find in a wife. She is well aware of my unorthodox choices, and how they will be viewed by others of our society. But Mother also knows that I am my own Master, with my own estate, and that I despise London society. It has taken extreme measures to force me to travel to Town, especially during the Season."

"Perhaps we should walk some more." Elizabeth stated, feeling out of sorts with all that this young man had said to her. *How can he think he has found the perfect wife, in just a matter of a few hours? We have not known each other a full day and he is talking of the future? I do find him appealing, and intelligent, but I wish to know him better.*

Darcy stood, offering a hand to aid Elizabeth in standing. As soon as she was on her feet, Darcy wrapped her hand around his arm and began to walk again. "So this is your favorite path?"

Elizabeth smiled. "It is. I love the flowers which grow through this area in the spring and summer. And at the top of Oakham Mount is the most incredible sight of the area. Sometimes, when I was young, I would pretend I was a princess, and all that I could see was my kingdom."

"And did you have a prince to come riding up the hillside to rescue you from dragons?" Darcy teased.

"I saved myself from the dragons, Sir. Though I did pretend the prince would rescue me from any mice in the kingdom. I am far from fond of mice."

Darcy openly laughed. "Miss Elizabeth, I am amazed to find you afraid of anything. As I have no difficulty with mice, I would be willing to come to your aid."

"So, Mr Darcy, tell me more about you. You attended school and university, correct? What were your favorite subjects? What sort of books do you prefer reading? Do you like music?"

A smile graced Darcy's lips. "I enjoyed history and languages at school, also reading and writing. I have written some poetry myself, though the pages are now locked away at Pemberley. No one else even knows of my attempts, so you now own one of my secrets. Reading, I would have to go with everything. I enjoy histories, of course, but I also find pleasure in reading poetry and other forms of literature. Here is another secret, I purchase novels for my library, claiming they are for Georgiana when she visits, but they are a delightful diversion from time to time. My library at Pemberley is incredible, the work of several generations. The book shop in Lambton is my favorite place to visit."

"Lambton? My Aunt Gardiner was born and raised in Lambton. Is it close to Pemberley?"

Darcy smiled again. "It is but five miles from Pemberley. What was your aunt's family name?"

"Moreland. I believe her father owned a milliner shop." Elizabeth said.

"Harlan Moreland? I remember him from my youth. He was a kind man. His wife always made sweet biscuits and gave them to us. They were delicious. Your aunt has two brothers, if I remember correctly." Darcy reminisced.

"Indeed, Robert and Andrew. Robert lives in Ireland now, with his wife's family. They are fabric manufacturers and my uncle imports the fabric to sell in Town. Andrew is a sailor, first mate on a ship, though I cannot remember the name. He was in London last summer and told us of his journeys all over the world. It was interesting to hear of the places I have read about over the years."

"That does sound enjoyable. I delayed taking a grand tour, but have always wanted to travel. From the sounds of your description of Mr Moreland's travel, you would find traveling a pleasure as well." Darcy watched Elizabeth for her reaction.

"I have enjoyed the traveling I have done, and look forward to more in the future. I went with my Uncle Gardiner to Ireland two years ago. I have a gift for languages, so my uncle says he will take me with him on future trips. His import business is quite successful."

"Well, I will hope for future trips, if that is what you wish." Darcy said with a smile. "Though I would be more content to take you on your travels."

"I do not think we should be thinking of our traveling together at this point, Mr Darcy. Unless it is making our way back to the house, for I am certain you will wish to make your way to Netherfield to rest."

"I was invited to break my fast with you and your family. If it meets with your approval, I would be pleased to remain at Longbourn to do so."

"Mr Darcy, you saw my mother and younger sisters at the Assembly. My mother can become agitated with my sisters and their exuberance, causing her to become vocal with her nerves. With them being tired from the Assembly, I am certain that my youngest sister, especially, will be far from her best behavior."

Darcy took Elizabeth's hand in his and brought it to his lips. "I have difficult relations as well, Miss Elizabeth. Your sisters are quite young, and it is normal for them to be excited. I wish to remain at Longbourn for breakfast."

~~~~~~~~ ** ~~~~~~~~
~~~~~~~~

CHAPTER 5

After breakfast, Darcy returned to Netherfield. He found Bingley was resting, after the housekeeper had cleaned his scratches and put on salve before bandaging. The housekeeper informed Darcy that the scratches were deep, she was shocked to see how bad they were, and stating she was hoping they would not become infected and the young man take a fever. There had been no word of Miss Bingley. It was believed that the young lady had fled to Town, hiding out with some of her friends. Knowing her brother would not announce to the world her behavior, Caroline would feel secure that he would not reveal what had happened at Netherfield.

Darcy went to his rooms, preparing to rest for an hour or two. His valet was standing ready to aid him. "Billings, have you been waiting all this time for me?"

"Sir, it was unknown when you would return, and, after all that happened here tonight, I felt it was necessary to be here to assist you. I wish to state for the record that I am deeply sorry for not being in the rooms last night. I know you released me for the evening, but if I had remained here, none of the events would have happened. Miss Bingley would never have been able to slip into your bed if I were in the room."

"You did as you were told, and you are not to be held responsible for anything that happened. Miss Bingley is insane, and she would have tried something else. She was angry with me for the way I spoke to her at the end of the Assembly, and I should have known her desperation was increased by her jealousy. Are you ready for this, Billings? I danced with a young lady I met last night. She was amazing, beautiful, witty, intelligent, and very kind. I plan to learn more about her in the coming days."

"My congratulations, Mr Darcy. It would be a pleasure to see you find the future Mrs Darcy. The staff had worried that Miss Bingley would somehow force you into marriage, so it will be a pleasure to see you with another young lady." The loyal valet had been with Darcy for nearly a decade and had been granted leave to speak openly with his master.

"The staff will be pleased with Miss Elizabeth Bennet. If I am successful, I wish to secure her hand before Christmas." Darcy said, a dreamy look upon his face.

"Very good, Sir. Now, when would you like me to wake you?" Billings said as he gathered Darcy's discarded clothing into a pile to be laundered.

Darcy pulled out his pocket watch at looked at the time. It was a quarter past eleven. "Wake me at two.

And have a bath drawn for me then. Thank you, Billings. That will be all for now."

Lying down on the bed, Darcy pulled the bedding over him and drifted off to sleep, with dreams of a certain young lady, her dark curls, and the sparkle in her eyes. A smile was permanently etched on his lips at the remembrance of parting from Elizabeth.

"Miss Elizabeth, I thank you for a most enjoyable morning. You are indeed a most charming companion for a long walk. Might I impose upon you to allow me to call on you again tomorrow?"

"You are a glutton for punishment, Mr Darcy. But, if you insist, I will ask you to meet me at Oakham Mount. I believe we can learn more about each other away from the house, where it is quiet."

"I look forward to our meeting. Would the same time as this morning's walk be a good time for you?" Darcy's heart was soaring.

"Yes, Mr Darcy, it will be perfect. Have a good rest and give Mr Bingley my regards for his speedy recovery."

"Do not forget to be careful, Miss Elizabeth. Miss Bingley is truly a threat to your safety."

"I will take your warning to heart. Susan is

pleased to be able to walk with me, for it gives her a break from her other duties."

"Then I am pleased to be of service to you as well, Miss Susan." Darcy then leaned over Elizabeth's hand and placed a gentle kiss on her hand. "Until tomorrow, Miss Elizabeth."

Darcy mounted his horse and rode off in the direction of Netherfield.

The memory of their time together that morning was enough to fill Darcy's dreams with warmth and desire for more.

~~ ** ~~

Caroline Bingley had arrived in Town just an hour earlier. She entered the Hurst townhouse, making her way to the rooms she used when she stayed there. She quickly washed up and changed clothing, then gathered some items into a travel bag and went to her jewel safe in the dressing room. She opened the safe with the key she kept in her desk drawer, retrieving the bag of coins and bills. She had approximately one thousand pounds that she had hidden away for emergency purposes. This would give her a start, and it was time to find a husband immediately. If she were to marry, her brother and sister could not force her to go anywhere. She would settle for a husband who was gullible and would believe anything she told him. It would not be difficult to find such a man.

Knowing her friend, Miss Armitage, was staying in her aunt's home, and had invited her to stay with her anytime, Caroline made her way to Regent Street. Miss Bingley was shown into the drawing room, where Miss Armitage and her aunt were taking tea.

"Caroline, I had no idea that you had returned to Town. What a pleasure to see you." Ruth Armitage exclaimed.

"Oh, Ruth, my brother has been absolutely horrible. I have never seen him be so awful. And Louisa was beside him in treating me poorly. They are determined to keep me a slave to the family, not allowing me to be courted by a gentleman who found me to be charming. If I have any hope of marrying and having a life of my own, I must do so away from them. They even threatened me with sending me to our aunt's home in Scotland if I did not live by their decisions for my life."

"But your brother is such a gentle and kind man. I cannot believe he would be so cruel." Miss Armitage exclaimed.

Caroline had tears welling up in her eyes. "The gentleman was a dear friend of Charles, and my brother would not have it. He is also angry because I spoke against the young lady he had claimed as his latest love, for she is a country nobody. His words were that if he could not marry where his heart lay, he would forbid me to be happy."

Miss Armitage was shocked. "You poor dear. Well, you are fortunate to have arrived when you did. We have a dinner party planned for this very evening. My aunt has invited several young men who are looking for wives. There is one in particular I was planning to write to you with regards to introducing you to him. Mr Geoffrey Goodman. He has an estate in Devon, and has a fortune close to that of your brother's. Mr Goodman is somewhat timid, though I think you would be perfect for him."

"Well, I would be willing to meet him." Caroline pretended to be shy about the situation. "Would there be a problem staying here with you for a fortnight? I do not wish to deal with my brother or sister, and I know the staff at Hurst's townhouse would inform them of every move I make."

"You are always welcome, Caroline. Is that not correct, Aunt?"

Mrs Armitage nodded her head. "You are welcome, Miss Bingley. I can remember being the youngest sibling and the officiousness of my brothers in particular."

"It is frustrating that they will not allow me to find

the same sort of happiness that they wish for in their own lives." Caroline stated, wiping at the tears.

"Let me show you to the rooms you may use while here." Miss Armitage said as she looped her arm with Caroline's.

~~ ** ~~

Viscount Anthony Fitzwilliam was furious when his brother arrived at their estate. Richard was a colonel in the regulars and was one of the most honorable men in England, only a hair below their cousin, Darcy. Their father's apoplexy attack had been during an argument with Anthony, and the heir knew that his proper brother would be a pain to live with.

"Richard, there is no need for you to be here. If Father's condition worsens, I can send you an express."

Colonel Fitzwilliam ignored his brother's obvious attempt to be rid of him. "I appreciate your offer, Anthony, but I am determined to be of assistance to Father. Aunt Anne sent for me, as she said Father wished me here. Until Father tells me to leave, I will remain here."

"I am just saying that it is not necessary. I am sure your time training the new men would be better than sitting around here."

"Oh, it is a pleasant holiday from my duties. I will enjoy riding about the estate and seeing what improvements are needed for the tenants. With the snow setting in early this year, it is necessary to ensure the tenants are safe and sound in their homes, though I am sure that it has slipped your mind. I will meet with the steward later to go over the books. I wish to assist Father in whatever way I can."

"You will not inherit the estate, what business is it of yours to tend to the affairs here? You are being nosy and presumptuous. I am more than capable of handling the estate matters until Father recovers."

Richard stood, extending himself to his full height. Being a tall and muscularly built man, the Colonel had learned to use his size to intimidate rather than fight his brother. "Anthony, until the day Father dies, you are not the Master of Matlock. You have already shown your inability to manage the affairs of your own life, let alone the estate. I will not stand by and watch the estate be destroyed by your frivolous life style."

Anthony became irate. "How dare you speak to me so? You are the second born, the spare, and you are worthless with regards to the estate. You should return to your unit and leave the important matters to the heir of the estate. And, in case you forgot, that is me."

"YOU WILL STOP THIS IMMEDIATELY!" came the voice of their aunt. Lady Anne had heard the conversation and had had her fill of her eldest nephew. "Anthony, you are a disgrace. If my father knew of your behavior, he would have cut you from the inheritance. As it is, your behavior has caused such a decline in the estate's income that it may be a moot point. Unless there are large surpluses of funds come to the estate, my brother may be forced to sell it in its entirety. Then you will be heir to what, a whole lot of nothing. Your mother spoiled you, and what good has come from it? You are to blame for your father's condition as well. I know you were arguing with him over your debts he was attempting to cover. You nearly killed your father. I have left strict orders that you are not to be left alone with my brother, for I do not trust you to not harm him further."

"Aunt, I will ask you to leave this house immediately." Anthony bellowed. "You have no standing to order me about, or to dictate to the staff as to who may or may not visit Father."

Richard moved towards his brother, grabbing hold of the Viscount's coat front. "You will apologize to Aunt Anne or I will beat you until you apologize to her. I will not allow you to treat our aunt with such disrespect."

"Take your hands off me this moment." Anthony demanded. "You will be cut from your allowance as soon as Father dies. You will not get one coin from me."

"There is no coin for you to give anyone." Richard stated loudly. "You have wasted everything our family built up over generations. I have saved money from my wages, and I still have my inheritance from Grandmother Fitzwilliam. You, on the other hand, have nothing after Matlock is gone. However will you live?" Richard really had no care what happened to his brother after their father was gone. At that point, Richard was determined he would wash his hands clean of his elder brother.

"I will marry. The dowry of my wife will be enough to sustain me and keep the estate from total ruin." Anthony was desperate.

"Who would be foolish enough to allow you to marry their daughter? Only a wealthy businessman who wished to rise in society and you would never stoop so low." Lady Anne stated.

"You could speak to Darcy again. I am sure that you can convince him to assist me with my debts. He has been comfortable for quite some time, and has more than he needs to run Pemberley and Darcy

House."

"He is also saving towards improvements to his estate, and preparing for his future children when he marries. Why should he throw away his future because you cannot control your indulgences? William deserves to be happy, to find a wife and have children. He has the right to pass on his inheritance to his heir, not bail out his cousin."

"And Albert is set against my marrying Georgiana in the future? Her dowry would save the family and the estate."

"My husband and my son agree that Georgiana will not be brokered in marriage to you. And I agree as well. Georgiana is only a child, it will be many years before she is old enough to marry anyone, but we will not arrange a marriage to someone who is irresponsible."

Fury overcame the Viscount. "None of you will lift a finger to assist me? I am to be abandoned to the streets, with no one to care whether I live or die?"

"You have made your bed, Brother. Now you shall have to lay in it." Richard stated as he let go of his brother's coat and left the room.

Once Lady Anne returned to her brother's side, Anthony stepped to the sideboard and poured a drink.

Seething, he took the drink and stood by the fireplace, watching the flames dancing about. "I will make each and every one of you pay for your treatment of me."

~~ ** ~~

It had been a week since Caroline Bingley disappeared from Netherfield, and still no word was to be had. Bingley had mended, but was still quite agitated with his sister's behavior. He feared her future attacks against those she was angered with, and prayed daily that she would behave. His greatest fear was any harm she might cause the Bennet family.

Each day had seen Bingley and Darcy visiting Longbourn and enjoying time spent in the company of the eldest Bennet sisters. The young men were delighted with the time they were able to know the young ladies better, and were often invited to dine with the family. Bingley was pleasantly surprised to see his friend so taken with Miss Elizabeth; he had never seen Darcy so taken with anyone. Darcy in love was most interesting, as the Master of Pemberley was like a young lad, making a fool of himself with his besotted ways.

Unknown to Bingley, Darcy had been meeting Elizabeth at Oakham Mount each morning. Their conversations had ranged from their favorite childhood memories to their dreams for the future.

They had each spoken of their favorite poets, composers, even their idea of the perfect day. Though Elizabeth was fighting hard to keep from admitting it, she was well on her way of falling in love with the bold man who announced his intentions towards her the first day of their acquaintance. She wished for more time to pass, to assure herself that it was not a passing fancy she was feeling. Marriage was a lifelong journey with someone else. And Elizabeth wished to marry for the strongest reason, a great love.

In her heart, Elizabeth knew she had found this love with Darcy. All she needed to do was convince her mind that it was true.

~~ ** ~~

George Wickham sat in a pub in London, drinking his ale. The man who sat near him was offering a job and a way to exact revenge against his longtime nemesis, Fitzwilliam Darcy. Wickham had grown up at Pemberley; his father was the steward for the previous Mr Darcy. Old Mr Wickham took care of the estate after Darcy's father died, making sure that Pemberley was protected for the prince of the estate to return to his throne. Wickham was furious with his father, taking care of the young master's interest rather than assisting his own son in taking over for Darcy.

Darcy's father had provided in his will for Wickham to attend school, just as the young prince, though Old Mr Darcy had decided on his godson taking orders and inheriting a comfortable living at the village of Kympton. This was the furthest thing from young Wickham's desires. He had grown accustomed to being important, flaunting the fact that he was the godson of the previous Master of Pemberley and demanding being treated as he felt he deserved.

Wickham had abused many of the young ladies who worked at the estate. From upstairs maids to tenant daughters, Wickham meant to conquer as many as possible, thinking he was a great lover who would be greatly desired.

His father died the year after Wickham and Darcy graduated from the University. Having seen Wickham's taste for the ladies, and his taking them willingly or not, Darcy decided to put an end to the young man's behavior at Pemberley. Knowing Wickham would never take orders, nor should he be in such a profession, Darcy settled the sum of three thousand pounds added to the one thousand that was written in Darcy's father's will. He gave the funds to his former friend and forbade Wickham to ever return to Pemberley.

Two years went by until Wickham was desperate

for assistance. He made his way to Pemberley and claimed his desire to take orders, wishing to accept the living at Kympton. Darcy refused to give him the living, stating he had already been compensated for giving it up. This infuriated Wickham. In his mind, he felt that he was owed more than a mere four thousand pounds. After all, it was Wickham's father who had kept Pemberley productive and strong. Wickham saw himself as the heir to Pemberley, not Darcy.

With Darcy's refusal to give Wickham more funds, the latter decided that one day, he would find a way to seek revenge against his childhood friend. This came in the form a young lady named Victoria Lawson. Victoria was the sister of one of Darcy's university friends, and Darcy took a liking to the young lady. Wickham was in London, attempting to find ways to acquire funds, when he saw Miss Lawson again. Though Darcy had come to think of Miss Lawson more as a sister, Wickham knew that he could strike at Darcy through her.

Charming the young lady was simple, Wickham was well versed in such behavior. When it came time for the innocent Miss Lawson to succumb to Wickham's seduction, she refused. That did not stop Wickham, as he had no compulsion in forcing himself upon young ladies. He took her virtue, leaving her battered in the process. He also left her with something else. Several months later, Wickham heard Miss Lawson had drowned. The truth was learned later, Victoria Lawson could not live with her disgrace and killed herself and the unborn babe she carried. Wickham made certain that Darcy knew that the babe had been his.

Now, this man before him wished to pay him to bring more misery to Darcy.

"My employer wishes to hire you to bring Fitzwilliam Darcy to disgrace. He wishes to make the disgrace publically known, ruining his good name forever." The man, calling himself Culiver, stated as he called for more drinks.

"And, just who is your employer?" Wickham asked.

"You have no need to know, all you need to know is that when you have accomplished your job, you will be rewarded handsomely. At the moment, Mr Darcy is visiting a friend of his in Hertfordshire. Mr Bingley, I believe you are acquainted with the man, has taken the estate of Netherfield Park, near Meryton. Mr Darcy will be staying there for some time. I have been authorized to purchase you a commission in the militia, which has recently arrived at Meryton and will be there for the winter. This will allow you the freedom to interact with the citizens of the neighborhood, as well as spread gossip against the man. But my employer requires Mr Darcy to be ruined, something that will permanently destroy his reputation. Do you think you can manage such a feat?"

"And how much is your employer willing to pay for my work?"

"We will give you five hundred pounds now, and when the job is complete, you will receive ten thousand pounds." Culiver said, reaching into his pocket and pulling out a leather folder containing the funds promised.

Wickham became quite pleased. "This is on top of the commission, you do not expect me to purchase it with this paltry amount. I will require this to buy my way into the confidence of others once I arrive in Meryton."

"Of course, as I said, my employer is prepared to purchase the commission as well. So, do we have an understanding? Oh, and my employer expects this to be handled quickly. When you arrive, begin investigating possible ways to destroy Fitzwilliam Darcy quickly."

"We have a deal, Mr Culiver. I shall leave for Meryton tomorrow. Will you have the commission purchased by then?"

"I will. And I will send word to you here when I have it ready for you." Culiver stood to leave. "Until later."

Wickham sat back and finished his drink. *Oh, yes, this will be sweet revenge.*

~~~~~~~~ ** ~~~~~~~~
~~~~~~~~

CHAPTER 6

Darcy was excited as he looked over his reflection in the mirror. There was a complete change in his looks, even his valet commented on the contentment that was visible in Darcy's features. Bingley had been wearing a similar look upon his face, the look of being in love with a wonderful woman.

Darcy had been at Netherfield for one and one half months, and the only days he had not spent in the delightful company of Miss Elizabeth Bennet had been days when the weather had kept the young men trapped at Netherfield. Those days usually found Darcy pacing about his sitting room or sitting in the library with an open book on his lap, not reading a word as he daydreamed of the young lady who had stolen his heart.

Bingley was surviving such days in better form than his friend, though he dearly missed his Miss Bennet, as well. Louisa and Hurst had remained at Netherfield, planning to stay until after Christmas. They had talked of returning to London to search for Caroline, but Hurst preferred to keep his wife safely away from her sister, especially after they learned of their family increasing finally. The Hursts had wished for a child of their own, and had worried that they would never be parents. When Louisa learned she was finally with child, Hurst announced that she was to remain as far from her sister as possible. With Caroline's unpredictable behavior, Hurst did not trust her near his wife.

Determining his future, Bingley had decided he would ask Miss Bennet for her hand in marriage. He knew he was in love with her, that she was the one woman who made him feel complete and brought joy to his life. Bingley had discussed the future with Jane, and was pleased to learn she had many of the same dreams and desires that he did. The past two days had been snowing, keeping Bingley and Darcy at Netherfield. Bingley had wished to ask for a private moment with Mr Bennet, but had to wait until the storm abated.

He was certain that it would not be long before Darcy was asking Elizabeth to marry him. The change in his friend was amazing. His natural shyness was hidden when in the presence of Elizabeth Bennet, allowing him to speak openly, smile constantly, even laughing openly in public. Never had Bingley seen such contentment in the Master of Pemberley, a man who carried the weight of the world upon his shoulders.

The weather had calmed, leaving behind a blanket of white across the neighborhood. Bingley and Darcy decided to make their way into Meryton before visiting Longbourn, wishing to take gifts to their ladies. They stopped at the mercantile, purchasing a box of confections, before stepping across the street to the bookshop. After Darcy chose two new books for Elizabeth, the men were planning to make their way to the milliner shop for some new ribbons for their ladies.

That had been their plan. It was quickly changed when a young man stepped from the mercantile nodding his head slightly towards Darcy. Wickham. Darcy's expression changed immediately, seeing the man who had been a thorn in his side for many years. *What is he doing here, of all places? I must do everything I can to keep him from Elizabeth. I will not allow him to cause her harm.*

Wickham strolled over to his former friend. "Darcy, what a pleasant surprise to see you here. Bingley, how are you? I have not seen you in years. What brings the two of you here, to this country village?"

"Bingley has leased an estate near here and I am here on a holiday. What brings you here?" Darcy attempted to keep his expression and voice neutral. Since learning of Miss Lawson's death, due to Wickham's violation of her, his dislike of Wickham had grown.

"As I have been in need of an occupation, I recently purchased a commission in the militia regiment which is encamped here, at Meryton. I am excited to be a part of the neighborhood, as it seems quite pleasant. There are quite a few pretty young ladies to keep me smiling as well." Wickham gave Darcy a wolfish sneer.

"If you bring about harm to any young lady in the neighborhood, Wickham, you will regret it. These are good people, not used to the likes of a scoundrel such as you." Darcy said with a low growl. "Do I make myself clear?"

"I have the right to flirt with the young ladies, Darcy. There is nothing you can do to stop me from doing so. If the ladies enjoy the attention I give them, that decision is for them to make, not you. Do no attempt to discredit me, or I will make certain your friend, Lawson, is mortified to hear the details of the night I spent with his sister. She was delightful, warm and tight as a virtuous maid should be."

Darcy could not stop himself as he reached out with his fist and connected with Wickham's eye. "You vulgar animal, how dare you speak of a lady in such a manner? She was a proper young lady, never causing you or anyone harm. And you destroyed her."

"She took her own life, Darcy. I had nothing to do

with her death." Wickham staggered back from the man. I was in Town when Miss Lawson died, so how could it be my fault?"

"You ruined her, forced yourself upon her. You took her virtue and left her with your child. When she learned of the babe, she could not live with the knowledge that the babe was yours. That is why she took her life. That is why she preferred death than to live her life with a part of you growing inside her." Darcy was furious and unable to reign in his temper.

"She may have told her brother and yourself such a story, but Victoria Lawson was pleased to be in my bed and granted me access to her most private delights. It does bother me that she could so easily kill my child. That was not right, though I was in no position to be a father. Too bad you did not offer to save her and marry her. You could have given her a proper name for her bastard child. But then again, the great and powerful Fitzwilliam Darcy could not be lowered to such behavior."

Wickham found himself on the ground. Shaking his head, Wickham tried to make sense of what had happened. Two men in red coats came running towards them. "Wickham, are you well?" one called out.

"No need to worry, Denny, I am fine." Wickham

replied. "Just a misunderstanding with an old friend of mine; I am fine."

The young man named Denny stood still, frowning at the situation before him. "Sir, I would suggest you refrain from further misunderstandings with Lieutenant Wickham. He is a member of our regiment and I would not wish you to regret your actions. We protect our officers."

"Denny, no need to threaten Darcy, he is a pillar of society and was momentarily overcome with emotion over a tragedy which happened a year ago."

"If you can forgive his behavior, Wickham, then I will as well. But if he causes you any further harm, I will have him arrested." Denny puffed out his chest, feeling he was important.

Bingley took hold of his friend's shoulders and turned him from Wickham. "Darcy, let us finish our shopping. We should be on our way soon."

Darcy's eyes moved from Wickham to Bingley, finally able to calm himself. "You are correct, Bingley. Let us finish and leave the village."

~~ ** ~~

Wickham watched his former friend walk with Bingley to the milliner shop. This was surprising to

Wickham, unable to think of a reason the Great Fitzwilliam Darcy, the prince of Pemberley, would be stepping into a milliner shop. Taking a peek through the window, Wickham was able to see Darcy choosing ribbons. This made Wickham's heart soar. *This will be easier than I thought, as Darcy must have a young lady he is in love with. I will need to do some investigating and learn all I can of her.*

Denny walked up behind Wickham and glanced in the window. "Ah, it appears the men are purchasing gifts for the young ladies of Longbourn."

"What can you tell me about the ladies?" Wickham asked.

"Five sisters, the two eldest are the jewels of the neighborhood. Miss Jane Bennet is currently being courted by Mr Bingley. Her next eldest sister, Miss Elizabeth, is believed to have captured Mr Darcy's attention. The man would have to be blind and an idiot to not be drawn to her. Miss Bennet is beautiful, do not mistake me, but Miss Elizabeth is beautiful and vibrant. I am partial to dark hair as well, so that adds to the young lady's charms."

"Miss Elizabeth Bennet. I must learn more about her." Wickham whispered to himself.

~~ ** ~~

Darcy and Bingley arrived at Longbourn, excited to see their ladies. Mrs Bennet was in the drawing room when the young men were escorted in.

"Gentlemen, what a pleasure to see you today, as your presence has been missed with the recent weather."

"Thank you, Mrs Bennet, for your kind and warm welcome. We have missed being in the company of your family, feeling as depressing as the weather was." Bingley stated. "Where are your lovely daughters this morning?"

"Mary is in the music room, learning a new piece with the master who has recently been hired to work with her. Kitty is reading in the study, with her father, as she is becoming nearly as well read as her sister, Elizabeth. Lydia is in her rooms, resting. But the two daughters you are most likely inquiring after are in the dry room off the kitchen. Jane is fond of making her own scented waters, and Lizzy is assisting her sister in the preparations of the flowers they had stored there. Lizzy also makes some of the best salves and poultices, so I am sure she is working with her dried herbs to make those."

Darcy was impressed. "It is pleasant to see the young ladies so productively employed in activities."

"Well, with the holidays only a month away, the

girls always enjoy being able to give some of the items to the tenants and staff as gifts. The little girls on our estate always enjoy receiving some of Jane's rose water or lavender water. And everyone appreciates Lizzy's talent with herbal remedies. She is often able to assist the apothecary in tending the sick and injured. And Mrs Hill says there is nothing better for her aching feet than the salve Lizzy makes to help with the swelling and pain."

"Your daughters are well liked by all who meet them, Mrs Bennet." Bingley stated. "You should be proud of them."

"I am, Mr Bingley, though it would be nice to see them well settled. I worry about their futures, and wish to see them as happily settled as I am. That is the hope of all mothers, I guess."

"And a noble wish for your daughters, Mrs Bennet. They have the perfect role model for a good mother and devoted Mistress of Longbourn." Darcy said, bowing over the hand of the woman who had created the woman he loved. "Bingley and I did some shopping today, and we could not stop ourselves from purchasing gifts for your family. You have been so kind as to feed us most days, and have been gracious enough to tolerate our constant attentions, so we wished to repay you in some small way."

"Oh, Mr Darcy, it is not necessary to bring us gifts. I do appreciate your generosity though. Let me call for the girls to join us."

Within a few moments, Mrs Bennet had gathered her daughters in the parlor. "Mr Darcy, it is a pleasure to have you and Mr Bingley return to Longbourn." Elizabeth said with a smile. "We have missed you recently."

"Bingley and I have missed you as well." Darcy said as he bowed over the hand of his beloved. "If the weather had not cleared, I believe I would have gone mad with despair."

"Miss Bennet, it is a pleasure to see you." Bingley said as he walked to Jane's side. The young men took seats near their lady loves, as the younger Bennet sisters found seats in the room.

"Ladies, we have enjoyed your company so much of late, when the weather cleared, Bingley and I decided to do some shopping to bring presents for you all." Darcy was holding a stack of packages. He handed out the confections to the oo's and ah's of all the ladies. "Miss Elizabeth, this is for you." He stated as he handed her the wrapped books.

"Mr Darcy, this is far too kind of you. I could not possibly accept such a gift."

"Lizzy, as I am well aware of you and Mr Darcy courting, I would say it is allowable to accept such a gift." Mrs Bennet declared.

Elizabeth and Darcy were in shock. "Mamma, how did you know of our courting?" Elizabeth asked.

"Do you find me to be a silly woman with no intelligence? Lizzy, Mr Darcy has been here almost daily, spending his time strictly with you. And, if that was not enough, I am aware that Susan has been chaperoning your meetings to Oakham Mount in the early hours of most mornings. What more rational answer could it be than the two of you are meeting quietly to court with no one to disrupt you?"

Darcy began to laugh. "Well, it was bound to come out sooner or later. Mrs Bennet, may I ask if you approve of our courtship?"

"I must say that I do not. You have been courting for over a month now, I believe it is time to move forward. Do you intend to ask my daughter to marry you?" Mrs Bennet was determined.

"MAMMA!" Elizabeth cried out. "We have not discussed becoming engaged, and I wish to take some more time before I am ready to commit. And I am not certain Mr Darcy will even wish to marry into such a family."

"Oh, I am finding your mother more and more endearing. I thank you, Mrs Bennet, for this is the direction I wish to take my relationship with your daughter. Have no doubt, I pray to win her hand before the holidays arrive." Darcy was openly laughing. "Now, here is another gift for all of you. We stopped by the milliner shop, and Mr Green stated that he had a new shipment of ribbons arrived on Monday, but the weather has kept you ladies away. Bingley and I took the liberty to purchase a selection for you to choose from."

Looking to where his friend was sitting, he was surprised to see Jane Bennet sitting alone. Curious, his eyebrow lifted questioningly at Jane. A blush appeared on her cheeks, attempting to keep from drawing attention, Jane moved her eyes towards the door to the hallway, then behind her. If Darcy was a betting man, he would have placed a large bet of his friend having made his way to Mr Bennet's study to have a discussion of importance to Bingley.

The sisters were thrilled at the selection of ribbons they were presented. "Mr Darcy, you are a generous man with good taste." Mrs Bennet stated. "Do I remember correctly, do you have a young sister?"

"I do, she is quite young, only twelve years of age. And yes, I do enjoy purchasing gifts for her, including ribbons. So I have had practice in choosing ribbons." His answer shocked even himself. It was rare that he would divulge such private information about himself. It was clear that he was becoming comfortable with the Bennet family.

"She must be pleased to have such a kind elder brother." Mrs Bennet stood and prepared to leave the room. "I will check on refreshments. I presume that you gentlemen will be joining us for dinner this evening. I am certain there will be some celebrating happening."

Elizabeth could not believe her mother's comments. Had she greatly underestimated her mother all her life? Mrs Bennet was quicker to deduce the truth of what was happening around her, far quicker than Elizabeth had given her credit.

Soon, Lydia and Kitty left the room, wishing to return to their activities, and Mary soon returned to the music lesson. Elizabeth, Jane, Darcy and Bingley found themselves alone in the drawing room. With Jane and Bingley having eyes only for each other, it was not long before Elizabeth and Darcy felt they were alone in the room.

"Miss Elizabeth, I have missed our meetings at Oakham Mount. I cannot begin to tell you how dear they have become to me."

“And to me, Mr Darcy.” Elizabeth replied. “I forgot to ask, have you any recent news on your uncle’s condition?”

“Mother wrote me that he is improving. She says he is better each day. She is worried though. My cousin, the heir to Matlock, is becoming almost cryptic in his behavior. Mother and my other cousin, Richard, are quite concerned with what Anthony might be planning. Richard is an honorable man; I have told you about his being a Colonel. His rank was not purchased, like many of the men of our society. He earned each promotion he has had.”

“He sounds like the sort of person worthy of friendship.” Elizabeth smiled. “So, the Colonel is concerned with regards to his brother’s behavior? What are they planning to do with their concerns?”

“As my uncle’s health improves, my cousin is speaking with Uncle of the need to protect the estate. If they can talk him into their plan, they will have the solicitor come to Matlock to sign papers for Anthony to be disowned. Then, when Anthony gambles and goes on his wild sprees, the estate will not be burdened with the losses. Richard should be the heir to the estate, he is much better prepared to take care of the estate, as he loves the land of his ancestors, as much as I love mine. Whenever he is visiting Matlock, Richard speaks with the steward and inspects the estate, making certain that any repairs which are needed are made. He takes care of the tenants, knowing they are the ones who make the estate profitable."

"He does seem to be the better of your two cousins. Your uncle has suffered greatly for his eldest son's actions. What will happen to the Viscount?" Elizabeth asked.

"Knowing my cousin, he will either be killed in a duel, drink himself to death, or end up in debtor's prison. Unfortunately, we can no longer watch over him and protect him. We have in the past and it has only caused further problems." Darcy was grieved by the situation.

Sensing the melancholy washing over the man beside her, Elizabeth attempted to change the subject. "Tell me more of your mother. What is she like?"

Smiling, Darcy instantly knew what she was doing. "Thank you, my dear Miss Elizabeth. Mother is a kind and loving lady, though she can be a most intimidating force to be reckoned with. She is slightly taller than Miss Bennet, with light brown hair, green eyes, and a smile that can make others feel at ease. She is the finest lady I have ever known, until I met a certain young lady from Longbourn who captured my heart." He raised a hand and gently placed it on her cheek. "You know that you have my heart, now and forever?"

Elizabeth blushed profusely. "Mr Darcy, I beg you, let us continue our discussion." Her eyes pleaded with him, yet they cried out to him that her desire be felt.

"Let me tell you of my father." Darcy took pity on Elizabeth. It was clear that she loved him, but she was having a difficult time being able to speak of it. "My father was the eldest, with one sister and one brother born after him. His sister died when she was five and ten, from a severe fever. Father was devastated, as he told me he doted on his sister. His description of her was that his sister, Rebecca, was all that was sweet and nice. There is a portrait of her on the wall at Pemberley. She was blonde, with curls, and bright, blue eyes. She had dimples when she smiled, which Father claimed was a family trait."

"I have seen your dimples, and find them quite intoxicating." Elizabeth said, her hand reaching for his cheek and touching the spot where the dimple was known to appear.

Darcy smiled, allowing her fingers to caress his left dimple. "My father had them as well. He said that his father also had them. My uncle was said to have had them, though I never saw the man smile. He was a sad man, as he lost his wife, in childbirth, the year after I was born. My uncle, Michael, died five years ago. He had become a recluse, not wishing to spend time with anyone, except a handful of servants who had been with him for years."

"How terrible, to lose the ones you love and shut yourself away from the world; such a lonely existence." Elizabeth declared. "So you are the last member of the Darcy family?"

"I am. Though, I look forward to marrying and having at least a dozen children to rebuild the family." Darcy could not help but notice the blush grow stronger in her cheeks.

Hearing a cough, Bingley attempted to draw attention to Jane and himself. "Darcy, let us take these young ladies out for a walk in the gardens."

"Bingley, my good friend, you have made a most wonderful suggestion. Ladies, do you approve?"

~~~~~~~~ ** ~~~~~~~~
~~~~~~~~

CHAPTER 7

After the walk, the men remained at Longbourn to dine before returning to Netherfield. Darcy was pleased for his friend, though envious of Bingley being able to openly declare his love for Jane Bennet. Darcy knew that Elizabeth loved him, it was clearly written in her eyes when she looked at him, but she was afraid of being in love. Everything was happening quickly, though she had come to express simple gestures, such as the sweet caress of his dimple. The simple touch spoke volumes of her heart. And he was certain, one day soon, he would have the joy of announcing to the world that he, Fitzwilliam Darcy, loved Miss Elizabeth Bennet.

Before leaving Longbourn, Darcy had a chance for a private meeting with Mr Bennet, informing him of Wickham's past behavior and warning Elizabeth's father of the danger the younger man posed to young ladies. It was advice Mr Bennet would soon wish he had heeded.

~~ ** ~~

It had been a week since Wickham had seen Darcy in Meryton, and he had also witnessed his former friend at a dinner held at Lucas Lodge. Darcy rarely left the side of Elizabeth Bennet, and Wickham took great joy in watching the man's behavior with the young lady.

Wickham had seen the look in his childhood friend's eyes. He knew that Darcy had developed feelings for this country miss, even if he had not acted upon them. Wickham also knew that this was the way he would strike back at Darcy. And he was certain he could convince some of the others in his unit to participate in Darcy's destruction.

Over the following days, Wickham learned all he could with regards to his prey. He learned that she was fond of long walks in the country, alone, in the early morning hours. And he had discovered Denny and Woods were also taken with Miss Elizabeth Bennet's ample curves. He knew he could supply them with drink and they would go along with his plans.

His employer wished to have Darcy ruined in public, and what better way than to have him involved in a scandal over the stolen virtue of a gentlewoman. Wickham planned the event to be done in such a manner that he could accuse Darcy of being the perpetrator, causing even more of a scandal. The one thing that Wickham wished the most was for Darcy to witness the ruining of his little chit. It would not be as painful to the spoiled and pampered Master of Pemberley, if Darcy did not see, with his own eyes, the fall from grace which the young lady would take.

Wickham determined to set his plan in motion on Friday morning, as his friends would have been up all night the night before on guard duty, so he would talk them into some fun before they rested for the day. He also planned to send a message to Darcy, requesting a meeting between the two of them, which would have the man arriving at the determined location nearly an hour after the group had begun to enjoy her favors.

Having watched Miss Elizabeth walking for two mornings in a row, Wickham concluded that the young lady held a preference for Oakham Mount. This would be their point of attack; the men would be waiting for her at the top of the hill. Wickham had no qualms with dealing with the maid who accompanied Elizabeth either, for she was young and pretty.

Wickham decided to tell Denny and Woods that they were meeting a young gentle born lady who wished to fulfill her desires with them. He described a wanton young lady who wished to be handled roughly as if she were fighting them for her virtue. The men laughed and agreed that it would be entertaining to take a young lady in such a manner, with Denny commenting he had never had a gentlewoman before.

~~ ** ~~

Elizabeth had left home that morning, planning to walk to her favorite spot in all the estate. Susan was not feeling well, but Elizabeth decided to meet Darcy anyway, as she had promised and had no way to send word to him of the change. Darcy had stated, as he left the night before, he had a surprise for her in the morning. She was certain he was going to propose to her, and she had finally come to the realization that she was ready to take this step forward in their relationship. As she approached Oakham Mount, Elizabeth was so deep in thought of Darcy's surprise, she was surprised to see three young men in red coats already at the top. "Forgive me, gentlemen, I will leave you to enjoy the view." She said as she turned to leave.

Wickham took hold of her arm and held tight. "Miss Elizabeth, there is no need to pretend with Denny and Woods. I informed them of your desire and they are here to assist us."

Elizabeth frowned. "Mr Wickham, is it not? I am not sure of what you speak, but it would be highly improper for me to remain here with three young men. I will return to my home."

Woods blocked her path. "Come, Miss Elizabeth, we all know you desire us, and you wish for us to become better acquainted. I, for one, am looking forward to knowing you much better." He stated as he leered at her, reaching out a hand to roughly caress her breast, through the fabric of her gown.

"Keep your hands off me." Elizabeth stated in a harsh tone. "And I insist you let me go to my home. If you do as I say, I will not inform my father of your behavior."

"You will not tell your father, for what would he say when he learns of your requesting our presence here." Denny said as he stepped up from behind her. He placed his hands on her waist, then moving them towards her womanhood. "I believe it is time to remove some of these clothes, so we can begin to enjoy your bounty."

With that, he began to tear at the buttons on the back of her dress. "Unhand me, immediately." Elizabeth shrieked. Mortified at what was happening to her, Elizabeth fought the men as best she could, even grasped hold of Wickham's hair and pulling. Wickham moved his arm, bringing it down roughly in a backhanded slap.

"There is some rope over by that bush." He stated to Woods. "Denny, tear a piece of her petticoats to use as a gag, we cannot have her ruin everything by crying out in her pleasures."

Wickham grabbed hold of Elizabeth's hair and began to drag her to an area where there were two small trees. Holding her neck with his hands, in her struggles, he felt his fingernails dig into her tender flesh. Wickham continued to hold her while the other men secured her, tying one of her arms to each of the trees, so she would not be able to use them while they took her favors.

Just as they had secured her arms to the first tree, they heard the sound of a horse approaching. Wickham could not imagine who it was, so early in the morning. He had not expected Darcy for at least another hour.

Elizabeth attempted to cry out from around the gag, causing Wickham to become enraged. He reached out his hand and struck her about the face several times before she could take no more and collapsed.

Turning around, Wickham found Darcy had come into sight at the top of the hill. "Ah, Darcy, I did not know Miss Elizabeth had invited you here as well. Well, I am sure that there is more than enough to go around, as she is quite a tasty morsel."

Since his first sighting of Wickham, Darcy had been carrying a new double barrel pistol he had recently acquired, keeping it with him each and every day. He knew Wickham was dangerous, though Darcy would never have imagined such an attack as lay before him. Darcy drew his gun and pointed it directly at the scoundrel who had plagued his life. "Let her go, and step away from her."

"But the young lady invited us to join her here. She wished for our attentions to her." Denny stated boldly.

"Miss Elizabeth did no such thing, for she is a gentlewoman. She would not behave so improperly. What have you done to her to cause her to be unconscious?"

"Come, Darcy, you know that young ladies are a fickle lot. This young lady requested us to meet her here, knowing what the outcome would be. You cannot blame us for indulging a fine piece of fluff that is so willingly given?" Wickham said with a smile.

"I know that she did no such thing, as I am courting her. I know the sort of young lady she is and Miss Elizabeth Bennet is a proper young lady, the daughter of a gentleman. You will now leave here, and speak of this to no one. If you dare to speak of your vile attempts on her, I will see that you are run through." Darcy spat the final words out.

"How dare you?" Woods growled. "You think you are so much better than the rest of us. If I were Miss

Elizabeth, I would prefer being with us to you."

"You heard me, step away from the young lady and leave. If you refuse, you force me to take measures to protect her." Darcy stated, his pistol moving to each of the men.

"You cannot believe you can take the three of us on." Denny said. "Pompous man, you think your money will protect you."

Suddenly, Woods lunged at Darcy. The pistol fired, leaving Woods dead on the ground.

"How dare you murder my friend?" Denny declared as he leaped at Darcy, knocking him to the ground. The fight continued, and soon, Wickham had joined in as well. The pistol fired a second time, and this time, the target was Denny. Wickham struggled with Darcy, managing to pull his own handgun, which became pinned between them. A shot fired, cutting through the skin of Darcy's shoulder. In the heat of the moment, Wickham ran from the scene.

~~ ** ~~

Without thinking of his own injury, Darcy quickly released Elizabeth from the ropes, and then gathered her in his arms. He removed the blanket from his horse and wrapped it around Elizabeth, before he mounted his horse with her still in his arms.

Riding quickly to Longbourn, Darcy took her in the back entrance to avoid being seen by her mother. Darcy did not knock, he opened the door and brought Elizabeth inside the house. Knowing where Mr Bennet's study was, and sure that the gentleman would be inside, Darcy made his way into the study.

"Mr Darcy, what is the meaning of this?" Mr Bennet demanded. He then noticed the bundle in Darcy's arms to be that of a young lady, and requested information.

"Sir, your daughter, Miss Elizabeth, was attacked by three men from the militia. Two of the men are dead, and the third ran from the area."

"Attacked my Lizzy? How dare they treat my daughter in such a manner? Who is the culprit who ran from the scene of his crime? I will send word to have him brought here immediately so I may dispense justice."

"Mr Bennet, I, too, wish to avenge Miss Elizabeth in seeing the man brought to justice. But if we do so, we will subject her to the most severe gossip and ridicule. Her reputation would be in ruins, as will the reputation of your entire family. Allow me to find justice for your daughter in a way that will not ruin your family."

"And what do we say as to the men who are dead

on my lands?" Mr Bennet was pale. "I fear that it is too late to fret over our family's reputation with the blood of these blackguards staining my grounds. How badly injured is my daughter?"

"She is unconscious, so I am not sure of her injuries. I am certain the other man will not speak up on the matter, as I believe he will have deserted his post and is long gone by now. As to the men who are dead, a simple explanation can be that they attacked me to rob me. Miss Elizabeth was walking in the area, and heard the commotion. In coming to my aid, she was injured by one of the culprits striking her."

"It appears that you are bleeding, Mr Darcy." Mr Bennet pointed to the stain blooming on the shoulder of his coat.

"Would you mind if I were to take a seat?" Darcy asked. Mr Bennet assisted him to the nearest chair, with Darcy refusing to relinquish his blanket wrapped bundle.

"I will send for the apothecary." Mr Bennet stated as he made his way to the door of the study, calling out for Mrs Hill.

Mrs Hill scurried inside the room as quickly as possible. The sight of Mr Darcy, bleeding through his coat, holding tightly to the bundle in his arms, brought Mrs Hill up short, as she suddenly realized the bundle was a person, particularly a young lady, and she recognized the skirt of the gown the young lady was wearing.

"Miss Elizabeth." The devoted housekeeper nearly whispered. Though she could not see the face of the girl she had helped raise since birth, Mrs Hill was sure she was correct. She also knew that Mr Darcy held a tender regard for the young lady, so, seeing how protective he was of the precious bundle, it only reinforced her notion of the identity.

"It is, indeed, our Lizzy. Mrs Hill, we need for Mr Jones to be called here. We will keep Lizzy here, in the study. Mr Darcy, perhaps we should have you place her on the sofa."

"I do not wish to cause her any further pain by moving her. Once Mr Jones arrives, I will move her, as he will need to examine her injuries."

Mr Bennet shook his head. "And he will need to examine yours as well, Mr Darcy. Where did this attack occur? I will need to send someone for the bodies."

Mrs Hill gasped. "What happened to our dear Lizzy, Mr Bennet?"

"Fortunately, not what the young men had intended." Mr Bennet knew he could trust Hill with the knowledge. "This cannot leave this room, and especially my wife cannot know what has happened as yet. We cannot have gossip spread about, and we know that my wife, though a good and loving lady, is fond of gossip. We will need some fresh water and cloths to wash the wounds, bandages, and bring your bag of herbs."

Mrs Hill nodded her head. "I will send my son to Mr Jones. Shall I send some tea or coffee to you while you wait? I believe Mr Darcy could stand to have something."

"Mrs Hill, you are indeed correct." Darcy stated. "And perhaps some dry toast, as this event has caused my stomach to be slightly queasy."

"And, Mrs Hill, would you send to Meryton for Colonel Forster. It was three of his men who were responsible for the attack upon my daughter and Mr Darcy."

"Yes, Mr Bennet. After Fred notifies Mr Jones, he can go to the encampment and notify Colonel Forster. Mr Darcy, would you wish for Mr Bingley to be brought here as well?"

"Perhaps it is wise. I will need his assistance when I leave here."

"Very well, Sir, I will see that he is also sent for."

Mrs Hill then left the room, closing the door behind her.

"Mr Darcy, I am not certain how we should approach the Colonel with the actions of his men. I am not sure with who we should share the true situation, rather than the story you suggested."

"The only person we have to worry about is Wickham. He escaped after wounding me. I would have given chase, but I was far more concerned with Miss Elizabeth. As I said, I am sure that Wickham has fled the area, for he is a coward. And I am sure that, as a Colonel, Forster can be trusted."

"I appreciate that, Mr Darcy. I know we can trust Mr Jones with the truth, he has known Lizzy since she was a babe and he has been fond of her for many years. She has assisted him many times, nursing some of the patients for Mr Jones."

~~ ** ~~

Jane knew something was wrong when she woke that morning. She could feel the tension in the house, though she was certain that her mother and younger sisters had no awareness of it. She made her way to her father's study, after searching the house for Elizabeth and not being able to locate her.

Mr Bennet went to the door and opened it himself.

"Ah, Jane, is there something you need?"

"I am concerned for Lizzy, Papa. I have been looking for her and cannot find her. My heart is telling me that something dreadful has happened."

"Come in the room, Jane. Your sister is in here with Mr Darcy and me." Mr Bennet stepped aside.

Mr Darcy was still holding Elizabeth in his arms, wrapped snuggly in the blanket. Seeing her sister's gown from under the blanket, Jane gasped. "What has happened? Is Lizzy alive?"

"She is alive, Miss Bennet, as I can feel her heart beating and her soft breathing. I do not wish to move her until we need to when the apothecary arrives."

"What happened to her? Is she badly injured?" Jane said as she moved closer to her sister's form.

"She was beaten by three men." Mr Bennet said. "You must keep a secret, Jane, for your mother cannot know the truth. Three of the soldiers attempted to force themselves upon your sister. Fortunately, Mr Darcy arrived to save her. The men attacked Mr Darcy, and two of the men are dead. Mr Darcy has been injured in the struggle with the last man."

"Who were the men?" Jane's eyes pleaded with her father.

"I believe it best to wait until Colonel Forster arrives, so Mr Darcy only needs to tell the tale once."

"Of course, please forgive me, Mr Darcy." Jane stated.

Another knock was heard on the door and Mr Bennet opened it to allow Mr Jones to enter.

"Young Fred Hill stated that there had been an accident. Who is injured?"

"We have two patients for you, Mr Jones. Mr Darcy has an injury to his shoulder and Lizzy has been beaten. I suggest we keep her down here for the time being, away from my wife and younger daughters. If you will assist me, we can aid Mr Darcy in standing with his bundle so he can carry it to the sofa."

"Beaten? Who would do such a thing to Miss Elizabeth? She is such a kind young lady, taking care of others before her own needs. Who are these blackguards?"

Just then, another knock announced Colonel Forster. Once Darcy placed Elizabeth on the sofa, he was assisted in removing his coat and short coat while Mr Jones examined Elizabeth.

"Gentlemen, now that we are all here, I believe it is time for Mr Darcy to tell us what happened this morning." Mr Bennet suggested.

~~~~~~~~ ** ~~~~~~~~
~~~~~~~~

CHAPTER 8

"Very well, Mr Bennet. It may come as a surprise to you, Colonel and Mr Jones, but Miss Elizabeth and I have been courting. We have been keeping the news quiet for the time being. This morning, I went for an early morning horse ride, to Oakham Mount, planning to meet Miss Elizabeth with the purpose of proposing to her. Miss Elizabeth favors the location, and we have taken in the sunrise several mornings of late, chaperoned by a maid. This morning, when I arrived there, I was shocked at the scene before me. Miss Elizabeth was unconscious, lying on the ground with her hands tied by ropes to two small trees. The ropes are still there, when you go there you will see them. As you can see, her dress is torn and she has been beaten about the head and face. There were three men, preparing to violate Miss Elizabeth. Mr Wickham, Mr Woods, and Mr Denny were all claiming they had been invited by Miss Elizabeth, and that she desired them to take their pleasure of her. I knew this to be a falsehood, and insisted they step away from her. Mr Woods attacked me, and I shot him before he could harm me. Mr Denny then tried the same, and met with the same fate. Mr Wickham struggled with me for the pistol, which fired, striking me. Wickham then ran off. I freed Miss Elizabeth and brought her here."

"As you can see, Mr Darcy is bleeding on the shoulder, and my daughter has obvious bruising and a cut lip from the beating. She has been unconscious since Mr Darcy brought her home." Mr Bennet stated.

"You claim that my men were responsible for this heinous crime, and that Wickham had fled the scene? When I left the camp to come here, Wickham was there, breaking his fast with other men."

"Wickham is the one who shot me. I am amazed he has not grabbed his belongings and run from the neighborhood, so there is some ultimate reason he has remained. You will need to arrest him immediately, before he has time to escape." Darcy stated.

"Miss Elizabeth also has marks on her arms from the ropes, Mr Bennet." Mr Jones stated. "She fought the brutes, as she has torn her fingernails in clawing at them. There are bits of hair under her nails, so she must have fought them hard."

"Elizabeth has always been a scrapper, Mr Jones. You, of all people, should know that she would not quietly stand by and allow the men to treat her in such a manner without a fight."

"I am concerned for her head injuries." Mr Jones stated. "Has she awakened at all?"

"No, Sir, she is as you see her." Darcy stated.

"Bennet, I would feel better to have a surgeon take a look at her. She should have made some response when I used the smelling salts in an attempt to wake her, and she did not even flinch when she was poked with a needle."

"I will send an express to London." Darcy immediately stated. "I will have my personal physician attend her."

"Mr Darcy, forgive me for making such a suggestion, but I believe it might be best if we were to take Miss Elizabeth to London. There is a surgeon who is well versed in head injuries from the battlefield. By the time we would send expresses, and the surgeon and physician arrive, we can arrive and meet them quite a bit earlier in Town." Mr Jones stated.

"Then we will use my carriage. I will have it prepared immediately. Mr Bennet, you and Miss Bennet are welcome to accompany us as well. And you are welcome to stay at my home in Town. Whatever is needed for Miss Elizabeth, I will see that it is done."

"Are you certain, Mr Jones? Would the travel cause her more harm?" Jane asked.

"The risk of greater harm from travel, as compared to quicker treatment by a specialist, should be weighed. I believe the threat of harm is far below the need for the treatment. If we position her in the carriage carefully, I believe there will be no risk of further injury."

"While you men see to Miss Elizabeth's care, I will see to Wickham's arrest. I will send word to you in Town as to what happens. And I will send a detail to collect the remains of Denny and Woods." Colonel Forster said, as he made his way from the room.

Another knock was heard at the door just moments after the Colonel had left. This time, Jane went to the door to learn the identity of the visitor. Mr Bingley was standing before her, nervously anticipating what he was to learn.

"Bingley, good, I need you do some things for me. First, I need you to have my carriage made ready for me immediately. Have it brought here. I will be traveling to London with Mr Bennet and his two eldest daughters. Miss Elizabeth has been injured and we need to take her to the surgeon for treatment. Do not let your sisters know anything until after we are gone."

Bingley nodded his head. "Do you need me to send expresses to your housekeeper and to your cousin?"

Darcy smiled. "You are reading my thoughts, Bingley. Yes, if you would. Let my housekeeper know to have several rooms prepared for guests, and inform Richard that Wickham is involved. We will need the surgeon from the military hospital, as Miss Elizabeth has suffered a head injury."

"If Mr Bennet would allow me to use his desk, I will prepare the letters immediately."

"Of course, Mr Bingley, and I can send Fred to have the carriage prepared for Mr Darcy."

"Thank you, Mr Bennet. Darcy, will you require your trunks packed before leaving?" Bingley asked.

"I believe my valet can achieve the packing and meet us in Town later."

Bingley nodded. "When I return to Netherfield, after you have left for Town, I will have Billings pack your belongings. He can travel in my second carriage."

Mr Bennet showed Bingley where the writing supplies were as he quietly gave his future son in law the basic information of what had happened that morning.

"Thank you, Bingley. Now, Mr Bennet, you and

Miss Bennet should pack some belongings to take with us, and, perhaps, some clothing for Miss Elizabeth as well." Darcy stated, wincing as Mr Jones was working on his wounded shoulder.

~~ ** ~~

Darcy was assisted into the carriage before Jane and her father, and lastly, Elizabeth was carried to the carriage and handed over to Darcy. Mr Jones then entered the carriage last. At first, it was thought to have Elizabeth placed between her father and sister, allowing them to keep her in the seat. Mr Darcy did not approve of this suggestion. "With all due respect, Mr Bennet, I intend to marry your daughter as soon as I can. I would ask to be allowed to hold Miss Elizabeth in my lap, as I did in your study. I believe it will be the most comfortable for her."

After a moment's hesitation, Mr Bennet nodded in agreement. "I wish for Lizzy to be as comfortable as possible. It would, also, protect her from any further bumping of the head."

As the carriage pulled away from Longbourn, Elizabeth began to stir. She was mumbling, her words unclear and slurred. When she finally opened her eyes, she was unable to communicate any better. Her left hand was outside the blanket that was wrapped around her, and Mr Bennet noticed she appeared to be trying to use her hand, but to no avail.

"Mr Jones, what is wrong with my daughter?"

"I believe there is a break in her skull and the blow caused bleeding in the brain. This is why I wished to get her to a surgeon immediately. To save her life, it may be necessary to operate. At the very least, they will need to drill holes to release the blood which is causing pressure inside her skull."

Listening to the words of the apothecary, Darcy's grip on his beloved grew. He whispered in her ear that all would be well, and that she would recover soon enough. He spoke of their future together, of Pemberley and the beauty of the estate. When her words could not be understood, Elizabeth became agitated. "Dearest, please remain calm. It will not be long before we arrive at Darcy House and the surgeon will arrive to make you better. If you understand my words, please squeeze my hand."

It took several moments, but she finally made an attempt at squeezing his hand. He could feel the tremors from her body, and his concern grew. The horses were changed quickly at the first stop. Wishing to travel quickly, no one exited the carriage and they were soon on the road again.

~~ ** ~~

They finally pulled up in front of Darcy House, and the carriage was quickly emptied, with Darcy exiting last, still holding tightly to the woman he loved.

"Mr Darcy, we have the rooms in the family wing ready, as requested. I have taken the liberty of preparing your mother's suite for the injured lady, as Mr Bingley stated you were engaged to her. It is also the best suite, as there are the adjoining rooms which can be utilized by the physician or nurses."

"Mrs Jenkins, you have always impressed me with your wisdom." Darcy climbed the steps to the next level, and entered the rooms of his mother. He placed Elizabeth gently on the bed, and asked Mrs Jenkins to bring fresh water and some cloths. "And we will need a maid to assist in preparing Miss Elizabeth for the surgeon's arrival."

"Your cousin has sent word that he will be arriving soon with the military surgeon. He received word from his commanding officer stating that they would allow the surgeon, as the young lady was injured by men from a militia regiment."

"Bingley has been thorough in his messages." Darcy smiled. Leaning over Elizabeth, he spoke calmly to her. "I will step from the room, allowing the maid to assist you into a night gown. Your sister will assist you as well. Once they have you situated, I will return. I will not be gone long."

Elizabeth gave a clumsy squeeze of his hand. This brought a smile to Darcy's lips. She could hear him and understand him.

By the time the maid and Jane had Elizabeth's clothing changed, Darcy heard his cousin coming up the stairs. "Richard, I cannot thank you enough."

"William, this is Doctor Josephson. He is the leading surgeon on head injuries for the army. Doctor, this is my cousin, Fitzwilliam Darcy."

"And this is Miss Elizabeth's father, Mr Thomas Bennet. His eldest daughter, Miss Jane Bennet, is in the room with her sister at the moment. And this is the apothecary who first attended Miss Elizabeth, Mr Jones."

"Mr Jones, what can you tell me of the patient?" Mr Josephson asked. Seeing the maid open the door to the bed chambers, the two men entered, with Darcy close behind them.

"Miss Elizabeth was beaten by several young men, as they subdued her for their own purposes. She was unconscious for nearly three hours, and since has had difficulty with speaking and moving her hands. There has been no breathing difficulty so far, nor bleeding from the ears. She seems to understand what is being said to her, she has responded to Mr Darcy by squeezing his hand."

"That is a good sign. But it sounds as if there is bleeding in the brain. Has she worsened since you have been with her or remained the same?"

"I have seen no worsening, and slightly improved when she regained consciousness." Mr Jones stated.

"Good, good, then let us examine her." Mr Josephson suggested. The surgeon placed his bag on the bedside table, opening it and extracting several instruments. He performed a thorough examination, and concluded that there was bleeding, most likely on the left side of her brain.

"I believe that we should watch her carefully over the next few hours. At any sign of worsening, we will need to drill holes in the skull to release the pressure the blood pooling is causing. As there are risks from such actions, I wish to delay it until I am absolutely sure it is necessary."

"How long a wait is needed to know?" Mr Bennet asked. The group had moved from the hall into the sitting room which connected the Master and Mistress suites. Mr Bennet sank into a nearby chair, becoming quite pale.

"The next four and twenty hours will be the most

critical. I suggest you prepare yourself for a long day and night."

Mr Jones approached his friend. "Mr Bennet, Doctor Josephson studied at the Royal College of Physicians in Edinburgh, under the esteemed Doctor Benjamin Bell. The reputation of Doctor Bell was extraordinary, and his son is carrying on his father's legacy. Doctor Josephson has also been an army surgeon for over twenty years. His vast knowledge is why we came to London. Lizzy could not be in better hands."

"Thank you, old friend. I trust in your judgment." Mr Bennet stated. Mrs Jenkins returned to the room, with a tray of refreshments, placing them on the table near Mr Bennet.

"Sir, I suggest you have something to nourish you while you wait. You cannot be of service to your daughter if you take ill from ignoring your own needs." She chastised the gentleman.

Mr Bennet chuckled. "Yes, Mrs Jenkins, I will do as I am told. Lizzy would be quite upset with me if I did not."

Darcy returned to Elizabeth's room, taking his seat in the chair next to her bed. Holding her hand, he raised it to his lips. "I love you, Elizabeth Bennet. And I am telling you now, I will not tolerate your leaving me. So you had best come to the conclusion that you will be recovering."

Elizabeth tried to smile. "Yyyyessss, missser Darrrrcccc."

"William, my love, I wish you to call me William."

Again, she tried to smile. Her exhaustion was clear, and Darcy knew from the surgeon that it was common with head injuries. They would keep her stimulated, keeping her from slipping back into oblivion. She could not be given anything for the pain, as they needed to keep her alert so they could determine any changes.

Colonel Fitzwilliam entered the room. "Forgive me, Miss Elizabeth, but I do wish to be introduced to you. You have stolen my cousin's heart and I cannot delay in meeting such an extraordinary woman."

Darcy shook his head. "Dearest, this is Colonel Richard Fitzwilliam, second son of Lord Matlock and a distinguished war hero. Richard, this beautiful lady is Miss Elizabeth Bennet, second daughter of Mr Thomas Bennet, and the love of my life."

"Ah, Miss Elizabeth, I can see now that we second born must stick together in the world. So you are not allowed to leave me to fend for myself against all first born." Colonel Fitzwilliam smiled.

“Yyyyyyeeeesssss ssssiiirrrrr.” She agreed.

“Now, if you do not mind, I need to speak with my cousin for a moment. I will not take him for long, but it is vital.” Richard informed her.

“JJJJaannnnnneee.” Elizabeth held a frightened look in her eyes.

“I am here, Lizzy.” Jane spoke from across the room. “I will stay with you while the men speak.”

Elizabeth smiled. “Kkkkkkk”

~~ ** ~~

Richard did not wish to speak so openly to his cousin, with Mr Bennet in the room as well. “Should we go to your study?” he asked.

“No, I remain here.” Darcy stated. “Besides, Mr Bennet is involved, as the attack was against his daughter and on his estate.”

“Darcy, they have captured Wickham. Unfortunately, he says that he fled the area in fear for his life after you killed Denny and Woods. He claims they came upon you, that you had injured Miss Elizabeth and they came to her defense. And he claims that you killed the other men in a fit of rage due to their interrupting you.”

"Why am I shocked that Wickham would turn this against me? He has done everything in his power to hurt me. You would have thought all he did to Lawson's sister would have been painful enough, as she was the sister of a close friend and Wickham believed I cared for Miss Lawson." Darcy stated. "He is determined to destroy me."

"But my daughter will be able to tell them the truth." Mr Bennet stated.

"Unfortunately, Miss Elizabeth has suffered a severe head injury. It could be turned against Darcy, that he has told her what happened and what to say rather than her remembering any of it." Richard explained.

"This cannot be." Mr Bennet exclaimed. "How can anyone believe such nonsense with regards to Mr Darcy?"

"Darcy has always been withdrawn from society, Mr Bennet. Some believe he looks down his nose at everyone, others think that he has been living a secret life. We are facing the possibility of this being taken to the courts. At the very least, it will be posted in the papers by tomorrow morning."

Mr Bennet was furious. "What if we were to tell our version before the lies become known?"

"This is a delicious scandal with one of the most eligible and sought after bachelors in all of England. Many would use it as justification as to why their daughters were overlooked by the man, and others would try to capitalize on Darcy's troubles, wishing to make him more legitimate. Those sorts would sell their daughters to him, giving him protection and they would have access to his wealth. There are many desperate families in the upper circles of society, due to mismanagement of their estates or the lifestyle of the family in gambling and overindulging."

"I cannot believe this is happening. Is it not enough that I am sitting here, waiting word as to my daughter's health? These blackguards nearly kill her and then it is turned against the man who rescued her? No, no, Mr Darcy, you must know that I will stand beside you all the way."

"My thanks to you, Mr Bennet, and I pray you know how dearly I love Elizabeth."

"I look forward to the day when I can call you my son." Mr Bennet stated. "So what happens now?"

"The general will be coming here himself to learn more of the dealings from all parties. Wickham is being brought here by Colonel Forster. From what was sent in the letter, Colonel Forster stated Denny and Woods had been on guard detail overnight, and the attack occurred less than two hours after they were relieved from their duty. The claim is that the men did not have ample time to find Miss Elizabeth and do all that Darcy claims before the men were killed. They say that the only way the evidence of the rope at the scene, tying Miss Elizabeth after beating her, tearing her clothes and such, can match the timeline is if Wickham's version is believed."

"Does the fool not think that Wickham had plenty of time to prepare for the attack, bringing the other two as they finished their duty?" Darcy stated. "Forster is a fool, if he chooses to believe the lies being set forth by Wickham."

Jane stepped out of her sister's room. "Papa, Mr Darcy, the surgeon wishes to speak with you."

The look on his eldest daughter's face told Mr Bennet something was not right. Before Mr Bennet could even stand, Darcy was at the door and entering the room.

Mr Josephson was leaning over Elizabeth, checking her progress. He looked up when he heard the men enter. "Gentlemen, I believe that the bleeding is worsening. She is having greater difficulty trying to speak, and cannot grip my hand at all. If we do not act quickly, I am doubtful of her survival."

Terror nearly overwhelmed Darcy, as he dropped

to his knees beside the bed. Taking hold of her hand, Darcy began pleading with Elizabeth not to leave him.

Mr Bennet stood still, watching the love the young man held for his cherished daughter. "Darcy, it is my opinion we should allow Doctor Josephson to do what is needed to save Elizabeth. As her betrothed, do you agree?"

Tears were streaming down Darcy's cheeks as he turned to the father of his beloved. "I am not her betrothed, Mr Bennet, as you well know. We are courting."

"As of this moment, I believe there is no doubt in my mind, you and Lizzy are betrothed. Do you wish to disagree with me?"

Darcy shook his head. "I agree with your judgment. Doctor, what will you need?"

"I assume that this is the Mistress' suite, correct?" Darcy turned red as the truth came out. He nodded his head in acknowledgement. "I then assume there is a birthing room nearby?" Again, Darcy nodded.

"Then I suggest we use the birthing room as an operating room. Your housekeeper has already gone to gather supplies that will be needed. We will need to shave the left side of Miss Elizabeth's head, and drill several holes for the blood to drain out. I must warn you, the blood will appear different than most injuries, as it will be darker. This is normal. And it will appear to be huge volume. Head injuries bleed more than other injuries, do not be alarmed. I will be keeping a close watch over the quantity. With all good luck, the swelling inside her skull will be relieved and she will recover. We will need to watch for how long the bleeding continues, for that could mean there is still bleeding going on inside. Hopefully, once this is drained off and the pressure is released, we will find the bleeding in her brain stops."

Mr Bennet turned quite pale and Darcy hurried to his side to guide him to a chair. "Elizabeth would find some sort of tease to make fun of losing her hair for the time being." Mr Bennet said, trying to ease the tension. "She has always followed her own style, perhaps she will find a way to start a new fashion."

~~~~~~~ ** ~~~~~~~
~~~~~~~

CHAPTER 9

Mrs Jenkins and a maid were to assist Doctor Josephson in his work. The housekeeper was saddened by the need to shave the beautiful curls of dark chocolate from her head. The young lady was beautiful, even with all the bruises on her face. And it was obvious that her master was in love with the young lady.

She had been the housekeeper of Darcy House since Master William was six, and she had never seen his heart so touched by anyone. Silently, Mrs Jenkins said many prayers for the survival of the young lady before her.

It was difficult to watch the surgeon in his work. As the holes were drilled in the side of Elizabeth's head, dark red blood oozed from them, pouring into the basin which was placed to catch it. Doctor Josephson stated he needed to be able to examine the blood to ensure that the bleeding was not worse.

Three hours passed, and the blood, which had slowed to a trickle from the holes, had nearly stopped. Doctor Josephson took a deep sigh of relief, as he was certain that the worst was over. The recovery would take time, but the most dangerous time appeared to be past. The greatest danger facing them now was if she were to take a fever or reinjure her head.

Doctor Josephson stepped into the sitting room to speak to Mr Darcy and Mr Bennet, only to find three other men present.

Mr Bennet stood and walked to the doctor. "What is the news?"

"The bleeding has nearly stopped. I believe the injury is clotted over. We will need to watch her carefully for signs of a fever and make certain that she does not bump her head for quite some time, but I believe the worst is over."

One of the strange men stepped towards the doctor. "Sir, I am General Stockwell. We are investigating the allegations made by both Mr Darcy and Lieutenant Wickham. May we ask you some questions?"

"Of course, General, I am sure that Mr Bennet will give me leave to discuss his daughter's medical condition with you." Doctor Josephson stated.

Mr Bennet nodded his head in agreement.

"Sir, we have information that the two suspects have different sides which is their strong hand, with the lieutenant being left handed and Mr Darcy being right handed. Can you tell, from the injuries, whether they were made by the right or left hand?"

"For that, General, I would have to take you into the room to see Miss Bennet for yourself. I warn you, it will not be a pleasant sight."

"I have fought in many battles, Doctor. I doubt very much if such a sight would be too difficult."

The men turned and stepped inside the bedchamber, with Doctor Josephson leading the General into the birthing room. "Doctor, I stand corrected. I am taken aback by this sight. What can you tell me of the injuries?"

"As the bruising is becoming more and more vivid, you can tell the outline of some of the strikes. Here, on the cheek, is what appears to be where knuckles struck. But the force and angle, I would say that it was from a backhanded blow. Being where it is, it would make the blow from a left handed person. Also, on her chest, is the impression of a man's hand. As Miss Elizabeth is quite thin, there is not much padding in that area to make an indentation, which would make the impression appear different size. If I were you, General, I would have the impression measured and even place some delicate rice paper over it and trace it. You can then have the two men in question place their hands next to the tracing and see which has the appropriate size."

The general was quite impressed with what was being shown him. “Anything else, Doctor?”

“Miss Elizabeth has scratch marks on her neck, here, on the left side. I would believe the person responsible for such injuries to have some of her skin under his fingernails. I have witnessed Mr Darcy’s hands, and he has not been alone since he brought Miss Elizabeth to her father’s home, from what I have been told. As concerned as the young man is over her well-being, I doubt very much if he has taken the time to tidy himself up and cleaned from under his fingernails. He has not even removed the bloodied shirt from his own wound. Mr Jones also spoke of hair being stuck in Miss Elizabeth’s fingernails and one of her nails being torn off. Do you see any visible scratch marks on Mr Darcy? The hair, according to Mr Jones, was light colored.”

“You are highly intelligent, Doctor. And you are certain of your findings?”

“I am quite certain. I am also certain that the love and devotion I have witnessed in Mr Darcy is not something pretended. And someone who is so much in love with such a young lady, would not treat his beloved in such a manner.”

“I hate to ask you this, but Lieutenant Wickham claims that the young lady was violated and he was sure that it was not the first time, as he had heard rumors of Darcy taking her virtue quite some time ago. Wickham stated that he witnessed Darcy violating her at the scene, and this was why he and the other men stepped forward to stop him."

"Before I operated on her, I gave Miss Elizabeth a thorough examination. Miss Elizabeth's virtue is still intact. She has not been violated by any man or object. This Lieutenant Wickham is lying to you. I will testify to all of my findings."

"That is all I need from you, Doctor. I have a few more questions to ask Mr Darcy, but I believe I am soon to be finished here. If you will be so kind as to make a tracing of the hand impression on her chest, I will take that with me."

"I will send for some rice paper immediately." Doctor Josephson stated.

As General Stockwell turned to leave, he had one more favor to ask. "Would you examine Mr Darcy's hands? I wish to know if you find any injuries to them which would account for Miss Bennet's injuries."

"I would do so gladly, for I am certain of the answer. As I said, I have watched Mr Darcy closely and witnessed his hands. If he had inflicted the injuries on Miss Elizabeth, he would most likely have bruising or scrapes on his hands."

~~ ** ~~

The General took the tracing of the hand impression and entered the sitting room. "Mr Darcy, would you be willing to hold up your hands for me?"

Darcy was confused, but did so easily. There were no cuts, scrapes, or bruising on either of his hands, the nails had no signs of scraped skin under them or damage to them from scratching someone in a struggle. Then he held the tracing to Darcy's hands. Fitzwilliam was a big man, and that included his hands. The impression was far smaller than the tracing.

"Mr Darcy, I agree with Doctor Josephson in his assessment. The injuries which were sustained by Miss Elizabeth appear to have been made by a left handed man, who should have some sort of injuries to his hands, and his hands are much smaller than yours. I can therefore rule you as innocent of the charges which have been laid so viciously. And I believe I know exactly what happened. As soon as Colonel Forster arrives with Lieutenant Wickham, I believe I will have my proof. I will send word to you when we make an arrest, as I will need you to make a formal statement."

"Other than being with my fiancé, and taking care of her needs, I have no plans to be anywhere else."

Darcy shook the General's hand. "Thank you for proving my innocence."

"I only wish we could keep the assault private, for I am certain Mr Bennet's family, especially Miss Elizabeth, will suffer." General Stockwell replied. "Mr Bennet, I will do what I can to downplay the situation as much as possible. These men were a disgrace to the militia and to every man in uniform. It will not stand lightly."

"My thanks, General, though we are aware that the chances of the papers and gossips having the news are great." Mr Bennet stated.

~~ ** ~~

Mrs Bennet could not believe her ears when she woke that morning. She was told, by Mrs Hill, of an accident involving Elizabeth, leaving her daughter in severe condition. Her husband and eldest two daughters had hurried to London, along with Mr Jones and Mr Darcy, who was said to have been in the area of the accident. There were two men from the militia dead on their property, and Mr Wickham was in custody.

All Mrs Bennet could think was that her family was in ruins due to her daughter's foolishness of walking early in the morning and alone. Now Jane would never be able to marry Mr Bingley, and the younger girls would be ridiculed and scorned due to their sister's having been compromised in such a manner.

Her sister, Mrs Phillips, came from Meryton to share the latest gossip. She told Mrs Bennet of the news that Mr Wickham was innocent of the charges and the militia had attempted to save Elizabeth from Mr Darcy's depraved actions. And Mrs Phillips told her that the statement from Mr Wickham was that Mr Darcy had taken Elizabeth's virtue long before the assault.

Mrs Bennet swooned, and had to be taken to her rooms. It would be many days to come before the lady could bring herself to leave her bed.

~~ ** ~~

The horses arrived at the encampment of the regulars. George Wickham and Colonel Forster were shown into the residence of General Stockwell.

"General, it is good to see you." Colonel Forster stated. "We came as soon as we could. Is there any word on Miss Elizabeth's condition?"

"She required surgery, where they had to bore holes in her skull to allow the built up blood to drain out. We can only hope that there is no permanent damage to her mind." General Stockwell stated. "I assume this is Lieutenant Wickham."

"It is, General. I have brought with us Wickham's written statement."

"Lieutenant, I would first like you to hold out your hands." General Stockwell requested.

Wickham was nervous. "My hands, Sir? I must admit, they look a fright after battling with Mr Darcy."

"I understood that you shot Mr Darcy, wounding his shoulder, and then fled the location."

"Oh, well, before we struggled for the gun, we were throwing punches. I am sure that his hands look worse than mine do though, after what he did to poor Miss Elizabeth."

"I find it odd that Mr Darcy had no injuries to either of his hands, or to his fingernails. Yet I see bruises, scratches, and even torn fingernails on your hands. There appears to even be some blood under one of the torn nails. Consistent with the scratch marks on Miss Elizabeth. Hold out your hands."

One of the General's aides came forward and took hold of Wickham's arms and forced them out. General Stockwell held out the tracing to Wickham's hand, a near perfect fit to the size of his palm and fingers.

"This is a tracing of the impression left on Miss

Elizabeth's upper chest, near the base of her neck. As I said, Mr Darcy's hands are uninjured, no damage to his fingernails. What I didn't tell you is that he has no other injuries to his face or body, except the gunshot wound, and his hands are far larger and could not have made the impression on Miss Elizabeth's chest. So, Lieutenant, I find that the evidence is against you and in favor of what Mr Darcy has stated. You and your partners attacked Miss Elizabeth, beating her near death, tied her up and attempted to rape her. Then you became a coward and ran away when someone stopped you, after you injured him. To add to the charges, you made a false report, accusing an innocent man of your depraved and immoral behavior. You, Lieutenant George Wickham, are under arrest. I will see that every possible charge can and will be laid at your feet, in addition, I will see that you receive the harshest possible punishment for your actions. Now, Colonel Forster, we need to have a chat about your future. As the commanding officer for the three men who assaulted Miss Elizabeth Bennet, you will be facing court martial for failing to command them properly. I do not hold you responsible for the lies Wickham told, or your desire to believe them, until we discovered the truth. I do hold you responsible for the actions of your men harming an innocent young woman, a gentlewoman, who is now ruined in society. Her family is also harmed by this taint, as is Mr Darcy. The sad part is that Mr Darcy is engaged to Miss Elizabeth. They will always live with this nightmare."

Wickham sneered at that news.

General Stockwell looked at the man in front of him. "That was your plan all along, was it not? You wished to harm this young couple, destroy their happiness."

"I do not care about Miss Elizabeth, she is just a means to an end. But Mr Darcy has been a thorn in my side far too many years. I knew they were courting, I did not know they were engaged. All the better. He will live with this for the rest of his life."

"You admit that you behaved in such a manner, harming Miss Elizabeth Bennet deliberately, to cause Mr Darcy harm?" The General asked, appalled at what he was learning.

"I was paid to do so." Wickham said, defiantly. "And I would do so again if it brought him greater pain."

The General turned toward his assistant. "Captain, remove the prisoner immediately. I will require you to give a statement regarding Wickham's confession and statements."

"I will return shortly, General." The Captain replied, pushing Wickham towards the door where other soldiers were waiting for the former lieutenant.

"And when they return, Colonel, we will further discuss your future."

~~ ** ~~

A message was dispatched immediately to the men at Darcy House.

Mr Darcy,

I have news regarding Mr Wickham. The man confessed his crimes, as the evidence had shown he was the culprit, though he made a startling statement.

It appears that, not only did Wickham purposely attack Miss Elizabeth Bennet, he did so to bring you pain and has claimed that he was paid to do so. We do not know the voracity of his claim of being paid, or who is alleged to have done so, and he refuses to inform us.

Mr Wickham insists that he will only speak to you on the matter, and if you will not come to see him, he will take the information to the grave.

Please send, word with my aide, if you wish to confront the man. With his confession, witnessed by my aide, and others, it will not take long until we sentence him and I see no need for more than a written statement from you, you will not be required to testify. My opinion is that he will be put to death.

Sincerely,

General Stockwell

"Paid to do this?" Richard cried out. "Who would have paid him to dishonor the woman you were courting? Not even Aunt Catherine is that low."

"Who knows if Wickham is telling the truth?" Darcy replied. "I cannot leave the house, though. What if something were to happen to Elizabeth while I was gone? I cannot take such a chance."

Mr Bennet shook his head. "Mr Darcy, you would be best to go, learn what you can. Lizzy is resting. Doctor Josephson is pleased with her progress. He and I will be here with her. I am sure she will be fine while you are gone. If there is any problem, any at all, I will send one of your footmen immediately."

Darcy stood and paced for a few moments. He went to the door to the bedchamber and knocked. Jenny, the maid who had been assigned to assist in Elizabeth's care, opened the door, then stepped aside to allow in the Master. Darcy then went to the door to the birthing room. When the door opened, Doctor Josephson stepped into the bedchamber.

"How is Elizabeth?" Mr Darcy inquired.

"She is holding her own. The blood flow is stopped, only a slight bit of bleeding from the scalp near the holes is seen in the past half an hour. And there are still no signs of a fever. We have bandaged her head, applying a poultice to keep any possible swelling down."

"Might I see her? I have been requested to leave for an hour or so, and I cannot do so without seeing her for myself." Darcy pleaded.

"Mr Darcy, I am at odds about allowing you to see her. She has been through a great ordeal, and I fear your reaction to seeing her in such a condition."

"I realize her appearance is not what I would wish to see, but I need to see her for myself. I need to see her breathing, feel her heart beating, feel the touch of her skin to assure myself that she is alive and will remain so while I am from the house, dealing with the man who caused her injuries."

Doctor Josephson thought about it for a few moments before finally allowing Darcy to enter the room.

Elizabeth was lying on her left side, with her head positioned for the bleeding to flow down if it continued. Heavy bandaging was wrapped around her head, hiding the holes which were placed there to save her life, as well as the skin on her head where the hair had been removed. There were bruises on her face, on her arms and on her chest. The latter was the most difficult, as Darcy knew the implications of the location. Gently lifting her hand to his lips, Darcy placed his lips against the inside of her wrist. He could feel her skin, not too hot or cold, the beat of her heart through the veins in her arm. He leaned his head lower, hearing her gentle breathing. She was alive. Would she be the lady he fell in love with? Would she be his Lizzy?"

A sudden shock ran through him as he felt her squeeze his hand lightly. "Mr Darcy." She whispered, her eyes remaining closed.

"William, my love. Please call me William. Your father has consented to our marrying."

"My William." She said with a smile on her lips.

"Yes, dearest, your William. I love you so dearly."

Finally, her eyes began to flutter. "I love you more." She teased. She was then gripped with a sudden pain.

"Elizabeth, where does it hurt?" He pleaded as she squeezed his hand tighter.

"My head, it feels as if a horse stomped on it."

Doctor Josephson had returned to the room just then and stepped closer to the bed. "Welcome to London, Miss Elizabeth. I am pleased to see you awake."

“London?” Elizabeth was confused.

“We needed to bring you to London to be treated, my love.” Darcy said and he gently caressed her bruised cheek.

“What happened? Why do I hurt?” Elizabeth was becoming agitated.

“We can discuss that later, when you are better. You have been battered, mostly about the head. There was bleeding inside your head, and the surgeon, this gentleman, has saved your life. It will take some time to recover completely, but you will recover.”

Elizabeth’s eyes were filled with unshed tears. “Mr Wickham did this. And the other men. Did they...oh, no, did they...?”

“No, Miss Elizabeth, your fiancé saved you from their intent. Two of the men are dead, and this Wickham has confessed his intentions. Mr Darcy rescued you, and took you to your home and sent for Mr Jones. Mr Jones determined quickly that you required more care than he could provide, and he came with your father, your sister, and your betrothed. I believe Mr Jones’ quick thinking contributed to our being able to save your life as well.”

"From what Elizabeth's father has told me, Mr Jones has known her all of her life, and is somewhat protective of her. For that, I will be eternally grateful." Darcy said with a smile. "As Doctor Josephson has said, the men did not succeed with their scheme, and you have not endured such horror. I will be forever grateful for my horse's speed and my desire to be at the Mount as soon as possible. But most of all, I am extremely grateful for seeing your beautiful eyes open and hearing your sweet voice. You are the dearest person in my life and I cannot begin to think of losing you."

Elizabeth smiled. "As you are to me, my William." It was obvious she was drowsy, and Darcy placed a gentle kiss on her lips.

"I will leave you to rest. I have to sign some papers for the army to prosecute Wickham, and as soon as I return, I will be at your side. By then, we may be able to move you to a more comfortable room, with a softer bed. This table you have been lying on must be quite uncomfortable."

"Hurry back." She whispered as she drifted off to sleep.

"I will be back before you wake."

~~~~~~~ ** ~~~~~~~
~~~~~~~

CHAPTER 10

Darcy was shown into the prison section of the encampment. He was taken to the cell where Wickham was being kept, and the guard stepped to the side to allow the men to speak through the bars.

"Wickham, I was told you requested to speak to me. What is it you wish to say?"

"Ah, the knight is shining armor, riding his trusty steed to save the damsel in distress. And how is the fair maiden? Though I should change that, as maiden she is no more."

"My betrothed is as virtuous as the day she was born. She was not sullied by you or your pack. But I will say this, Miss Elizabeth is alive and will recover. She spoke to me just before I left to come here. Now, what is it that you have to say to me? Make it quick or I will know you are still lying and leave."

"Lying? Unfortunately for you and your family, I am not lying of this. One of your beloved relatives wished you to be ruined, how do you like those apples?"

"My relative? And just which of my relatives are you speaking? Which of my family members wish to see me destroyed?" Darcy asked, his anger brewing just under the surface.

"Ah, I will tell you, but there has to be a reward for my breaking the trust this person had with me. My life is in jeopardy, I wish to continue living. And I believe some funds to begin a new life would be appropriate."

"You are a fool, Wickham. Do you truly believe I am able to save your pathetic life? Or that I would give you one coin? What a joke you are. You are attempting a last effort to save your skin, and I would not trust a word from your lips. Good day, Wickham. Enjoy the few you have remaining."

With that, Darcy turned and marched out of the prison. When he reached his carriage, he could still hear Wickham crying out for him to return. *No, I will not give him another thought. It is time to return to Elizabeth.*

~~ ** ~~

By the time Darcy had returned to his townhouse, he was exhausted. It had been a long day, filled with such emotional uproar, which drained his energy. He entered the bedchamber of his betrothed, not even bothering to knock. A smile graced his lips when he found Elizabeth lying on the bed, a sweet smile on her lips. Doctor Josephson turned to see who had entered and acknowledged Darcy's arrival.

Whispering, Darcy inquired as to Elizabeth's

condition. Before the doctor could speak, Elizabeth's sweet voice spoke out. "I am better, William, now that you have returned. Are you well?"

"Hearing your voice is like a breath of fresh air in my longs. It has been a long day, and you should be sleeping."

"Not until you returned. I needed to see you, to know you were well." Elizabeth closed her eyes. "I pray that your meeting went well."

"It is of no importance, Elizabeth. Now, I plan to sit here in this chair and read, while you sleep and have peaceful dreams." Darcy stated, as he placed a kiss on the bandaging on her head.

~~ ** ~~

When Mr Bennet checked on his daughter later, he was surprised to find his future son in law, fast asleep in the chair. He thought it was wise to allow the young man to sleep, after all that had happened that day and it was becoming late in the evening.

Near nine that evening, Mr Bingley appeared at Darcy House. He had found the note that had been delivered to Netherfield, from Wickham, asking him to meet him at Oakham Mount that fateful morning, directing a time as well. Though Wickham had sealed his own fate, this was icing on the cake. Richard knocked on the door of the bedchamber and was allowed to step inside quietly. When he stepped to his cousin's side, he attempted to wake him. Only Darcy did not wake. Richard noticed the heat coming from his cousin's body and placed the back of his hand to Darcy's forehead.

"Good God, he is burning up." Richard called out. Elizabeth woke to the sound and quickly became agitated by the news.

"William, wake my love. Please, William, wake for me." She cried out.

Richard scooped his cousin into his arms and carried him across to the door leading to the Master's bedchamber. Lying Darcy on the bed, Richard was removing his coat and waist coat before Doctor Josephson entered the room.

"He has a high fever." Richard explained. "And I could not wake him."

"His wound must have taken an infection. From what Mr Jones explained, Mr Darcy would not allow his injury to be tended until after the man examined Miss Elizabeth. Even then, he has not rested since the incident, leaving him less resistant to fight an infection."

Mrs Jenkins entered the chambers as Richard

called out for a basin of the coldest water they could furnish, as well as cloths to use to cool his body down.

From the Mistress' chambers, Elizabeth was sobbing, her fear of losing the man she had come to love was shattering her heart.

~~ ** ~~

Lady Anne was sitting beside the bed of her brother, reading to him. His recovery was slow, but each day he was improving.

After papers were signed with the solicitor, naming Richard as the heir to Matlock, and disowning Anthony, Richard had left for London to prepare to resign his commission.

When Anthony learned he was disowned, he was furious. His father gave him a small property in Norfolk, though the property was protected against Anthony being able to sell it or use it to procure a loan. He was also given one thousand pounds with which to begin his new life, and Anthony was assured there would be no further assistance coming from any member of the family.

Learning of his family's determination to desert him, Anthony flew into a rage. Before leaving for Town, Richard made sure his brother was removed from Matlock, sending two footmen who were loyal to

Lord Matlock, to escort Anthony to Norfolk. This further infuriated the former heir. As he entered the carriage which would take him from his home, Anthony cried out that he would exact his revenge against everyone in his family.

Richard had informed all the staff of the change in heirs, and of his brother being evicted from the estate. They were to report immediately if Anthony was seen in the area, and the man was not to be allowed to enter the house for any reason.

Lady Anne knew there was a guard outside Lord Matlock's room at all times. Another precaution Richard had left in place when he traveled to London. This brought her a sense of peace. Looking up, Lady Anne noticed her brother had dozed off again. She quickly left the room, making her way towards her own suite of rooms.

The butler stepped towards her. "Lady Anne, an express just arrived for you."

"My thanks, Alfred." She took the express and continued to her sitting room. Opening the letter, she began to read.

Aunt Anne,

I beg you to come to London as soon as you possibly can. There has been a situation which has occurred and William needs you to come immediately.

I cannot go into details, it is far too extensive to tell the entire story. William, I am certain, has spoken to you of Miss Elizabeth Bennet. Wickham and two other men attacked her, beating her severely. William came upon them, and in the struggle, he was injured. He has developed a severe fever and the surgeon fears for his life.

Please hurry. I will make certain that extra security is added to watch over my father in your absence.

Your nephew,

Richard

Lady Anne Carrington nearly collapsed. How could this have happened? Wickham, the man was a plague to her son. She prayed that his evil would finally come to an end. She called out to her maid to have her trunk packed and ready for her to leave within the hour. Stepping to the hallway, Lady Anne saw the butler nearing the staircase.

"Alfred, have my carriage prepared and brought to the front of the house. I must leave for Town immediately."

"Yes, my lady. I will have the kitchen prepare a basket of food and drink for you as well."

Lady Anne nodded her thanks and then turned back towards her rooms. Going to her desk, she pulled out some parchment and wrote a message to her nephew informing him she was on her way, followed by a letter to her husband to inform him of the situation. At the end of her husband's letter, she asked him to come to London, bringing Georgiana.

Once the letters were given to a footman to be sent express, Lady Anne returned to her brother's rooms. Lord Matlock was beginning to stir as she approached his bed.

"Henry, I must leave for London in a few moments. I received a letter from Richard telling me William is very ill with a high fever. I have sent a message to

Albert to have him bring Georgiana to London as well. Will you be well without me?"

"Anne, go. I have staff here to care for me. Send word of William as soon as you know how he is." Henry Fitzwilliam stated.

"I will, Brother. Pray for him."

Nodding his head, Lord Matlock said he would.

~~ ** ~~

For nearly four days, Richard sat at his cousin's bedside, assisting the surgeon who was tending Darcy. For days, Darcy's fever raged on and on. The young man was fighting, but the fever had taken a strong hold of him and refused to let him go.

Elizabeth had to be sedated, her fears for him had been so great and she had tried to come to his side when her maid was retrieving fresh water. Fortunately, she had not caused further harm to herself. Mr Bennet and Jane had determined it was best if one of them was with Elizabeth at all times. When she was awake, all Elizabeth could think of was seeing Darcy. All she wanted was to know he would survive and be well.

Bingley had assisted wherever he could, sending messages, making requests for more supplies, having food and drink brought to everyone when they needed it, and even being forceful in making sure they took nourishment to keep themselves going. He would sit beside Darcy when Richard needed to refresh himself.

The door opened suddenly, and Lady Anne entered the room. She rushed to the side of her son's bed, lifting his hand to her cheek. "Richard, has there been any improvement?"

Richard shook his head. "None. He is growing weaker each day. The fever is making him delirious."

"What of Miss Elizabeth? Where is she?" Lady Anne asked, as she kept her eyes trained on her son.

"She is in the Mistress' chambers, I have not checked on her since yesterday." Richard felt guilty for ignoring the young lady who loved his cousin, but he was riddled with fear and grief at the thought of losing the man who was more a brother to him than Anthony ever was.

"I will check on her." Lady Anne knew that news of Elizabeth would be of comfort to her son.

"Aunt Anne, I must tell you what has happened before you enter the room." Richard's eyes came up to meet his aunt's. "Wickham and the other men, they were planning to force themselves on Miss Elizabeth.

The beating Wickham gave her caused a crack to her skull and blood to build up pressure in the brain. The surgeon, Doctor Josephson, was required to drill holes in her skull to drain the blood, or the pressure would have built until it killed her."

Lady Anne gasped. "Is she to live?"

"Yes, though she will need to be taken care of for quite some time. Fortunately, your son saw to all of her needs, taking all the care possible. He was given permission from Miss Elizabeth's father to be her betrothed. William was planning to ask her that very morning, which was why he arrived when he did. He was meeting Miss Elizabeth there. In the struggle, William was able to kill two of the men, leaving him to deal with Wickham. In their struggle, William received a bullet wound. It was treated, but, due to his concern for his betrothed, he did not take proper care of himself."

"This is the reason for my son's fever, an infection from the wound he received? What has happened to Wickham? Is he in custody?"

"The scoundrel attempted to accuse William of being the one to have attacked Miss Elizabeth. We had to deal with a scandal that was brewing as well, as Wickham claimed my cousin had violated Miss Elizabeth many times. All of that blackguard's accusations were proven false, but it does not protect Miss Elizabeth from the humiliation of being the victim of the assault by these men." Richard looked at his cousin momentarily before he continued. "Wickham claims he was paid to destroy William, ruin him in society. We cannot prove it, but Wickham had a large sum of money hidden in his belongings at the militia camp in Meryton. It was found after Wickham was arrested."

"Who would do such a thing?" Lady Anne was sickened at the thought of someone behaving in such a manner.

"Can you not think of someone who has declared to avenge himself against William? Who would enjoy seeing William suffer?"

"No, I cannot believe he has sunk to such depths." Lady Anne was shocked. "Anthony does not have access to money, and William's ruin would do no good to your brother."

"I am not sure why he would do something so cruel, but it was clear that Anthony was angry at William for not assisting with paying off his debts." Richard took the cloth from Darcy's forehead and rewet it, returning it to Darcy's face.

"I would like to see Miss Elizabeth, meet the young lady who is to be my daughter soon." Lady Anne said as she stood. “When I return, I will take over tending to William, as I can see you are in need of rest.”

Richard nodded his head in agreement.

~~~~~~~~ ** ~~~~~~~~
~~~~~~~~

CHAPTER 11

Lady Anne knocked on the door to the Mistress' bedchamber, and was permitted to enter. Mr Bennet was sitting in the chair, beside the bed, holding his daughter's hand. Elizabeth was laying on the bed, pale and thin, the bandages and bruises making her appear quite fragile.

"Are you Mr Bennet?" she asked as she approached the bed. Seeing Mr Bennet nod, Lady Anne continued. "I am Anne Carrington, Lady Covington. I am Fitzwilliam Darcy's mother."

"I would say that it is an honor to meet you, but I would wish it were under better circumstances." Mr Bennet said.

"I am guessing this is Miss Elizabeth, my son's betrothed?" Again, Lady Anne witnessed Mr Bennet's nodding. "How is she fairing?"

"She is weak, and I fear that the sedation is keeping her from recovering. But when she is awake, she is distraught at Mr Darcy not being at her side."

"Mr Bennet, I wish to make a suggestion to you. I know my son well enough to know he needs to know your daughter is alive. From the sounds of it, your daughter needs the same reassurance. I know it is highly improper to make this suggestion, but from the looks of both, it is time for taking a drastic step."

Mr Bennet frowned as he listened to Lady Anne. "What are you suggesting?"

"We should move your daughter into William's bedchamber. We can either place them on the same bed, though separated by the bedclothes, or another bed can be taken into the room and be placed beside his. I believe their being able to reassure one another will give them the strength to recover from all they have been through."

Looking down upon his beloved daughter, Mr Bennet knew that she was giving up her will to live, her fear for the man she had come to love was wearing her strength down. Keeping her sedated was causing harm to her as well. "Very well, Lady Anne, I will agree to the plan. Shall we have Lizzy carried into your son immediately?"

"The sooner the better, I believe. Which would you prefer, a second bed or on William's bed? As you are most likely aware, the bed is large enough for four people to lie side by side."

Mr Bennet chuckled lightly. "It would be just as improper either way, so we might as well place her beside him."

Lady Anne stepped over to the door which

separated the two bedchambers. "Richard, would you come here, please?"

Richard came quickly to the door, entering the room and looking at Elizabeth. "Has something happened? Is Miss Elizabeth worse?"

"Richard, Mr Bennet and I have discussed the need William and Miss Elizabeth have to know the other is alive. It is my belief that if they can be together, they will be able to rally their strength and recover. Mr Bennet agreed with my suggestion. Would you be kind enough to carry Miss Elizabeth to your cousin's bed?"

Shocked by his aunt's suggestion, but willing to do whatever he could to assist his cousin recover, Richard moved to gently lift his future cousin. She began to stir as she was being moved, and Richard spoke softly to her. "Miss Elizabeth, stay calm. I am taking you to see William. Be still, you will be with him in a moment."

As she was placed on the bed tenderly, Elizabeth turned towards the fever riddled body of the man she loved. In a quiet voice, barely over a whisper, she began to beg Darcy to stay with her. Her hand reached up to the wet cloth on his forehead, removing it and asked for someone to refresh it. Once ready, Elizabeth took the cloth and gently dabbed it to his fevered brow. "I love you, William. Please fight your way back to me. Do not leave me."

Though weak, it was plain to see that Elizabeth was calmer than she had been in days. She continued to do what she could for Darcy, all the while allowing others to tend to her as well. When Mr Bennet insisted his daughter take some broth and bread, she did as she was told. Elizabeth knew she needed strength to care for Darcy, and she had no desire to be removed from his side due to her own frailty. And Elizabeth had no desire to be sedated again, so she would behave to the best of her ability.

The entire day and well into the evening, Elizabeth, Richard, Lady Anne, and Mr Bennet did all that they could to bring Darcy's fever under control. Finally, near midnight, Darcy began to cool. The fever had broken. Darcy began to sleep peacefully, for the first time in a week. Exhaustion finally overtook Elizabeth, and she, too, fell into a natural sleep. Lady Anne remained with her son and future daughter, allowing the others to go to their own rooms to sleep.

Just before dawn, Lady Anne heard her son beginning to stir. "William, stay calm. You would not wish to wake Miss Elizabeth, would you?"

"Lizzy?" Darcy looked first at his mother, then at the woman beside him on the bed. "Am I having a bizarre dream?"

"No, dear boy, you are truly lying beside the woman you love. Nothing else seemed to work to help you fight the fever you developed, and they were forced to keep Miss Elizabeth sedated to keep her from rising from her bed to come to you. The sedation was not aiding in her recovery, so Mr Bennet agreed to my plan to have her brought to your side."

"Thank you, Mother. I am pleased you are here."

"Where else would I be, William? You and Georgiana are the dearest part of my life. Albert and Georgie will be here tomorrow. We wish to be here for you and for Miss Elizabeth." Lady Anne smoothed back some curls which were on her son's forehead. "Now, if you ever scare me like this again, I will be forced to have Richard take you behind the stables and tan your hide."

"Forgive me, Mother. I had not planned to end up in this manner. But I would do it all over again to protect Elizabeth from what was happening to her."

Wiping tears from her cheeks, Lady Anne smiled. "Your cousin told me what happened. I am so proud of you, William. You saved Miss Elizabeth from being killed by those men. I cannot wait to get to know her better. From everything you wrote to me, and the devotion she showed yesterday in tending to you, she is indeed a most amazing young lady and deserving of your love."

"Thank you, Lady Anne." Came a soft voice beside Darcy. It was another few moments before her eyes opened, but Elizabeth was feeling stronger than she had since she was attacked.

"Welcome back to the world, Miss Elizabeth. I am pleased to see a little color in your cheeks, compared to yesterday. How are you doing? Is there anything you need?"

"Everything I need is beside me, here on the bed." Elizabeth smiled. "I am grateful for your speaking to my father and convincing him to allow me to be at William's side."

"I am grateful that my ludicrous plan worked." Lady Anne chuckled. "Now, I will send to the kitchen for something to be brought up for you. You both need to eat something to build your strength."

In unison, Darcy and Elizabeth smiled and said "Yes, Mother."

~~ ** ~~

The arrival of Lord Covington and Miss Georgiana Carrington was met with appreciation. Lady Anne welcomed her husband and daughter, insisting they remain at Darcy House rather than open their own townhouse. As there were plenty of rooms available, Lady Anne felt it would be ridiculous to allow her husband to withdraw from her son's home.

"Albert, it is time that whatever issues have been between William and us are resolved. I have never understood why William resents you or our marriage, but it is time to work it out. I nearly lost my son, and the young lady he loves. It is time that we act like a family." Lady Anne had tears flowing down her cheeks.

"Anne, I will do whatever is needed to see the breach mended. I love you, and our daughter. William is your son, therefore, I cannot help but care for him. I have never truly understood his animosity towards me, but I wish for it to come to an end as well."

Georgiana came into the room. "Mother, how is William?"

"He is much better. And he has exciting news for us."

"Is he to marry Miss Elizabeth?" Georgiana's eyes widened. "Each letter I have received from him has spoken of the young lady."

"Yes, your brother is indeed engaged to marry

Miss Elizabeth. Once they have both recovered sufficiently, they will have a wedding." Lady Anne said with a smile, her hand caressing her daughter's hair.

"Both? Was Miss Elizabeth ill as well?" Georgiana was frightened. Albert was interested in knowing what had happened to Miss Elizabeth Bennet, as Anne had not been able to tell him.

"Miss Elizabeth was injured badly, and she was brought to Town to be treated by a surgeon. They were fortunate in being able to save her life. After she was doing better, William fell ill with a fever."

"Anne, you are not telling us the full story. I know you would wish to protect Georgiana, but I feel it is important to be honest with her." Lord Covington stated.

Lady Anne looked into her husband's eyes, tears continued to flow down her cheeks. Her eyes returned to looking into her daughter's eyes. "Your father is correct. Miss Elizabeth was attacked by three men, with the intention of violating her. William arrived in time to save her from the worst, though she had been beaten severely. In protecting Miss Elizabeth, your brave brother was forced to defend himself and Miss Elizabeth. Two of the men were killed, the other injured William when he struggled with your brother for control of a gun. The wound was treated, but with his concern over Miss Elizabeth and dealing with the issues of the men, he did not rest as he should have."

Georgiana was shaken. "How badly was Miss Elizabeth injured?"

"Due to blood pooling in her brain, the surgeon was forced to make holes in her skull to release the pressure. Otherwise she would have died."

A gasp was heard from both Georgiana and her father. Albert reached out a hand to his wife, who eagerly gripped it for strength. "As Miss Elizabeth began to improve, William was finally overcome with fatigue. After he had slept for some time, Richard discovered William was running a very high fever."

"The fever has broken now?" Albert asked in a soft, caring voice.

"Fortunately. He was very ill for several days. It was the love that he has for Miss Elizabeth, and her for him, which made him fight his way back to us. It was improper for us to take Miss Elizabeth to William's bedside, but it was worth it to see both of them truly begin to recover. They had to sedate Miss Elizabeth during William's illness, or she would have harmed herself trying to get to his side."

"Mother, they do love each other. It is so romantic." Georgiana embraced her mother. "William has found a lady who will love him as you do Father."

"I am pleased to know the depths of Miss Elizabeth's regard for your brother. I was sure of his feelings towards her, his letters were quite telling to one who knows William as I do."

"Anne, I could not be happier for your son. I look forward to meeting Miss Elizabeth when she is stronger." Albert said with a smile.

Lady Anne nodded her head. "Well, let us get you two settled into rooms. I wish to return to check on our two patients."

~~ ** ~~

Two days after Darcy's fever broke, a message arrived for Richard from General Stockwell. Wickham had been found guilty of conspiracy, attempted murder, attempted rape, abduction, false report, and several other lesser charges. He was sentence to death, and was hanged the following morning. Even as he was led to the gallows, Wickham cried out for Darcy, begging to speak with the man, claiming he had information as to the person who had hired him. His dying words were cursing Fitzwilliam Darcy and Elizabeth Bennet, for leading him to his death.

Though relieved to be rid of Wickham forever, the thought remained that the man claimed to have been hired by someone close to Darcy, to ruin Darcy in the eyes of society. It was believed Anthony had been the one behind hiring Wickham. Richard could not fathom where money would have come from, as his brother had very little.

~~ ** ~~

With both Darcy and Elizabeth recovering, Elizabeth was returned to her own rooms for propriety's sake. Though they were saddened by the separation, Darcy was granted the freedom to sit beside her often, so long as he did not overtax himself.

Elizabeth had convinced Darcy to return to his bed to rest just an hour before Lady Anne came to visit her. "Lady Anne, I cannot thank you enough for all you have done for my family."

"Goodness, my dear girl, you are soon to be my family as well. And I know how precious you are to William."

"Might I ask you a question, Lady Anne?" Elizabeth asked nervously.

"You may ask, if you start calling me Mother." Lady Anne smiled as she squeezed Elizabeth's hand lightly.

"Did you love William's father?"

Lady Anne was not expecting such a question. "I loved him dearly. Gerard was one of the kindest men I have ever known, and handsome. William looks so much like his father, including those incredible dimples. Whenever Gerard smiled, showing his dimples, my heart melted. He treated me as if I were his princess, making me feel cherished and loved. When he died, a part of me died with him."

"William does not believe you loved his father. He told me that he felt you would not have married again if you had truly loved his father." Elizabeth divulged.

Shocked, Lady Anne stood and began to pace. "This is why he has held such dislike for Albert? He believes my marriage to his own father was of convenience?"

Elizabeth nodded her head.

"Oh, my poor boy. All these years he has felt such pain and for nothing. If I had only known, I could have told him the truth. Gerard taught me what it was like to love openly and generously. Elizabeth, you cannot know how grateful I am to you for telling me this. Now I can speak to William, tell him about my marriage to his father. Hopefully, we will be able to mend the relationship between William and Albert."

"I pray that it can be so." Elizabeth said with a smile.

~~ ** ~~

Bingley decided to leave Darcy House to do some shopping. Jane had explained to him that Elizabeth's hair had been shaved from one side of her head, and he wished to find something to cheer his future sister in law. The bandaging would be in place for another week, and then she would most likely desire something to wear to hide her lack of hair.

Lady Anne had suggested a milliner who might be able to design something to be of comfort to Elizabeth, as she was already self-conscious about her looks. Not only was the hair missing, but she also had scars from the holes in her skull, and it would be some time before her hair grew back enough to cover her head.

After speaking with the milliner, and ordering several fashionable covers which would hopefully bring Elizabeth comfort, Bingley stepped out of the shop and headed for the confectionary shop next door. Entering the door, Bingley could not believe his eyes. Standing before him was his missing sister. "Caroline, where have you been? We have been trying to find you for weeks now."

"Oh, Charles, it is a pleasure to see you again. What brings you to Town?"

"I am here with Darcy and some of the Bennets. I wish to speak with you." Bingley was looking around for a private area in the shop to allow him to speak with his sister.

Just then, a man stepped to Caroline's side. "Is all well, Dearest?"

"Dearest? Forgive me, Sir, but I insist you not speak to my sister so informally." Bingley declared.

"Ah, Charles Bingley. A pleasure to meet you at last. Has my dear Caroline not written to you about me?"

Bingley was confused. "I have not heard of you Sir, nor have I been introduced to you."

Caroline placed a hand gently on the other man's arm. "Charles, allow me to introduce you to Mr Geoffrey Goodman. Geoff, my love, this is my brother, Charles."

"Caroline, you are behaving most improperly, and in public. I need you to come with me immediately, as we have much of which to speak."

Mr Goodman placed a hand gently, though firmly, over Caroline's hand on his arm. "Forgive me, Mr Bingley, but my wife does not require your assistance or shall you force her to join you for a private conversation."

"YOUR WIFE?" Bingley nearly shouted to the entire shop. "When did you marry?"

"Why, just last week." Caroline stated. "It was a lovely ceremony, and we then spent three days at Geoff's townhouse. Today is one of the first days we have come out of the house, as my dear husband insisted on taking me to order a new wardrobe. He is so very kind to me." Caroline was practically salivating as she spoke.

"I am here to inform you, Bingley, I will do all that I can to protect my wife from you and your other sister. I plan to see my solicitor, to see what is needed to be done to release Caroline's trust fund. I will warn you to refrain from further contact with my wife, especially without me present." Goodman was adamant.

"If this is what you wish, Caro, I wish you great joy in your married life. I will speak to my solicitor and have him prepare the papers to release the trust to you, Goodman. Have no fear, I have no plans to stand in the way of your happiness. The trust was set up for my sister's protection, it is her money to do with as she sees fit." Bingley found it difficult to hide his frustration with his sister. "I will leave you now, Mr and Mrs Goodman. God bless you both."

Bingley then turned and walked away from his sister. *How had this come to be? His sister was married, she was no longer under his protection.* Having had enough for one day, Bingley returned to Darcy House.

~~~~~~~~ ** ~~~~~~~~
~~~~~~~~

CHAPTER 12

Mrs Bennet was finally pulling herself together again. Fortunately, her husband had the presence of mind to send her brother and sister in law, Edwin and Helen Gardiner, from their home in Town, to look after Fanny and the younger three Bennet daughters.

When the rumors were expanding on the lies Wickham had started, before leaving Meryton with Colonel Forster, Mrs Bennet feared for her family being ruined. She continued to have nightmares of Elizabeth dying, and Mr Bingley refusing to marry Jane. She also had nightmares of the younger girls having to become scullery maids and never being able to marry. All of the ruination because of the rumors of Mr Darcy having forced himself on Elizabeth, or worse, Elizabeth was giving herself to him willingly, without being married.

Mr Gardiner had learned the truth before leaving London, as Mr Bennet had sent for him while they waited for the surgeon to relieve the pressure building inside Elizabeth head. The General had just left the Darcy townhouse, pronouncing Mr Darcy innocent of being the perpetrator of Elizabeth's injuries, when Mr Gardiner was shown to the sitting room.

Mrs Bennet was relieved to learn that Elizabeth

had not been violated, but her fear grew when she learned how severe her daughter's injuries were. Her heart ached for Mr Darcy as well, as she was certain he loved her daughter completely. And she ached to comfort her husband, for she knew how dear Elizabeth had always been to Thomas Bennet. Helen Gardiner sat beside Mrs Bennet's bed, talking with her, encouraging her to eat and rest.

Two days after the attack, word arrived from two sources. First, an express arrived from Mr Bennet, explaining Darcy's fever and the need to sedate Elizabeth to keep her from harming herself. The second source of information was from Sir William Lucas, and he came with news that Colonel Forster had been taken into custody in Town for his failing to command properly. A new commander had been sent to Meryton to take over the militia regiment, a Colonel Watkins. It was from Colonel Watkins, who had been given the information directly from General Stockwell, that Sir William learned the true events of the fateful morning.

According to Sir William, everything Wickham had claimed, before he was taken to London, was false. It had been Wickham who had instigated the attack, bringing his friends Woods and Denny, with him. They had intended to ruin Elizabeth, and blame Darcy, thereby ruining him as well. Fortunately, Darcy had arrived in time to rescue Elizabeth before the men could violate her, and Darcy had killed Woods and Denny in self-defense. When Wickham struggled with Darcy for the gun, the latter was shot, which had led to his taking a fever. The evidence had cleared Darcy, and convicted Wickham. Wickham faced a list of charges and would, most likely, be hung, if found guilty. Colonel Forster was most likely to be demoted or even dismissed from the militia. Sir William was remorseful for all that had happened to his neighbors and friends, he was fond of Elizabeth, who was his eldest daughter's closest friend.

Sir William promised Mr Gardiner that he would contact all of the families in the neighborhood and inform them of the true nature of the events, in an attempt to protect the Bennet family from ruin.

~~ ** ~~

Darcy had been resting in his room, waking late in the evening. "Ah, my son is awake." Lady Anne said with a smile. She leaned towards him, reaching out her hand to caress a lock of hair which had fallen on his forehead. "How are you this evening?"

"I am well, Mother. Is Lizzy well?" Darcy rubbed the sleep from his eyes.

"She is much better and resting peacefully. I would like to have a little bit of your time. There is something important I wish to discuss with you."

Darcy looked at his mother with concern. "What is wrong?"

"Nothing is wrong, my dear boy. But there is something important I believe we should discuss. It is my understanding you believe I did not love your father, that our marriage was one of convenience."

A blush grew on Darcy's cheeks, and he knew Elizabeth had spoken with his mother. "It is not important, Mother. I know that marriages of convenience are common in our society."

"William, how can you think that I did not love your father? Can you not remember all the times you saw Gerard and me together? Can you not recall our constantly touching each other, holding hands, his arm wrapped around my waist as we walked? We never held with the society view on having separate bedchambers, and I never slept a day in the Mistress' bed in my married life. Your father and I shared a passion that was beyond words. You are proof of our devotion. And it appears that you were not aware of the three other times I was with child by your father. I lost those children, the last one died at birth. Your father was devastated, as he knew how dearly I wished for more children to love."

"But, if you loved Father so dearly, how could you

marry Lord Covington so quickly and be so happy with him? It is clear that you love him."

Lady Anne laughed. "Do you believe I love you?" Seeing her son nod his head, she continued. "And do you believe I love Georgiana?" Again, Darcy nodded his head. "It is possible to love more than one person, my dear boy. The love I shared with your father was intense and powerful. The love I share with Albert is comfortable and soothing. Albert and I have known each other since we were children, so he knows everything about me. He has always been in my heart, though as a dear friend when I was married to your father. Albert has nothing but respect for your father, and for you. I cannot believe that all these years, you have held Albert in disdain because you felt I did not love your father. You were so young when your father died, perhaps I should have realized you needed to hear from me how much I loved Gerard, I hope you can forgive me for failing to do so."

"It is I who should be asking for forgiveness. I have made a fool of myself all these years, treating Lord Covington so abominably. Will he ever forgive me for my behavior?"

"You should spend some time with Albert, talk to him openly. I believe he is more than willing to have you be a part of our family. And I think that your father would approve as well." Lady Anne leaned forward and placed a kiss on her son's forehead. "Now, I will have a tray brought up for the two of us to share, and then you will sleep some more. Doctor Josephson will be here in the morning to check on you and Elizabeth."

~~ ** ~~

Doctor Josephson was pleased with the progress that both Darcy and Elizabeth had made. The stitches on the side of Elizabeth's head were removed, as it had been nearly a fortnight since the attack. Hair had started to regrow, though Elizabeth was self-conscious of anyone seeing her head without bandages. When the surgeon was examining her, Elizabeth insisted on everyone leaving the room, except the maid, Hannah, who was to tend her while Elizabeth recovered and be her lady's maid after the wedding. Not even Jane was allowed to see her sister's head.

After the stitches were removed, Doctor Josephson did not return the bandages. "Miss Elizabeth, there is no need for bandages any further. The incisions are healed, and there is no need to worry about bleeding from them."

"Doctor, I cannot be seen with half my head nearly bald. I would be mortified for anyone, other than you and Hannah, to see me so."

"You realize it will take quite some time before your hair is grown out?" Seeing Elizabeth nod and look down at her hands, Doctor Josephson took pity on her. "Miss Elizabeth, I must tell you that the young man waiting on the other side of that door cares not a bit for your hair. The fact that you are alive and love him is all he needs."

Tears began to overflow from Elizabeth's eyes. "I know he loves me, but will he wish to have me seen on his arm, in public? People will know by looking at me that something happened. He will come to be ashamed to be betrothed to me and will wish to call off the wedding."

"Miss Elizabeth, Master William would never do such a thing. He loves you so much, nothing would change his mind with regards to marrying you." Hannah attempted to soothe her lady. "And Mr Bingley had some special scarves made for you, to cover your head."

"Mr Bingley did?" Elizabeth was amazed.

"He said that you will be his sister when he marries Miss Bennet, and he wished to do something to ease your mind. Granted, you will wish to only wear it while in the house." Hannah went to the dressing room and returned with several pieces of cloth. "They are somewhat like a gypsy head covering, only not as colorful. Mr Bingley thought soft pastel colors would be preferred for this."

Hannah assisted Elizabeth placing the covering on her head. Elizabeth looked into the peer glass and was frustrated with the view. Half of her head was covered with long curls, even when pulled back and pinned, curls escaped and hung down. And under the cloth the curls could be seen. The other side of her head was obvious in showing no curls or hair at all.

"Hannah, would you bring the shears please?"

Confused, Hannah did as she was asked. Doctor Josephson watched, praying his patient would find a way to cope with the change in her appearance.

Elizabeth took the cloth off her head and unpinned her hair. Taking the shears in hand, she took hold of her hair and cut it short. "Miss Elizabeth, what are you doing?" Hannah shrieked. There was pounding on the door, as Darcy was concerned after hearing the maid cry out. Fortunately, Elizabeth had insisted on the door being locked, or her betrothed would have entered the room.

"I will not have my hair long on one side and stubble on the other side. This way, as the hair grows in, it will not be in such contrast with the other side." Elizabeth stated with slightly more confidence than she truly felt. The hair was now cut to the bottom of her ear. "Hannah, would you assist me in tying the cloth on my head again?"

"Of course, Miss Elizabeth." Hannah said, taking the cloth and tying it carefully about her lady's head. After the initial shock, Hannah was proud of the courage it had taken for Elizabeth to cut her hair as she did. Hannah collected the remnants of hair and removed it from the room.

Once Elizabeth was prepared to face her family, she allowed the door to be opened. Darcy nearly fell into the room, and rushed to Elizabeth's side. "Dearest, are you well? I heard Hannah cry out, is something wrong?"

"No, William, everything is fine." Elizabeth said, though she could not look him in the eyes. She was nervous as to how Darcy would react to her appearance.

Darcy looked at Elizabeth, and then turned his attention to Doctor Josephson. The surgeon smiled slightly as he motioned with his eyes towards Elizabeth's head. Darcy noticed the cloth his fiancé donned. He then looked at Hannah who was standing several steps behind Elizabeth. Hannah held up a single, long curl and the shears. This enlightened Darcy as to what had happened. His beloved Elizabeth was concerned with how she appeared to him and others. She had cut her curls off, making her lack of curls on the other side more consistent. Darcy was proud of his courageous love. To him, she had never been more beautiful than at that moment.

"My dear Elizabeth, I must commend Bingley on his suggestion of wraps for your head. That color brings out the sparkle in your beautiful eyes. Are you ready to come to the drawing room? Everyone is waiting to see you."

"Remember, Mr Darcy, I only allowed you to take her to the drawing room for one half hour. Then she is to return to her bed and rest. And you are to rest as well. I do not want you doing too much either."

"Of course, Doctor." Darcy stated. "Are you ready, Elizabeth?"

Elizabeth looked up and into Darcy's eyes. Seeing the love and devotion which was clearly written in his eyes convinced her to stand and leave her room, holding on to his arm for support.

There were cheers of delight and praises when Elizabeth and Darcy entered the drawing room. Mr Bennet gave his daughter a kiss on her cheek. "Lizzy, you look wonderful. And Doctor Josephson is pleased with your improvement?"

"He is, Papa. The stitches were removed and he

said that other than rest and being careful not to re-injure my head, I should be fine." Elizabeth smiled.

Jane was next to her sister. "Oh, Charles, you were correct. The cloth is perfect. And the color, it is so flattering to her complexion and eyes. Lizzy, you are beautiful. Your eyes are shining again."

"Your sister is worried that we will think less of her because of her lack of hair. I think she is quite beautiful, no matter how much hair she has on her head." Darcy said as he lifted her hand to his lips.

"They say that love is blind, William. But I cannot be seen outside the house. It is difficult enough to be seen by all of you." Elizabeth's concern was obvious.

Lady Anne stepped up to her future daughter. "Elizabeth, you have no reason to be shy around us. We love you, no matter what has happened. In fact, I believe I love you more because of what happened, and what you have done to recover. As I have never seen what you looked like before the attack, I find no difference in your looks. And I agree with Jane, the color of the cloth wrap is quite flattering on you."

Moving behind his wife, Lord Covington smiled. "Anne is correct, you are a beautiful young lady who has a strength I have rarely seen before. William, you are a fortunate man. When are the two of you going to set the date for the wedding?"

Elizabeth's eyes grew wide with fear. "We must wait, I cannot be seen looking like this at my wedding."

"My love, you need not worry over your appearance. We can purchase a special license and marry here in the house. No one, outside of our loved ones, needs to be invited. And I think a wreath of flowers for you to wear upon your head would be quite fetching. What say you, Mother?"

"I agree, William. The gown I wore would only need a few alterations to fit you, Elizabeth. And we have a seamstress on staff that can fit it to you." Lady Anne said, encouragingly.

Mr Bennet joined in the fray. "I will add my opinion. Elizabeth, you will be a beautiful bride, no matter what you wear or having hair pulled back in a bun. Your mother would insist on your wearing a wedding bonnet or a beautiful piece of lace over your hair anyway. Mr Darcy's suggestion of a wreath is a wonderful suggestion."

Elizabeth was overwhelmed. "Can we discuss the wedding date later? I am still coming to terms with my appearance, I need to think."

"Of course, Dearest." Darcy smiled as he spoke. "Now, we should discuss our plans for Christmas. As it is only a fortnight away, we should decide what we would like to do for the holiday."

"My brother, Gardiner, suggested he and his wife bring Fanny and the younger girls to Town, to their home. I will move to the Gardiner home, leaving Jane here with Lizzy. We can come visit the girls sometime during the day on Christmas. This would allow all of you to enjoy the holiday in your own fashion as well."

"Thomas Bennet, we will be family when my son and your daughter are wed. I will not tolerate a separation of the two families. Our Christmas celebration will include your family from this year forward." Lady Anne insisted.

"Mr Bennet, I suggest you not argue. My wife is quite tenacious when she wishes to be." Lord Covington said with a laugh.

"I will insist we stay at the Gardiner home though. We can easily join all of you here. I would like to provide Lizzy with some peace and quiet to continue to heal." Mr Bennet was adamant.

"Very well, Papa, you may stay with Aunt Helen and Uncle Edwin. I must say I am surprised, as I would not have thought we could pry you from the library here at Darcy House."

"Your betrothed has given me leave to borrow any of his books, so I will still be able to enjoy the books, if not the room." Mr Bennet smiled. "Though I am looking forward to the journey to your future home in Derbyshire, for I am told that it is three times the size of this library."

Darcy smiled. "We will have a bed moved to the Pemberley library, so that you will not have to leave it. Your meals can all be sent there as well."

"Do not encourage him, or we will never see him again." Elizabeth laughed.

It was clear to everyone Elizabeth was becoming fatigued. "Elizabeth, I promised Doctor Josephson you would only be in here for a half an hour. I believe it is time to return you to your room. You promised to rest."

"I did promise, and I find I am quite sleepy. I do not understand why."

Mr Bennet embraced his daughter. "You have been through a major event, my dear girl. Your injury caused you to lose a tremendous quantity of blood. It will take time to build your strength."

"Thank you, everyone, for your kindness to me. And Mr Bingley, I am truly appreciative of your gift of the cloths. It was very thoughtful."

"You are my future sister, Miss Elizabeth. It is only

fitting that I would wish to be of service to you. I am pleased to know you like them."

Darcy led his fiancé back to her bedchamber. She decided to lay down in the morning gown she was wearing, and Darcy draped a coverlet over top of her. Before taking his leave, Darcy stoked the fire and placed another log on it. "Now, Dearest, sleep. I love you, Elizabeth." He said as he kneeled beside her bed, one hand caressing her cheek.

"I love you, William. Off with you, to your bed, as you also promised to rest."

Darcy leaned forward and placed a gentle kiss on Elizabeth's lips. "Yes, my love, and I will keep my promise."

~~ ** ~~

Mrs Bennet was pleased when she received an express asking her to bring her younger daughters to Town for the holidays. Mr and Mrs Gardiner were overjoyed with being able to return to their home, as their children were with their nanny, and they missed the children tremendously. All were grateful Elizabeth was on the mend as well.

Mr Bennet had also written to his wife to counsel her discretion when she saw Elizabeth for the first time. It would be shocking to see Elizabeth with the cloth wrapped about her head rather than her unruly dark curls. He also explained his daughter's nervousness for the way others would react to her. Determined to be a comfort to her daughter, Mrs Bennet thought of ways she could soothe her daughter's worries.

Lydia was being her natural self, wild and foolish, when her mother tried to speak on the matter. "La, Lizzy with no hair. What a good joke. It is best she is engaged, otherwise no man would have her."

Mrs Bennet walked to her youngest daughter and firmly shook the girl's shoulders. "Lydia, you are cruel. You sister was nearly killed, and her hair had to be shaved to save her life. We are fortunate Lizzy is still alive, as those men nearly took her from us forever. I will not tolerate your saying such cruel things about your sister, and you will be kind to her when you are in her presence. If you cannot control your silly ways, you will remain at the Gardiner home with the children, in the nursery."

"Mamma, Lizzy's hair will grow back, and we will all look back on this and laugh. It is funny to think of her with no hair on half her head. She will be lopsided."

Walking to the nearby cupboard, Mrs Bennet picked up a few items and returned to her youngest daughter. Reaching behind Lydia, Mrs Bennet took hold of the girl's bun and cut the hair with a pair of shears.

"MAMMA! What have you done?" Lydia cried out.

"I thought it would be funny to see you with your hair cut short. You seemed to think you would be laughing to see your sister, now you can see how she feels. Be grateful I do not shave part of your head as well. Your foolishness has now guaranteed your remaining in the nursery, as you cannot act as a proper young lady. Perhaps, when you finally learn to behave, your hair will have grown back."

Mrs Gardiner sat in her chair, watching the entire scene before her, attempting to keep from laughing. Lydia had always been carefree, no matter what anyone said or did to correct her. To see Fanny behave in such a manner was commendable.

Lydia ran from the room, tears streaming down her cheeks. Kitty looked on, shocked at her mother's behavior. Yet Kitty was also relieved. Though Lydia was her closest friend, Kitty was also offended by her younger sister's behavior. Hearing Lydia speak so carelessly towards Elizabeth had made their sister wish to strike the youngest.

"Now, let us plan for our trip. We should be able to leave tomorrow." Mrs Bennet said as she picked up the hair she had cut from her daughter.

"Bravo, Fanny, bravo. I am proud of you for putting Lydia in her place and making her see her foolishness." Mrs Gardiner said as she embraced her sister in law. "Mary, Kitty, let us begin to pack."

~~~~~~~~ ** ~~~~~~~~~
~~~~~~~~

CHAPTER 13

Mr Goodman was at his desk in his study when his wife came to the door. "Caroline, is something wrong?"

"No, I was just wondering if we were going to remain in Town for the holidays or if we would be traveling to your estate?"

"I thought we would remain in Town until after Twelfth Night. We have invitations to dinners and I thought it would be pleasant to take an evening at the theater. Does this meet with your approval?"

"Yes, though I hope that your friends are not friends of my brother or sister. I would hate for any uncomfortable situations."

"I have never run in the same circles as your siblings, so I doubt they will be invited to the gatherings we are. If, for some reason they are, we will leave immediately. You must know I will protect you from their maliciousness."

"Of course, my dear husband, and I cannot express to you how grateful I am to you." Caroline sidled up to her husband, though she had no affection for the man. He had been a means to an end.

"After the holidays, we will be able to enjoy

staying at the estate until the summer. In the summer, I wish to do some traveling to check on a piece of property in Scotland I wish to purchase. It will be pleasant to spend the summer in the north, where it will not be miserably hot."

"That sounds delightful. Well, I am planning to do some more shopping. I wish to have some new gowns made." Caroline simpered, knowing her husband would deny her nothing.

"Enjoy yourself, my love. I will see you at dinner this evening." Mr Goodman smiled and returned to his work.

~~ ** ~~

Mrs Bennet was nervous when she arrived at Darcy House. She did not wish to upset her daughter, yet she was frightened of the reaction she might have when she saw the cloth covering her head to hide the lack of hair. The footman escorted her to the drawing room to meet with her husband and eldest daughters.

Mr Bennet walked to his wife to welcome her, after the footman announced her arrival. "Fanny, I have missed you. Are you well?"

"I am, Thomas. How is Lizzy? Is she truly healing?" Mrs Bennet asked, her eyes seeking the truth in her husband's face.

"She is doing much better, my dear. She is in her rooms at the moment. I am afraid that she is nervous of your reaction to seeing her."

"I thought she would be. I left our other daughters at my brother's home, as I did not wish for Lizzy to be overwhelmed. May I see her?"

Mr Bennet took hold of his wife's hand and placed it on his arm. "I will show you to her rooms."

When they reached the Mistress' suite, Mr Bennet knocked on the door. Hannah opened the door and Mrs Bennet halted her husband's steps to enter. "Allow me some time with Elizabeth." she asked.

Nodding, Mr Bennet stepped back and returned to the drawing room. Mrs Bennet entered the room, finding her daughter sitting in a chair near the fireplace. "Lizzy, may I join you?"

"Certainly, Mamma." Elizabeth responded, though she kept her face turned from her mother. Mrs Bennet could see her daughter was being timid, something Elizabeth had never been. Before stepping to her daughter's side, Mrs Bennet asked Hannah something in a whisper.

"Lizzy, dear girl, may I look at you?" Mrs Bennet asked her daughter, wishing to ease her discomfort.

"There is no need, Mamma. I can tell you I am ugly. I am mortified to have anyone see me, and if they saw me without the cloth covering, I know I would die from the humiliation."

"Well, my sweet, smart, funny girl, you will have to get over such feelings. The most important aspect is that you are alive. I would rather have my daughter alive with no hair at all, than taken away from me forever with all those curls still intact. As a matter of fact, Hannah, do you have what I asked for?"

"Yes, Ma'am." Hannah stepped forward and handed something to Mrs Bennet. Fanny Bennet reached up and pulled the few pins she had placed in her hair to hold it in a simple bun that morning. Once her hair was down, Mrs Bennet reached to take hold of her hair, and taking the shears Hannah had handed her, cut her own hair.

"MAMMA! What on earth are you doing?" Elizabeth cried out.

"I wish to show you that hair is not the important thing here. You are beautiful, with or without your dark curls. You have the most amazing eyes, that dance with life and find the good in most everything. Your smile could make the world come to life with joy. And I love the way your cheeks look when you blush. If you are to live with your hair being gone, then it is only fair you are not alone. I wish to show my support to you as you recover."

Tears were streaming down Elizabeth's cheeks. "Mamma, you should not have cut your hair. Papa has said many times how much he loves your hair."

"And he will love me even without it. Now, I wish to see you without the cloth on your head." Mrs Bennet took a deep breath as she lifted her hand to Elizabeth's head.

Elizabeth's hand came up to halt her mother's progression. "Please, Mamma, no one, other than the surgeon and Hannah, has seen me without the covering. I would be mortified."

"I am your mother. I carried you inside me for so many months, feeling you move inside me. When you were only a year old, you took ill with a fever and we nearly lost you. I stayed at your side until the fever broke, nursing you the best I could. Nothing I see here will ever change the fact that I love you, and will be at your side through this. Please, Lizzy, allow me to see for myself."

Finally, Elizabeth lowered her hand and closed her eyes, as her mother slowly removed the cloth from Elizabeth's head. The hair on the left side of her head was beginning to grow back, though it was barely more than stubble. Mrs Bennet reached her fingers to caress the scars from the incisions and could feel where the holes had been made in the skull. "I wish I had been here for you, Lizzy. Your father was wise, though. Had I been awake when you had first been brought to the house, I would have been frantic. I have never been good with my first response to tragedy. It takes a little while for me to regain my balance and be able to pull myself together. And the rumors that started, claiming such wretched lies about you and Mr Darcy, oh, I fell apart. But now I can be here for you, Lizzy. Now I can be strong for you."

Elizabeth opened her eyes, looking into her mother's, finding the comfort her mother had to offer her. Sobs began to wrack her body, as Elizabeth fell into her mother's embrace. Soothingly, Mrs Bennet caressed her hand over her daughter's head, speaking softly with words of comfort.

~~ ** ~~

For two hours, Mr Bennet and Darcy paced about the drawing room, waiting for Mrs Bennet to return. Finally, they heard the door from Elizabeth's rooms open and the sound of Mrs Bennet and her second daughter laughing.

When the two ladies entered the drawing room, Mr Bennet stopped for a moment when he saw his wife. "Thomas, I decided to join Lizzy in making a fashion trend. Oh, and Lydia wished to know what her elder sister was experiencing, so I cut her hair as well. She is also to be spending time at the Gardiner house's nursery, with the other children."

Elizabeth was shocked at her mother's confession. It was clear that Lydia did not wish to know what it was like for Lizzy, but that Lydia was being callous and foolish in her behavior and Mrs Bennet was finally putting her foot down with her youngest daughter.

Mr Bennet smiled and walked to his wife, embracing her in front of everyone. "Fanny, you could not look lovelier than you do at this moment."

"I think I am quite fetching, if I do say so myself." Mrs Bennet said, touching the bottom of her hair.

~~ ** ~~

Lord Matlock sent letters frequently to his sister, telling her of his improvement and his joy in Darcy finding Elizabeth. Though he wished to be with the family for the holidays, he did not feel strong enough to make the journey. Richard determined it was best if he were to join his father at Matlock. The latest reports from Norfolk, Anthony was keeping himself inebriated, though he never left his house. Richard was concerned, as the amount being spent on libations was far exceeding Anthony's finances.

The housekeeper for the house in Norfolk informed Richard that the spirits were being paid for with jewelry, evidently pieces which had been left to the heir when their mother died. Anthony had evidently stolen the jewels and sold them for his personal comfort. Richard was determined to recover as many pieces of his heritage as possible, and asked his cousin to be on the watch for any of the jewels. Lady Anne knew of most of the pieces, as they had belonged to her mother prior to the last Lady Matlock, and she was able to give detailed descriptions of the items.

Richard also learned from the housekeeper in Norfolk of Anthony's growing hatred of Darcy. Since learning of Darcy's engagement, Anthony's anger had become extreme. Fortunately, since the attack against Elizabeth, Richard had the housekeeper and footman monitor all mail which Anthony sent or received.

~~ ** ~~

Preparations were made for Christmas at Darcy House. Though Elizabeth was unable to shop for gifts for her loved ones, she gave Jane a list of items she wished purchased on her behalf.

The decision had been made that there would be a double wedding on Christmas Day. Lady Anne and Mrs Bennet began the planning, though it was to be a simple event, with only family and very close friends, as Elizabeth was still shy about being seen by others.

Lady Anne sent for her favorite modiste to come to Darcy House. Madame Fontaine had been creating gowns for Lady Anne since she prepared to marry Gerard Darcy. Though Elizabeth was nervous, Lady Anne convinced her of Madame Fontaine's discretion.

When the modiste arrived at Darcy House, Lady Anne spoke in private with her before taking to her to meet Elizabeth. Madame Fontaine was pleased to meet the future Mrs Darcy, and put the young lady at ease. "Ah, Miss Elizabeth, you have the figure that men truly enjoy. All the ladies who claim otherwise are jealous for they have no curves such as you do. You will be a pleasure to design gowns for. Your betrothed is a fortunate man, and will be envied by many. While we are designing gowns, we will also create pieces for your head to match. Have no fear, my dear girl, you will be the toast of London society."

~~ ** ~~

Bingley was pleased to have Louisa and Hurst returned to Town, as Hurst would stand up for Charles during the wedding ceremony. Jane decided to have Mary stand up with her, which thrilled the middle Bennet sister immensely.

Elizabeth asked Kitty to stand up with her, causing

joy with Kitty and envy with Lydia, who was told she would not be allowed to attend the wedding. Lydia would be remaining at the Gardiner house in the nursery, with a governess which had been employed to watch over the young girl.

This left Darcy with a conflict. Richard would have been his first choice, but Richard was at Matlock and would not be returning anytime soon. Bingley would have been his second choice, but, of course, he would be marrying at the same time. After much deliberation, Darcy decided there was only one choice.

After a recent talk with his mother, Darcy had spoken with Albert Carrington. Though Darcy still had feelings he needed to work through from the past, something Elizabeth had said to him helped to put him on the correct path. She had told Darcy to remember the past as it brought him pleasure. Wisely, Elizabeth suggested it was time to let go of his anger towards Albert, saying that it was wonderful that Lady Anne had not lived the rest of her life alone, mourning her lost love, after Gerard died. "Besides, if Lord Covington and your mother had not married, your sister would not be here. You love your sister dearly, and Lord Covington helped to create her."

"You win, you win. I will try to change my ways with regards to Lord Covington." Darcy laughed as he conceded defeat.

~~ ** ~~

"William, I hope you do not mind my borrowing one of your books. I have wanted to read this one for some time, but have been unable to procure a copy for my own library." Lord Covington remarked when Darcy entered the library.

"You are welcome to read any of the books I have at either of my libraries." Darcy said as he approached his stepfather. "I wondered if I could have a word with you."

"Certainly. Is anything wrong?" Albert asked.

"No, everything is well. I was wondering, since Richard will not be able to be here for the wedding, would you be willing to…to stand…with me?"

"You wish me to be your witness?"

Darcy nodded his head. "I can understand if you would prefer to not. After all, I have treated you poorly for so many years."

"William, I would be honored to be at your side when you marry the woman you love. Elizabeth is a wonderful woman, and I know you will have a marriage filled with love. Thank you, William, for asking me." The two men stood, and Albert placed a hand tentatively on his stepson's shoulder.

Suddenly, without a word, Darcy embraced the man who had given his mother many years of happiness and love. It was brief, and Darcy quickly broke the embrace and stepped back. It was then that Albert saw the tears welling up in Darcy's eyes.

"Well, now, shall we see into what sort of mischief your mother is? She has been so overjoyed with your finding Elizabeth, and Anne tends to make the world around her brighter when she is so happy."

"Yes, it is interesting to watch Mother's enthusiasm. It becomes contagious." Both men smiled at Darcy's words. "Al...Albert, I am grateful. Not only for accepting my request, but for loving Mother and Georgiana, and for all you have tried to do for me over the years. I treated you very poorly, and I am grateful for this second chance."

Albert had tears of his own starting to build. It was the first time his stepson had called him by his name. "I am grateful as well, William. Let us find the ladies we love."

~~ ** ~~

Christmas Eve was a joyous affair. The engaged couples were nervous, and the older men were enjoying being able to tease the younger men.

Elizabeth and Jane were in a constant shade of deep blush, hearing the impertinent remarks from the men in their family. After enjoying a delicious dinner, the ladies took turns performing on the pianoforte.

Later, the men separated from the ladies. The married men decided to celebrate with the grooms, pouring libations generously, as they teased and joked mercilessly.

While the men were showing no mercy to Darcy and Bingley, Lady Anne and Mrs Bennet were speaking privately with Elizabeth and Jane, respectively.

Elizabeth was quite nervous as she listened to her soon to be mother in law, though she was grateful to have Lady Anne speaking to her rather than her mother. Several times, Elizabeth's mind wandered to her dearest sister, sure that Jane was mortified by all their mother was telling her.

The evening ended early, as the morning would be filled with excitement and joy.

~~~~~~~ ** ~~~~~~~
~~~~~~~

CHAPTER 14

Elizabeth woke just after sunrise on the day of her wedding. So many thoughts ran through her mind, though the one of utmost importance was that in a few short hours, she would be married to Fitzwilliam Darcy, the man she loved and with whom she would spend the rest of her life. She was sitting at her vanity table, holding her brush in hand, looking at herself in the mirror when Hannah and Mrs Jenkins entered. Not hearing the ladies, Elizabeth was lost in her thoughts of being in her betrothed's embrace the night before, when he wished her sweet dreams.

"Miss Elizabeth? Miss Elizabeth... are you well?" Hannah asked.

"Forgive me Hannah, I was wool gathering. I am well." Elizabeth blushed to be caught in such a state.

Mrs Jenkins stepped forward. "Are you ready to prepare for the day? I have come to assist Hannah."

"Thank you, Mrs Jenkins. I am nervous, but very excited for the day to begin."

"Miss Elizabeth, we have prepared a bath for you, and will have a tray brought up here. I have asked Cook to fix some special items which will aid in calming your nerves and soothing your stomach, which I am sure is in knots." Mrs Jenkins said. "I can remember the way my stomach felt when I was preparing the morning of my own wedding. And I was with my daughter when she wed. I recommend some tea with peppermint and chamomile in it. And the food I have requested is rather on the bland side, so as not to cause any strain to you."

"You are thoughtful, Mrs Jenkins. And Hannah, you are such a dear, the way you take care of me."

"Miss Elizabeth, you are a wonderful woman, and it will be joyous to have you as our Mistress. Mr Darcy could not have chosen a better lady for his wife."

The ladies helped Elizabeth prepare for the day, and as they finished, Mrs Jenkins stepped into the next room and returned with a box. "Miss Elizabeth, this is a gift, from Hannah and me, for your wedding day."

Elizabeth opened the box and gasped. They had given her the most precious gift she could imagine.

~~ ** ~~

Mr Bennet was waiting outside his daughter's rooms, as everyone else entered the drawing room for the ceremony. Jane had already joined her father, and the two were waiting for Elizabeth to make her appearance. Hearing the sound of the door opening,

Mr Bennet turned to see his precious second daughter. Jane gasped at the sight of her sister.

"Lizzy, you are beautiful. Oh, my dear sister, we are about to marry two of the best men in all of England." Jane cried out.

"Elizabeth, I cannot begin to tell you how incredibly beautiful you appear today. I am pleased that you have found a man who will treasure you every day of your life." Mr Bennet placed a kiss on his daughter's cheek. He then turned to Jane and kissed her as well. "Now, once you two are married and will no longer be living at Longbourn, there will be no intelligent conversation from here on."

The sisters smiled at their father's attempt to lighten the moment, as tears welled in his eyes. Jane took hold of one of his arms, as Elizabeth took hold of the other. Looking at her younger sister, Jane nodded as she spoke. "It is time to lead us to our husbands, Papa."

The footmen opened the doors to the drawing room and the sisters were escorted towards their futures. Mr Bingley was entranced by the sight of Jane, in her natural splendor, blushing becomingly at the intensity of his looks.

It was the gasp that could be heard when Darcy saw Elizabeth for the first time that caught everyone's attention. It was easy to see why. The gift that Mrs Jenkins and Hannah had given to their Mistress was a gift of love for the young lady. They had taken Elizabeth's hair that had been cut or shaved from her head, and taken it to a wig maker. Elizabeth walked towards her betrothed, wearing her dark chocolate curls, elegantly fashioned upon her head, with several curls hanging down. The wreath of flowers Darcy had asked to be fashioned for her was placed delicately upon the curls, making her appear to be a fairy princess.

Darcy could not wait for his bride to meet him at the temporary altar, he nearly ran to her and kidnapped her from her father's arm when they were almost halfway up the aisle. Mr Bennet laughed openly, as did the other men. The other family members smiled as they watched Elizabeth, her confidence intact, take her vows with Darcy, side by side with Jane and Bingley.

The bishop declared the couples to be husbands and wives, and Darcy needed no prompting to seal his vows with a kiss, which was far from chaste. Laughter broke out through the drawing room. Bingley and Jane had been sedate in their exchange, though the passion was visible in their eyes.

After signing the register which the bishop had brought with him, the couples took a few minutes alone, Darcy and Elizabeth in his study and the Bingleys in the library, before they joined their guests in the dining room for the wedding breakfast.

Pulling his wife into his arms, Darcy claimed another kiss from her. "My goddess, you cannot imagine how I felt, the moment you began to walk towards me. How did you manage to surprise me in such a manner?" His hand reached up to touch one of her curls.

"Mrs Jenkins and Hannah saved all the hair that was removed for the surgery and what I cut off. They took it to a wig maker and presented it to me this morning as a wedding gift. I was so surprised, and thrilled. Do you like?"

"Very much so, though it was the look of confidence, the Elizabeth in which I had fallen in love, that I liked the most. You are beautiful no matter what, but today, you showed the strength and poise I have always known you to have. I could easily believe you to be one of the fairy princesses from tales I heard as a child."

"It was extremely thoughtful of them to have such a gift made for me. It must have cost them dearly." Elizabeth said as she reached a hand up to touch her hair.

"They did not care, for it was done with love. They

think highly of you, my dearest love. My Lizzy. And have no fear, they will both be receiving a generous bonus for Christmas, larger than I had already planned to give them."

"Do you really like it?" Elizabeth asked, timid at the possible answer.

Darcy cupped his wife's face in his hands and leaned in to kiss her again. "My beautiful Lizzy, I would love you no matter what. As much as I like the look of your curls, I love the way you feel with the wig more. And I love the kindness of the ladies who were so inspired as to have it made."

"I love you, William. You are the best of husbands." Elizabeth wrapped her arms around her husband's chest, luxuriating in the feel of his strong embrace.

~~ ** ~~

The wedding breakfast was enjoyed, though the newlywed couples were ready to be rid of their guests. Mr Bennet was enjoying torturing his new sons, prolonging their agony by not taking his family and returning to the home of Mr and Mrs Gardiner.

Lord Albert and Lady Anne had decided to have their townhouse opened for a fortnight, before they would return to their home. Georgiana was looking forward to visiting some art exhibits that were in Town from the Continent, as well as attending the opera. Knowing Darcy and Elizabeth wished for privacy, Lord Albert convinced his wife and daughter to hurry along so they could take their leave.

Finally, Darcy had bid farewell to their guests, with the exception of Jane and Bingley, who would be staying on the third floor of Darcy House, in the guest wing, far from the family wing on the second floor. The Bingleys had already made their way upstairs to their rooms. Darcy felt a twinge of jealousy at his new brother's freedom, while he was host who had to wait.

As soon as the door shut behind the Bennet family, Darcy took his wife into his arms, kissing her lips in such a manner as to leave no confusion where his thoughts lay.

Leading Elizabeth to their rooms, he opened the door to her dressing chamber. "Shall I give you some time to change clothing?"

"Give me an hour." She replied, in a nervous voice. "William, I have to ask, would you prefer for me to wear the wig or one of the hair coverings?"

"I would prefer you wore neither, but I wish you to be comfortable. You may choose whatever you wish." Darcy said, leaning in for one more kiss before he turned towards his own rooms.

~~ ** ~~

Darcy knocked on the door to Elizabeth's rooms, and, when there was no answer, he opened the door and peeked inside. Not seeing Elizabeth, he walked over to the dressing chamber, where he had left her an hour before. He knocked lightly on the door and received no answer. He opened the door, finding the room vacant except for Elizabeth sitting in front of the vanity. She had taken the wig off, and placed one of her wraps on her head.

Elizabeth looked up into the mirror, seeing his reflection there, looking at her with such love and devotion. It was clear to see her fear rising in her, nearly overwhelming her.

"Lizzy, my dearest, what is wrong?" Darcy quickly made his way to his wife and knelt beside her.

"I want to start our marriage correctly, without holding back the truth, but I am frightened that you will run away from me and wish to never see me again." Elizabeth said, her hand involuntarily reaching for her head.

"I wish to see you, to see how you look. Nothing could disgust me, nothing could cause me to run away or wish to never see you. If you are willing, I would like to see your head."

Reluctantly, Elizabeth nodded her head, her hand shaking as she reached it to the cloth and tugged on the fabric until it came off her head. It had been long enough that there was hair beginning to grow, and was about as long as the first joint on his index finger. The right side of her head was filled with curls, as the weight which was released when Elizabeth cut the hair on that side of her head had unleashed the unruly curls. Darcy was sure that the left side would begin to curl soon, as it grew longer. He reached his fingers up, allowing them to roam through her hair, caressing her head. He could feel the scars from the surgery, could feel where the bone had been punctured by the surgeon's efforts to save her life. Darcy did not care. This was his beautiful wife, the woman he loved more than anyone else in the world. She was his life, and she was his wife.

"Elizabeth Darcy, my beloved wife, you could not be more beautiful. I love the wild and untamed nature of the hair on the right side. I would place a bet that it will not be long before the left is in the same state of curls. You have no way of knowing just how long I have wished to run my fingers through your hair, feel your curls wrap around my fingers. It is everything of which I have ever dreamed. I love you, Elizabeth. You are beautiful, remarkable, intelligent, and the most amazing young lady I have ever met. I am grateful to have you as my wife. Now, let us spend some time in our sitting room. The fire is roaring, there are some refreshments waiting there for us, and I thought you might enjoy my reading to you for a little while. We are both nervous, and it would do us both good to spend some time, just the two of us, talking as we used to."

"How is it you know just what I need?" Elizabeth smiled. "I like the suggestion of talking."

"Come with me." Darcy took hold of her hand, leading her to the sitting room. The two cuddled together, in front of the fireplace, sharing the treats the kitchen had prepared for them, talking and reading, for nearly three hours.

Darcy ended up with his wife in his arms, seated on his lap and his arms wrapped around her. His lips found the tender skin of her slender neck irresistible, and could not be contained any longer. The kisses started gently, as Darcy kissed and tasted his wife's neck, ear, and jawline. Her head turned instinctively, her lips searching for his. The first kiss was gentle, though grew desperate, wanting more. While his lips took possession of hers, his tongue gently persuaded her lips to part, allowing him to taste the delights of her mouth.

All the while, his hands began to wander the curves of her body. Surprisingly, he realized that her hands had also craved to discover more of him. Breathless, Darcy pulled back from her barely. "My love, perhaps we should make our way to the bed."

Elizabeth nodded her head. "William, I am ready to become your wife."

~~ ** ~~

For the next three days, the household only knew their Master and Mistress, as well as their guests, were in the house due to requests for bath water and refreshments. Neither of the newlywed couples came from their suites, only their personal servants were allowed into the area. Finally, on the fourth day after the wedding, late in the evening, the couples came from their suites. They had planned to attend the theater with their family members that evening, and dine at Lord and Lady Covington's house afterwards.

Reluctant to leave their rooms, Darcy and Elizabeth had a difficult time even parting as long as it took to prepare for the evening. Jane and Bingley were nearly as bad, though they were more covert in their behavior.

When they arrived at the theater, the Bennets, Gardiners, and Carringtons had already arrived. Mr Bennet and Mr Gardiner smiled behind their hands as they saw newlywed men and the longing looks they gave their wives when everyone greeted each other.

Mr Bennet walked over to his new sons clapped each on the shoulder and whispered, "You have the look of men who are deeply in love. Now, allow the rest of us to give our girls a moment of our time and you can have them back."

Darcy blushed readily. "Is it obvious?"

"Son, you look as if it has been weeks since you last held Elizabeth, yet it has been a few moments that she has been embracing her family members. Yes, it is obvious to not only me, but to anyone here who has ever felt the arrow from Cupid's bow." Mr Bennet smiled before chuckling. "Have no fear, it is actually heartwarming, as it affirms your love for my daughter. I take it all is well between you."

Dimples were clear for everyone to see, as Darcy grinned from ear to ear. "I would say that everything is so far beyond well. And I have even been able to convince her not to wear the cloths on her head when we are home. When you next visit, do not be shocked to see your daughter's short hair rather than the cloths or the wig she is donning at this moment."

"That is indeed a magical feat. I am pleased to see Elizabeth feeling more confident and more like her old self. You have worked wonders in restoring her. After all that happened, she could have been destroyed forever."

"I feared that happening, though I believe she is stronger than the rest of us can even imagine. We are planning to do some shopping next week. I was surprised to see her willingness to accept this. I told her I wish to see her with a proper wardrobe, and that means more than a dozen or so gowns. She needs to have a larger selection available to her and warmer clothing for when we travel to Pemberley in a few weeks. We decided to leave on the fifteenth of January, so we will be here for a little over a fortnight."

"Would it be too much to ask that we visit in the summer, for I look forward to seeing this vast estate?" Mr Bennet asked.

"You are always welcome, though I believe it is the library at Pemberley to which you look forward to seeing, rather than the estate." Darcy laughed. "The Bingleys will be joining us in July, perhaps you could come with them. The Gardiners are even thinking of making the trip this summer, as Mr Gardiner is looking forward to some fishing and Mrs Gardiner wishes to visit some of her friends in Lambton."

"Fishing? My, it has been years since I have enjoyed a bit of fishing. Perhaps Edward and I could try our hands at some fishing."

Darcy smiled. "The ponds are well stocked and

the streams are usually quite active that time of year. We keep a supply of poles and gear for fishing, so there is plenty for all of us men to use."

"Mrs Bennet might be difficult to remove, once she sees the grand house. She has been pleased with the sight of Darcy House, so if the estate is even half as nice, you may regret having your mother in law visit."

Shaking his head, Darcy chuckled. "Never could I regret Mrs Bennet's visit. After how she treated my wife after the attack, the loving manner which she gave my dearest Elizabeth courage and strength, I will be forever in your wife's debt. It is pleasing to me to see how much love mother and daughter share. Though I have heard, so many times, that Elizabeth is so very much like you, I think there is a bit of Mrs Bennet in Elizabeth as well."

"Her kind and generous heart is her mother, Fanny has always been a caring lady. Most people have not seen that side of her, so they do not know the real Fanny Bennet." Mr Bennet smiled at his wife, who in turn gave him a familiar look with an arched eyebrow.

Darcy smiled at his own mother and stepfather. Knowing about his parents having a loving relationship, and that the love Lady Anne held for each of her husbands, had made a difference in how her son saw her current relationship. Seeing Anne and Albert sharing smiles, and innocent looking touches they shared, Darcy was pleased to know that his mother was deeply loved. He also knew that his father would have wanted Lady Anne to be happy.

"Well, shall we make our way to our box?" He asked everyone. All agreed, and they started towards the stairs leading to the upper level. Suddenly, Darcy noticed to his right, were Caroline and Geoffrey Goodman. The sneer on Caroline's face spoke of her displeasure in seeing the Bennets with her brother and Darcy. She stepped towards her brother, with her husband close behind her.

"Charles, we meet again. You are being seen in public, with those people?" Caroline spoke just above a whisper.

"Caroline, may I introduce you to my wife. Jane and I were married on Christmas Day, in a double ceremony with Darcy and Elizabeth." Bingley gestured towards his wife.

"I will never acknowledge that chit as my sister, and that family will be the ruin of everything our parents and grandparents built. How could you betray the Bingley family name in such a manner? And ruin your friend at the same time? You have no consideration towards the way your actions will affect so many others."

"Caroline, my dear, let us go to our seats." Goodman said, taking hold of his wife's arm.

"I cannot stand by and allow my friends be ruined because my brother is incompetent. That family is evil, they will be the ruination of all they touch." Caroline hissed.

"My love, we should make our way to our seats. Or would you prefer to return home?" Goodman could see the fury building in his wife. Never having seen this aspect of her, he was concerned for her well-being.

"I will not give them the pleasure of running me off. We came here to enjoy the performance, and we shall do just that." Caroline took hold of her husband's arm and walked off, though not before giving Elizabeth a look of daggers being thrown at the new Mrs Darcy.

Seeing the look given his wife, Darcy quickly ushered his family up the stairs and to their box. There were two rows of seats, and he led Elizabeth to the seats to the furthest right side on the front row. Darcy took the seat next to his wife's, and held tightly to her hand. "Forget her, my dearest Lizzy. Caroline is a sick woman, and her husband has yet to see what we have for so long."

Elizabeth looked him in the eye. "William, I was just thinking. Everyone believes that Wickham was hired by Anthony. What if it was not Anthony, but Miss Bingley...I mean... what is her name now?"

"Mrs Goodman. She does have a better flow of funds than Anthony, and we were concerned with her possibly attacking you after the Assembly. I will speak with Bingley after dinner tonight."

"Thank you, my dearest. Now, let us both put it from our minds and enjoy the performance. I have been excited all day to come tonight, and I refuse to allow anyone to ruin my happiness."

Darcy lifted her hand to his lips, placing a kiss on the back of it, which left no doubt as to where his mind was more pleasantly wandering.

From a box across the way, the newlyweds were being watched. "They will pay for their treachery." Uttered a whispered voice, to no one.

~~~~~~~ ** ~~~~~~~
~~~~~~~

CHAPTER 15

At dinner, Lady Anne informed her son of a recent letter she had received. "Catherine has made her disapproval well known. First she was upset with Anthony being disowned and sent away from Matlock. She has always doted on him. I am actually shocked that she did not assist him financially when he could not acquire the funds from you."

"I do not think Lady Catherine's estate is as financially set as she wishes everyone to think." Darcy said.

"I know she still harbors resentment that her dear Anne died several years ago, as she wished young Anne to marry you. I believe it was to combine the two estates, bringing Rosings under your protection."

"Mother, I have never considered Cousin Anne to be a potential wife for me. She was sickly and not a kind person. Lady Catherine did her daughter no favors, indulging the girl in fantasies."

Lady Anne nodded. "Well, in Catherine's mind, you should be mourning your long lost betrothed, even though you were not betrothed. This brings me to her other complaint. She is furious at me for making no attempts to destroy the wedding between you and Elizabeth. As a matter of fact she was furious over the connection between you and Lizzy, especially after the rumors which circulated after Wickham's attack."

Darcy nearly choked on his bite of potato. "What would she have me do? Would Lady Catherine prefer me to abandon the woman I love due to someone hiring Wickham to ruin me? Was I to just abandon Elizabeth, leaving her alone in the world, while I remained destroyed by her loss? I love my wife, and would move heaven and earth to protect her and keep her close to me."

"You know how Catherine is, she has always been difficult to please. I believe she will never be happy until everyone else is as miserable as she is." Lady Anne said.

"Is she still at Rosings?" Darcy asked.

"She was planning to spend the holidays with her poor, exiled nephew. Richard has not sent me any news, so I am not sure if she went to Norfolk."

"Anne, let your son enjoy his meal. There is time later to discuss such matters. Do not give William digestive problems by speaking of your sister." Lord Albert said with a smile.

Lady Anne chuckled at her husband. "You are correct, my dear. William, Lizzy has told me she will do some shopping before you leave for Pemberley. I am so pleased to hear such news. Where do you intend to shop?"

"We will go to your modiste and to Johnson's for footwear. I was trying to decide to which furrier to take her, which do you suggest?"

"Lawrence's is the best, though I find Jameston's to be better quality stitching and their prices are better. You should take her to Wilson's for other supplies she will need. Elizabeth will need hair accessories, gloves, handkerchiefs, bath scents, personal stationary, and such." Lady Anne rambled off the list.

"Could you do me a great service, Mother, and make a list of what Elizabeth will need? I know my wife well enough to believe she will never tell me, for she will believe I am spending too much on her needs."

Lady Anne smiled. "Of course, William. After dinner, I will go to my study and prepare a list. I know Lizzy is concerned with the cost, but she needs many items she never did before. She is now Mrs Darcy of Pemberley."

"I have already spoken to her on that fact. But you know how she is. I married a country miss, not a lady of the *ton*. And she does not appreciate the wealth that is now at her fingertips." Darcy looked down the table to his wife. Elizabeth was in a discussion with her father and mother, all three of them smiling and laughing.

~~ ** ~~

Lady Anne excused herself from the other ladies when they removed to the drawing room. "I will join you shortly, I need to take care of something first."

The other ladies all nodded their heads, as discussions of Twelfth Night were held. The Darcys would be joining the Bingleys at a party which was being thrown by a friend of Bingley's late parents. It was highly anticipated, and the first time the new wives had attended such an event.

Upon her return to the drawing room, she found Elizabeth looking at the sheet music. "Lizzy, will you honor us with a song this evening? William has informed me of your talent at the pianoforte, and he said your voice is quite pleasant."

Elizabeth took a deep breath and looked at her mother in law. "Your son exaggerated my talents, Lady Anne. My skill is mediocre at most, and my voice is far from being pleasant, unless you consider shrieking cats to be pleasant."

"Do not believe her, Mother, she has always undervalued her talents and worth." Darcy said as he entered the drawing room, walking straight to his wife.

"William, I must say you are prejudice when it comes to my talents." Elizabeth said.

Lady Anne laughed. "Very well, I insist you perform a song so I may judge for myself."

"Very well, but I must insist that my husband endure my performance at my side at the pianoforte, as I will require his aid to turn the pages."

"Such torture, Wife, however will I survive such agony?" Darcy smiled as he leaned over to place a kiss on her cheek.

Elizabeth's performance was enjoyed by all, especially those who could see the love which radiated from the newlywed couple, especially in the stolen glances and slight touches.

Shortly after the song was over, the Darcys decided it was time to return to Darcy House. They left the Bingleys to enjoy their family, with the Bennets promising to deliver their eldest daughter and her husband safely to Darcy House.

Upon arriving at Darcy House, both Darcy and Elizabeth dismissed their servants for the night. Darcy was more than pleased to be his wife's maid that evening, as Elizabeth was a more than willing valet for him.

~~ ** ~~

Caroline Goodman was furious, and she would not stand for what she perceived as a slight given by Darcy and her own brother. Geoff had tried to calm her, especially after they returned to their home. Nothing would sooth her anger, she could not wait until she could exact some punishment on the two newlywed couples.

Taking out paper and pen, Caroline began to write a letter. She was determined to contact someone who could come to her aid, someone who would do anything she asked, so long as there is a good sum of funds available to him. He had been her lover for several years, but he also had expensive tastes. Since her marriage, she finally had access to the funds to satisfy his needs.

Finishing the letter, Caroline smiled. *Ah, yes, that will do nicely. He will come to my aid.*

~~ ** ~~

Lady Catherine was furious when she received a letter from her sister. Lady Anne complimented the young lady who had tricked, Lady Catherine was certain it was trickery of some sorts, Darcy into marriage.

How can my sister be such a fool? Does she not see that her son has been lured into a trap, and by a woman of questionable reputation? The rumors that have spread about the chit were clear, speaking of the use of her arts and allurements to ensnare the Master of Pemberley.

Anthony had described the situation to Lady Catherine, how the country nobody had stolen Darcy's heart with her loose ways. He also pled his misery being at the hands of Darcy, as his cousin had refused to come to his aid when Anthony needed it the most. In his pleas of wrong doing towards him, he accused the new Mrs Darcy of prejudicing her husband against helping Anthony.

Lady Catherine was beside herself, her beloved nephew had been tossed from his home, his heritage, and robbed of his inheritance due to this country whore who had trapped Darcy. Her influence had spread, like a plague, throughout their family. Lady Anne, Lord Matlock, Richard, and others, all influenced by the deception of someone who was unworthy of their notice.

Sitting at the desk in Anthony's study, Lady Catherine pulled out paper and pen. She began a letter to a man she had known for most of her life, a man who held all of her secrets, as he was the man who did Lady Catherine's bidding. He would come to her aid once again. She was sure of it, especially if she offered him a handsome reward. Lady Catherine knew what that reward would be. And it would be a reward to herself as well.

~~ ** ~~

Mr Culiver had been nervous since the debacle with Wickham and Darcy. Though there had been rumors surrounding Darcy and his new bride, the Master of Pemberley had been able to deflect the major damage to his reputation when it was proven that Wickham was responsible for the attack against Elizabeth Darcy, nee Bennet. Fortunately, Wickham was dead, and it did not appear that he had given Culiver's name to Darcy.

He knew it was only a matter of time before his employer contacted him again, as they would wish completion of the assignment. Culiver was attempting to plan another attack, and who to use, but it would be difficult to get close to the newlyweds. For several months, Culiver had attempted to find someone employed at Darcy House or Pemberley who would be vulnerable to blackmail into doing his dirty work, but Darcy's employees were devoted to their master.

Finally, Culiver found someone who would be perfect to keep him updated on the Darcys, their comings and goings, and their preferences. He would soon move forward with his next plan to ruin Darcy. For Culiver knew that if he did not act soon, his own employer would soon find someone to eliminate Culiver.

~~ ** ~~

Richard was in his study at Matlock, when there was a knock on the door. A footman was bade to enter, and he was carrying an express.

Opening the letter, Richard began to read.

Colonel,

As you requested, I have been investigating your brother. You were correct in your assumptions that your aunt, Lady Catherine de Bourgh, has been aiding your brother financially. Recently, she deposited ten thousand pounds in an account for Mr Fitzwilliam to use. I have also learned that your brother has been drinking heavily, and in his inebriated state, is making threats against you, Lady Anne Carrington, and Mr Darcy.

It also appears that Mr Fitzwilliam has put out the word of his desire to hire someone to assist him in making his threats come to life. His housekeeper is turning away anyone who is not on the list you gave her, though Lady Catherine has interceded many times *when guests have arrived at your brother's house in Norfolk.*

I will continue to investigate and keep you informed of any developments. Please keep watching over your shoulder, Colonel.

Your friend,

P. Randall

Richard wrote a letter to Lady Anne and another to Darcy, informing them of the news of Anthony's activities. He knew it was coming to a time that it would be necessary to confront Lady Catherine, and it would take all of them to deal with the Mistress of Rosings.

Richard then walked down the hall and up the stairs, arriving at his father's bedchambers. Lord Matlock had improved immensely in the past fortnight, and he was pleased to know that Darcy and Elizabeth were recovered and happily married.

"Good morning, Father. How are you today?"

"Better." Lord Matlock stated. "Ate well, and walked down the hall twice. My hand and arm are stronger as well."

"I am pleased to hear this. I knew you would recover, especially with the nurse we hired. She is quite knowledgeable in her field."

"Indeed, she is. Now, what is the latest from London? You have that look about you which tells me that something is wrong."

Richard chuckled. "You have always known how to read me, Father. It was not news from London which has me concerned. I received word from my investigator. He had news from Norfolk. It appears that Anthony is making threats against the Darcys, Aunt Anne, and myself. I would not trust him not to threaten you as well."

"But he has no access to funds to enact his threats." Lord Matlock was concerned. "Let me guess, Catherine is sticking her nose in the middle of everything and supporting Anthony's habits."

"How did you know?" Richard was surprised.

"My sister has always stuck her nose where it was not wanted. Does Anne know?"

"I sent expresses to Aunt Anne and Darcy. I pray that they will be safe."

Lord Matlock pulled back the covers of his bed and sat up. "Richard, have the carriage prepared. We are for London."

"Father, you are not strong enough for such

travels."

"Be a good boy and do as you are told. I am strong enough to make the trip and to be at my family's side as we contend with Catherine and Anthony." Lord Matlock called out for his valet to have his trunks packed for the journey. The valet was as shocked as Richard was, though, after seeing the determination of Lord Matlock, both men did his bidding.

~~ ** ~~

The Carrington family dined at Darcy House on New Year's Eve, welcoming the New Year with joy. A footman entered with two expresses, one had been redirected from the Carrington townhouse. Lady Anne and Darcy took their letters and began to read. Once everyone learned the news of Lady Catherine's involvement and Anthony's threats, the situation was discussed. All agreed it was wise to remove from Town after Twelfth Night. Lady Anne asked her husband if they could spend some time at Pemberley, as she wished to be of assistance to Elizabeth as she was learning her position as the new Mistress. Albert was not of a mood to deny his wife, he loved her dearly and was pleased with the change in his relationship with her son.

"If William and Elizabeth invite us, Anne, I am more than happy to visit Pemberley. But remember, they are newlywed, they may wish for some time alone."

"Nonsense, Lord Covington." Elizabeth replied. "You are always welcome at Pemberley. Is that not correct, William?"

Darcy smiled. "Indeed, my love. Mother, you and Lord Covington, and of course, Georgiana, are welcome to join us at Pemberley. Though I will state that if we disappear from time to time, you will not hold it against our hosting abilities."

"William, I insist that you and your wife call me Albert. I cannot abide my stepson and his wife calling me by my formal title."

"And you must call me Elizabeth or Lizzy." The new Mrs Darcy declared.

Bingley and Jane had been planning to travel after Twelfth Night, and they decided they would join the party making their way to Pemberley. As the main house at the estate was quite large, and the dower house was available for the Bingleys to enjoy some privacy, the second newlywed couple felt certain they would be able to enjoy their stay.

Mr and Mrs Bennet would be visiting Pemberley in the summer, and decided it would be best to have some time at home to bring peace and quiet to their family, after all that had happened the previous months.

Kitty was invited to travel with the Darcys, and she was overjoyed when her parents agreed to allow her to make the journey. It was decided that she would travel in the carriage with Lady Anne, Lord Albert and Georgiana. Darcy and Elizabeth would ride in their newest carriage, and the Bingleys would travel in the Darcys' other carriage. Bingley needed to meet with his business partner the day after Twelfth Night, in the morning, so he and Jane would leave by midday.

Kitty and Georgiana would keep each other company when the couples enjoyed the ball for Twelfth Night. The ball was being held at the home of Lord Sherman Malcolm. Lord Malcolm had remarried a year ago, after being a widower for two years. He had no heir, and his estate had been suffering financially from several years of bad crops. His second wife was a young lady whose fortune had been derived from trade, her father being one of Bingley's father's friends from their younger years. It had been many years since Bingley had seen the Jefferies, and had been unable to attend the wedding of Arabella to Lord Malcolm, so he looked forward to introducing his wife and family to Mr Jefferies. Lord Malcolm and the Carringtons had known each other for many years, and Lord Albert was looking forward to introducing his stepson and new daughter to his friends.

The ladies had already ordered their gowns made for the ball, and were excited to attend. Elizabeth had finally regained her former zest for life, her strength and personality had been restored. The harm which had been plunged upon them by Wickham had been dealt with, and was now in the past, and the future as Mrs Darcy of Pemberley was a very exciting time for her.

~~ ** ~~

The arrival in Town of Lord Matlock and Richard was surprising to their entire family. As preparations were being made for everyone to journey to Pemberley, the men were also keeping close tabs on where Lady Catherine and Anthony were and what they were doing. A messenger arrived, just hours after Lord Matlock, at Darcy House. The messenger brought news that Lady Catherine and Anthony were traveling to London, planning to stay at her townhouse. They would be arriving in Town the following day.

This was news which the family was pleased to hear, as it would allow them all to confront Lady Catherine and Anthony at one time, a united front against the pair.

~~~~~~~~ ** ~~~~~~~~
~~~~~~~~

CHAPTER 16

Lady Catherine was surprised to see her brother and sister, as well as Richard and Darcy, at her townhouse. "I do not wish to speak with you, as I have many appointments today."

Lord Matlock stepped towards his elder sister. "Catherine, we know you are involved in assisting Anthony, and we need to discuss it immediately. My eldest son is ill, and he requires treatment to keep him from harming himself or others."

"Anthony would never harm another person. I am sure that Darcy and Richard have filled your mind with all sorts of lies about my dear nephew, for they are jealous of him. Richard has even gone so far as to take his brother's title and inheritance from him. Poor Anthony has been ill used, and I cannot believe you have taken Richard's lies and acted against your heir."

"Richard has not lied, Catherine. Anthony has nearly destroyed all that our father and grandfather built. With his gambling and spending habits he has nearly bankrupted me. I had to sell off part of our estate to cover his last spree."

"And Darcy was selfish in refusing to come to Anthony's aid to cover the debts. Pemberley is financially sound. There is no reason for Darcy not to come his cousin's aid."

"I did assist Anthony, Lady Catherine." Darcy stated. "I assisted him many times. It never made a difference, as Anthony would only go out and spend more and gamble more. I will not lose my estate to support Anthony's habits."

"You selfish boy. And what of you, Anne? Your husband is wealthy and could surely afford to come to Anthony's aid. Why did you not plead our nephew's case before Lord Covington?"

"As my son said, no amount of assistance to Anthony would have helped the situation. He only continued the behavior over and over, no matter how much help he was given. And why should we be the ones to continuously bail Anthony out? Why did you not come to his aid each time he was in need? You are pitying him now, but where were you when our brother had to sell part of our father's estate to cover Anthony's debts? What you do not understand is that William did come to his cousin's aid, as he was the one who purchased the land, to keep it in the family. He could not allow our heritage to be destroyed."

Lord Matlock was surprised. "William, you purchased the lands?"

"I did, I had Mr Farnsworth do it for me. I thought

you would be upset in my doing so outright."

"I wish I had known, my boy." Lord Matlock shook his head. "I cannot tell you how grateful I am to you."

"There is no need, Uncle. You would have done the same for me, if the situation were reversed." Darcy did not like being in the center of attention. "The point is that the land is still part of the estate, and Richard will see that I am repaid as the estate is returned to its previous glory. We have already discussed the matter."

"Now, Catherine, let us return to the matter at hand." Lord Matlock stated, turning his attention to his sister. "Anthony is out of control, and he has become dangerous. The attack against Darcy's wife was done after someone hired Wickham. Wickham was hired by someone to discredit Darcy, to make him a laughingstock in society. The plan was to blame Darcy for the attack against Elizabeth. It could have worked, but fortunately there was plenty of evidence to contradict Wickham's version of the event. Three men are now dead, Darcy and Elizabeth were both critically injured. You may not care about the new Mrs Darcy, but Darcy nearly died from the fever he took after being shot by Wickham. Does that mean nothing to you?"

Lady Catherine scrunched up her forehead as she

scowled. "You are lying. I heard no such information, only that the chit had taken advantage of the situation and forced my poor nephew into marriage. He was honor bound to marry the country nobody, as the rumors were abounding."

"I beg to differ, Lady Catherine." Darcy was attempting to control his anger. "I was courting Elizabeth when Wickham was hired to perform his vile duty. I was planning to ask her to marry me the very morning of the attack, only to arrive to find her beaten near death. The woman I loved, on the ground, battered and broken, with three men preparing to violate her. They attacked me, forcing me to shoot the first two. Then Wickham and I struggled over the other gun, and I was shot. The scoundrel accused me of vile behavior, stating I had violated Elizabeth, and that I had been carrying on an affair with her for some time. She was still pure until we married, and I am grateful that the vulgar deed had not been accomplished. It was proven, beyond a shadow of a doubt, that it was Wickham and his friends who were the perpetrators of the attack, and he finally admitted the truth. I would not save his sorry carcass from the noose, so he would not admit to the name of his employer, though he claimed it was a relative of mine. There are only two relatives who would treat me in such a manner, the first one is Anthony, and the other...well, we are well aware of your feelings towards me, Lady Catherine."

"How dare you, to accuse your poor cousin of such a foul action. You should be ashamed of slandering the good name of such a fine young man. Anthony has always acted in a proper manner, I have kept a close watch over him all of his life."

"A proper manner?" Lady Anne exclaimed. "Is it proper to gamble away the family fortune and to fornicate with every young lady he meets? Is it proper to spend money as if it grew on trees, all the while ignoring the conditions of the estate which supplies the funds which supports his living? I am ashamed to call you my sister, if this is your idea of what is proper manners."

"You think your son is so perfect, Anne, you always sided with him over Anthony and even Richard. Why, I remember when the boys were little, and your son accused Anthony of killing the cat which was my dear Anne's favorite. Anthony swore to me that he had done nothing to harm the cat, as he knew how dear the sweet animal was to his beloved cousin. I am certain that it was your son who committed the vile act, putting the blame on his cousin."

"You are a fool, Sister." Lord Matlock bellowed at Lady Catherine. "I overheard Anthony laughing at his being able to pull the wool over your eyes. Anthony has always known how to manipulate you, and you protect him. That makes you a simpleton, believing such nonsense from the mouth of my eldest son. Anthony laughs at you, behind your back. He ridicules you and belittles you, knowing full well that you will continue to believe him."

"Anthony is a dear boy, he has always looked after me. Especially after my Anne died, he kept in touch with me and came to see me."

"You are daft if you believe he came out of the kindness of his heart, Lady Catherine." Richard stepped forward. "He only came there to see what he could get from you to cover his debts. You may not be aware of it, but he stole several pieces of art from you and sold them. The landscape that hung in the blue parlor and the statue of the maiden with her water pitcher, they were stolen by Anthony. I have the signed statements attesting to who sold the items to the pawn broker, and how much Anthony received for the pieces."

"My former footman stole those items, I learned later that he stole some of Anthony's clothes and posed as my nephew to sell the items." Lady Catherine was furious.

"No, Sister, my son stole those items. He admitted that information to me, and I recovered the stolen pieces. I purchased the items from the pawn broker myself, and have them waiting at Matlock for you. No servant was involved, it was Anthony who committed the crime." Lord Matlock could see that it was a losing battle, his sister would never admit that she was wrong. "Anne, it is obvious that our sister is a fool and will continue to be so, where it concerns Anthony. Therefore, it is time to take more stringent steps in dealing with my first born."

Lord Matlock turned to leave, summoning the others to follow him, when Lady Catherine called out to him. "What steps are you planning to take? How do you plan to harm my nephew?"

"You have no need to know at this moment, Catherine. It is between us and Anthony, not you. But know this. If you do anything to assist him in the future, we will hold you just as culpable as he is for his actions. And if any further harm comes, to any member of our family, you will be held responsible as well."

The group turned and left the room, with Lady Catherine de Bourgh gaping like a fish out of water.

~~ ** ~~

Lord Matlock decided to stay with his beloved younger sister and her family rather than open Matlock House. Richard decided to spend the time with his cousin at Darcy House. Though the newlyweds were still spending a great deal of time apart, they had begun to spend time together discussing their planned trip and the properties which the Bingleys were planning to inspect in Derbyshire and the nearby counties. They had decided to give up the lease of Netherfield, and the Bennets had planned to add on to Longbourn, thereby making a second estate unnecessary for family gatherings.

Richard had many questions to ask his cousin, as there were many repairs which were required at Matlock. Tenant homes in need of repairs, one of the bridges was near collapse, the kitchen in the main house needed updating before there was a fire, and the roof over the east wing was leaking. They also needed to plan the crop rotation. Bingley was taking notes on all that was discussed, for he knew it would soon be him in need of advice on managing an estate. Darcy also recommended a young man who had been training with the steward of Pemberley, as the steward at Matlock had died in the past year and Lord Matlock had been unable to hire anyone before his health declined.

While the men were speaking of estate matters and business, the ladies were discussing their new wardrobes. Items had been arriving almost daily, and

Elizabeth could not remember so many items having been ordered. She had a sneaking suspicion that her husband had ordered items without her being aware. There were more gowns than she had ever thought of owning in her life, as well as undergarments, outerwear, night clothes, coats, shawls, bonnets, boots, slippers, and much more. All the while, Elizabeth was concerned with the amount of funds which had been required to afford so many items, especially the quality, which was far superior to what she had ever owned before. Though the Bennets were not poor, they did not shop at the elite shops of London. Mrs Bennet preferred quality which was durable and long lasting rather than quality because of beauty and charm.

Elizabeth was concerned that she was costing her husband far more than she was worth. She would need to speak with William, tell him that he should refrain from spending any further on her. He had told her that she would have a generous allowance each month, but she could not see ever having need of it. She would not need anything for years to come, she was sure of that.

Jane was also shocked with all the items which Bingley had purchased for her. She was certain that she was being treated as if she were royalty, as Bingley could not resist purchasing anything he saw which he thought would bring his wife joy.

~~ ** ~~

Twelfth Night arrived, and everyone prepared for the ball that night. The ladies were decked out in their finest gowns and jewels, their maids had outdone themselves.

The gown which had been fashioned for Elizabeth was a pale mint green, with slightly darker stitching on the bodice and around the hem. The stitching was in an elegant floral design, with vines and smaller blossoms trailing around and up to a large set of blossoms at her generously proportioned bosom. Darcy stood gaping at his wife, then shook his head.

"No, no, my love, I cannot take you in public in such a gown. All I can think of is to take you upstairs and tear the gown from your tempting body and ravage you the entire night through. I do not wish for any other man to see you in such a gown, for I know where their eyes will be the entire evening. I am a jealous man, my dearest Lizzy. I refuse to share you with anyone, even if it is only their seeing your beauty. And heaven help me, if any man even thought of dancing with you, I would be forced to call them out."

"But, William, whenever we are in public, all the ladies ogle you. Rather than being jealous, I delight in knowing you are mine and mine alone. Let them look, it is my bed you come home to." Elizabeth whispered in her husband's ear. Rather than helping soothe him, it only made his desire intensify.

Nearly growling in her ear, Darcy was frustrated. "Do we truly have to attend tonight? Can we not stay home, alone? Please, my love, do not torture me by making me see you in such a temptation and have to control my need for you."

"You will survive, my handsome husband. And I will only dance with members of our party. You, of course, will have the first set. Albert has secured the second, Charles the third, and Richard the fourth. By then, I am certain, you will be unable to refrain from having the supper set."

"I know what I wish to dine on, and I wish to have my dessert first." Darcy nipped hungrily at her ear when no one else was watching. "I have a necklace to present to you, but I know that it will only intensify the effect that the gown has on me."

Frowning slightly, Elizabeth did not understand.

Darcy opened the box he had removed from his coat pocket and held out a beautiful pearl necklace, with a teardrop shaped pearl hanging in the center. It would be nestled in the fold between her swells. He leaned again to whisper into her ear. "I might as well paint a sign on your chest saying 'look here'."

Elizabeth giggled. "My poor, dear husband. You will be in such misery until we return home."

"I truly will be, for I will be unable to stand properly from just looking your direction. It will be quite painful. Again, I plead that we remain home and enjoy our own celebration. I have a mask, I can wear it when I come to your dressing chamber."

His wife's giggles only grew. "William, you are just going to have to behave for a few hours. Then, tomorrow, we will be secluded in our carriage as we make our way to Pemberley."

"No one is allowed in our carriage the entire trip. If I must share you tonight, I insist on having you all to myself as we travel." Darcy's voice was pleading, nearly childlike.

"I agree, my darling husband. Now, let us delay no further."

~~ ** ~~

The party from Darcy House met Lady Anne and Lord Albert at the front doors of the Malcolm townhouse. Lady Anne gushed her praises for her daughter in law. "Lizzy, you look simply wonderful. I am amazed you were able to escape the house. My son did not attempt to have you change gowns to a simple morning gown?"

"I am certain he thought of such, as he was not pleased that other men would see me wearing this gown. As a matter of fact, I believe the gown will no longer exist when we arrive home, for he stated he intends to destroy it." Elizabeth stated.

With a giggle, Lady Anne embraced Elizabeth. "My dear girl, I cannot begin to thank you for bringing my dear boy to life. I feared for him for so long, and it is a pleasure to see this side of him. You are truly a blessing."

"Mother, you could not have spoken truer." Darcy stated as he stepped behind his wife. "Though you could have spoken to her with regards to her gown. I believe something plain and boring would have been more appropriate for such an occasion."

"Fitzwilliam Darcy, there is no chance I would not encourage my new daughter to dress beautifully. If you were intelligent, you would use this time to brag of such a treasure and make the other men jealous of your good fortune." Lady Anne spoke as she swatted her son on his arm.

"The two of you will be the toast of the ball." Richard offered. "If I were you, William, I would revel in the knowledge that this beauty is all yours."

"I do not wish to have any other man looking at my wife's beauty and have inappropriate thoughts of her. She is my wife, and I know what that gown is doing to my self-control. This is going to be the longest night of my life." Darcy shook his head.

The couples made their way towards the refreshments, wishing to procure some punch. "Lizzy, Jane, I would suggest you drink the lemonade, as I am sure that the punch has been added to by Malcolm." Lord Albert stated. "He is notorious for adding some brandy to the punch, as he enjoys seeing young ladies unwittingly imbibe."

Jane gasped at such an announcement. "That is quite evil of the man. Thank you, Lord Covington, for enlightening us to this information."

"It is all done in good humor, my dear girl." Lady Anne stated, taking Jane's hand in her own. "Malcolm would never allow a young lady's virtue to be at stake after she were to imbibe. He has footmen and maids prepared to come to the rescue of any young ladies in need."

After all had their glasses, they turned to find some seats. Elizabeth accidently bumped into another lady, spilling her cup of lemonade. "Forgive me, I should have used more caution."

"Indeed, Miss Eliza, you should have." Caroline

Goodman replied angrily. "You have no manners at all. What could be expected, you are a country nobody, unable to comprehend how to behave in such a setting."

"It was an accident, Mrs Goodman. I meant no disrespect."

"You are not worthy of shining my shoes, let alone arriving at such a gathering. How dare you show your face in polite society? You are a disgrace to all around you."

"Mrs Goodman, forgive me, but I must follow my party. I am truly sorry for your gown being damaged. Please send the bill to my husband, he will reimburse you for the damages."

"You filthy little chit, how dare you speak to me in such a manner?" Caroline reached forward, grabbing hold of the shoulder of Elizabeth's gown and ripped it. "Everyone will see you for the disgrace you truly are."

As Caroline reached towards Elizabeth's head, intending to yank the wig from her nemesis, Darcy took hold of her hand, arresting it from further movement. "You will keep your hands to yourself, Mrs Goodman. I suggest you find your husband, and refrain from further attempts to harm my wife." He took off his coat, draping it over Elizabeth's shoulders to cover the damage to her gown. "Come, my love.

We will return home."

Darcy led his wife to their party, making their excuses as they prepared to leave. Lady Anne was furious, as was Bingley, and it took several moments to calm them before the Darcys could leave.

Upon settling in their carriage, Darcy gathered his wife into his arms. "Forgive me, my love. I should have prevented Mrs Goodman from her assault on you. I will say I am grateful for one thing though."

Confused, Elizabeth looked at her husband. "What are you grateful for?"

"Now I will not feel as guilty when I tear this gown from you, for it is already damaged." The sly grin on his face told her they would soon be enjoying a pleasant evening and the ball would not be thought of until the following day.

~~~~~~~ ** ~~~~~~~
~~~~~~~

CHAPTER 17

The following day, the carriages pulled out from Darcy House, after Lord Matlock, Richard, and the Carringtons arrived. Bingley and Jane bid everyone farewell with the promise of meeting them the following day when they stopped for the evening.

The carriage ride was comfortable, as the Darcys enjoyed the privacy of their carriage while Georgiana and Kitty entertained each other in the Carrington carriage.

The first night was spent in a pleasant inn which Darcy had used whenever he traveled between Pemberley and Town. The girls had decided to share a room, and everyone decided to eat dinner in the private dining room that night. Elizabeth had not slept much the night before, so she decided to turn in early. Being ever concerned for his wife's health, Darcy bid everyone a good night before following his wife.

~~ ** ~~

The morning of the Darcys' departure, no one was aware of a man standing across the street, watching over Darcy House. The man had arrived at the park and concealed himself amongst the bushes, hoping that he had not missed the Darcy carriage leaving.

Two footmen were carrying trunks to the carriage, loading everything appropriately. One of the footman spoke. "When we are finished here, we will need to prepare the second carriage. Mr Darcy stated that the first carriage will be traveling early, while the second will leave around midday, as the gentleman has business with the solicitor."

"The Missus said the second carriage should meet up with the rest of the party by tomorrow when they all stop for the night. Old Joe will have to push the horses to make up the time if they are to meet up."

"Ah, it is no problem for Joe, he could drive the team in his sleep. Jimmy is taking the first carriage to meet with Lord and Lady Covington, so it will take them a bit longer to start, if Lady Covington is the same as she was when she married Mr Gerard. She was a good mistress, but was always late getting started on a journey."

"Well, one more trunk and this carriage will be ready to go. Once it has left, Old Joe will bring the other up to have it ready for the family."

The footmen returned inside and the man across the street smiled. He would wait for the second carriage to leave, as he was being paid to stop the Darcys from reaching Pemberley. He decided to make his way down the street to the tea shop and purchase something to eat. He would be back in time to see the second carriage off.

Little did he know, the Darcys were leaving in the first carriage, and, as the man left to take some nourishment, he failed to see the newlyweds enter their carriage. When he returned to his position, the second carriage was in position in front of Darcy House and had already been loaded with trunks. Walking past the carriage, the man stopped long enough to take a knife from his pocket. Seeing no one was nearby, he leaned down and made several cuts to the spokes on one of the carriage wheels as well as prying at the axle. He then left the area, fully confident that his work would be successful and he would be well compensated.

~~ ** ~~

The second day of travel began late for the Darcy caravan. Lady Anne woke with a headache. After some chamomile tea and a cold compress on her forehead for an hour, she finally felt well enough to travel. By then, there was a problem with one of the horses on Darcy's carriage and they needed to wait for another hour before a replacement horse could be put in place.

Near eleven that morning, the carriages left for the next section of the journey. It was expected that the

Bingleys would catch up with them long before making the inn.

~~ ** ~~

The carriages arrived at the inn where the group would be staying the second night of the journey. The ladies decided to rest for a little while before dinner was served, hoping that the Bingleys would have arrived by then.

Everyone was becoming concerned when there was no sign of the Bingleys after dinner had been eaten and the dishes removed from the sitting room. Darcy was beginning to feel something was wrong, though he did not wish to alarm his wife. Stepping outside, Darcy spoke to one of his footmen. "Roberts, I want to hire a horse and have you make your way back the way we came until you find the other Darcy carriage, which Mr Bingley and his wife were using. They should be here by now, and I am concerned. Once you find them, if they need assistance, see to aiding them. If they are just slow, bring news back to me so my wife will not worry for her sister."

"I will hurry as fast as I can, Mr Darcy. I am sure they are fine." The footman hurried to the stables and chose a horse while Darcy made arrangements with the stable owner.

~~ ** ~~

Near three in the morning, a knock came to Darcy's bedchamber door. He grabbed his robe and quickly donned it before opening the door and stepping to the hallway. Roberts had returned with news of the second Darcy carriage.

"Sir, forgive me, but the news is not good. The carriage lost control as it was coming down a hill, causing it to overturn. Old Joe is dead, as is Joshua. Mr and Mrs Bingley, they are in a bad way. They are only a few hours from here, and I made arrangements to have them brought here in a wagon. The apothecary who has been tending them is overwhelmed, and he felt it was wiser to move them to the inn. I made sure the wagon had padding before the couple were loaded on. They should arrive within the hour, I rode ahead to let you know."

Darcy was in shock. "Thank you, Roberts. Are they bringing Old Joe and Joshua here as well? We should have their bodies taken to Pemberley, to be buried there."

"I made arrangements for the bodies to be taken straight to the estate. Joshua's wife just had a young one last month. This will be quite difficult for her."

"I will send an express to Mrs Reynolds to prepare for the bodies. What of Peter?"

Roberts nodded his head. "He is on the wagon

with Mr and Mrs Bingley. He was thrown clear from the carriage, and has broken his arm bad. It was Peter who was able to get help for the Bingleys."

"I will wake the innkeeper and have rooms prepared. I am not sure if there is a physician here, if not, I will need to send a rider to bring one here." Darcy's mind was overwhelmed with the news.

"Sir, Peter told me…the wheel came off which caused the accident. When he looked at it, after the accident, he could see cut marks on the spokes and the axle. Peter is sure that it was damaged on purpose."

Darcy's eyes were wide with shock. *Why would anyone deliberately harm the Bingleys? There was no reason, as the couple were the most amiable people Darcy had ever known. Was this meant to be the Darcys in the carriage and mistakenly it was the Bingleys in the sabotaged carriage?*

Once Darcy sent his footman down to assist when the wagon arrived, he returned to his bedchamber to his wife. Elizabeth had awakened with the absence of her husband's warmth next to her in the bed. "William, is everything well? Have Jane and Charles arrived?"

"My love, there has been an accident. Their carriage overturned. I sent Roberts back to look for them and he had Jane and Charles loaded into a wagon. They should be here shortly. They are injured, Elizabeth. And Roberts said that their injuries are severe. Old Joe was killed, as was Joshua."

A cry escaped Elizabeth as the thought of her beloved sister dying. "William, they have to survive."

Darcy wrapped his arms around his wife. "I know, my love. I will go down and wake the innkeeper. A physician will be sent for as well. Get dressed and meet me downstairs as soon as you can. Roberts said they should be here within the hour."

~~ ** ~~

Darcy knocked on his stepfather's door, informing him of the accident, before he went downstairs. Mr and Mrs Baines had owned the inn for more than twenty years and knew Darcy and the Carringtons well. When they were roused from their slumber by Darcy, they were instantly alerted to something terrible having happened.

They sent the young boy who assisted around the inn to fetch the physician, and the maid was awakened to prepare two rooms and bring fresh water to heat. Blankets were hung by the fireplace to warm before the injured arrived. Darcy also requested the magistrate be sent for, as he wished to have the accident investigated thoroughly. Then he wrote a message to Mrs Reynolds, and asked to have it sent express to Pemberley. Not only did he inform her that the bodies of the two loyal servants were being brought to the estate, he wished her to be prepared when they brought the Bingleys to the house.

By this time, Elizabeth and Lady Anne had joined Lord Albert and Darcy in the dining area of the inn. Finally, the sounds of the wagon arriving in front of the inn were heard. The men went outside to bring the injured inside. When the makeshift stretcher carrying Jane Bingley was brought in, Elizabeth burst into tears. Had she not known it was her sister, she would not have recognized her.

Jane had cuts and bruises on her face, her left eye was swollen and there was blood all over. Her leg was displaced, with the lower section protruding in an unusual position.

Bingley was not much better. He had a severe cut over his left eye and on the base of his neck. The men who brought the couple to the inn stated that Bingley had lost a large quantity of blood, which accounted for his extremely pale appearance.

Elizabeth followed her sister into the first room, while Lady Anne followed Bingley. Each of the ladies began to clean the couple of the blood, as well as removing some of the clothing to make it easier for the physician when he arrived. Jane was shivering, so Elizabeth wrapped the warm blanket around her sister's body.

"Charles…where is Charles?" Jane whispered.

"Jane, remain calm. You are both at the inn. The physician is coming to tend to you and Charles." Elizabeth said, taking hold of her sister's hand and squeezing carefully.

"Charles, I need Charles." Jane began to cry, unable to open her left eye from the swelling.

"Dearest Jane, calm yourself. Charles is in the next room, and he needs to be tended to by the physician. You will see him later, after you have both been seen by the physician."

"Lizzy, what happened? How did we get here?"

"You were brought here in a wagon. The carriage had an accident." Elizabeth said, wiping tears from her cheeks. "Stay with me, Jane. The physician will be here soon. Stay strong, my dear sister."

"Tired…so very tired." Jane was beginning to drift. "Tell Charles I love him."

"You will tell him yourself." Elizabeth exclaimed. "You will see him shortly, Jane. Please, my dear sister,

I love you. Stay with me."

A knock was heard on the door and Elizabeth cried out for the person to enter. Mrs Baines entered with the physician. "Mrs Darcy, your husband asked for you to step out to the dining room. I will assist Mr Wall tend to your sister."

Elizabeth left the room reluctantly, her hands covered in blood. Seeing her husband nearby, she flung herself into his open arms. Darcy led his wife to a nearby chair, sitting her down as he knelt in front of her. "Be strong, Lizzy. Jane and Charles are healthy and young. They will survive, I am sure of it."

~~ ** ~~

The following day, an article was found in the London paper.

The carriage of Fitzwilliam Darcy, of Pemberley in Derbyshire, was found having been overturned multiple times down a hillside. The carriage was destroyed. All reports have declared there were no survivors.

Mr Culliver was pleased with the news. His employer would finally pay him what he was owed and he could escape England for the Americas, where he could begin life anew. He wished to be away from people such as his employer, and live a quiet life.

~~ ** ~~

The report spread quickly throughout London and beyond. Longbourn was soon in receipt of the article from the paper. Mrs Bennet's sister, Mrs Phillips, had brought it to everyone's attention, causing Mrs Bennet to have an attack of nerves and having to take to her bed.

Fortunately, later that very same day, an express arrived from Darcy, explaining the situation to the Bennets and relaying the news that the Bingleys and the Darcys were alive, though the Bingleys were injured. Darcy extended an invitation for his in laws to join them at Pemberley, which he hoped to move his family to within the next day or two.

Unfortunately, in her state of agitation, Mrs Bennet suffered an attack of apoplexy. The physician was called, but there was nothing to be done. Mrs Bennet died later that night.

~~ ** ~~

Jane Bingley woke in a strange room, with an unknown lady standing nearby. "Where…where?" she whispered, her throat raw and dry.

"Mrs Bingley, let me get you a glass of water." The lady stated as she scurried to the nearby table to pour a glass from the pitcher. Carrying the glass to the bed, she held it as she aided Jane in sitting up enough to drink some of the cool water. "Allow me to call for your sister."

The lady stepped to the door and spoke to someone in the hallway. When she returned, Jane tried to speak again. "Where am I?"

"Jane!" she heard the familiar voice from the opened door. Elizabeth rushed to her sister's bed, taking her hand in her own and placing a kiss on the back of it. "Oh, Jane, you have had us so worried."

"Lizzy, where are we? Where is Charles?"

"Charles is in the next room, and the physician is tending to him at the moment. He will be so pleased to know you are returned to us. As to where, we are at Pemberley. William and the physician determined it would be the best place for both of you, as the inn was limited on space and staff. Here, you are receiving the best care possible. William has turned these suites into a makeshift hospital."

"What happened?" Jane asked, as she took some more sips of water, this time her sister held the glass.

"It was a carriage accident. Oh, Jane, we nearly lost you. All because someone thought you and Charles were William and me. All they saw was that it was a Darcy carriage and they sabotaged the wheel and axle. They were trying to kill William and me, and you got in the way." Elizabeth was sobbing. "Can you ever forgive us? Because of us, you were nearly killed. I would do anything to make it better, to have taken the pain you experience to myself."

"Lizzy, you did not cause the accident. How could you have known what was done to attempt to kill you? You would never purposely have caused me or my husband pain, I know that. Calm yourself, dear sister. I will hold none of this against you." Jane spoke softly as she allowed her hand to squeeze Elizabeth's. "Would you check on Charles? I wish to know how he is doing."

"Of course, dearest Jane." Elizabeth wiped the tears from her cheeks. "I will have some broth sent up. You will need to regain your strength, though it will take some time."

~~ ** ~~

Elizabeth knocked on the door to Charles' room. Her husband answered the door, stepping into the hall to speak with her. "Lizzy, is something wrong?" he asked as he took her into his arms. He had sent her off to her bed to rest, after spending day and night at her sister's side for nearly five days straight.

"Jane is awake. She is exhausted, weak, and in some pain, but she seems better than I could have expected."

Embracing her in his strong arms, Darcy let out a sigh of relief. "I am pleased to hear the news."

"What of Charles? What does the physician say?" Elizabeth asked. The news of her brother in law's injuries had not been good.

"He has no feeling in his legs or his body. His hands have some feeling, and we are exercising them and his arms. Mr Bolton believes that the damage is most likely permanent. Charles refuses to speak or even look at anyone. He just lies there, staring off at nothing. If he continues in this manner, Mr Bolton fears for his life."

"Oh, Will, this cannot be. Do you think my telling him Jane has returned to us would make a difference?"

Darcy shook his head. "I am not sure anything can make a difference at this point. It is like he has already left us, and only this shell was left behind."

"I must try. For Jane's sake, I must make an attempt to get through to him." Elizabeth said, her head resting against her husband's chest.

"Very well, but give me a moment to make sure he is ready for a visitor."

A few moments later, Darcy returned to the hallway and took his wife by the hand, leading her to Charles' bedside.

Elizabeth sat on the side of the bed, holding Charles' hand. "Charles, I have wonderful news. Jane is awake. She has been asking after you, and I know she wishes to see you."

There was no change in Bingley's expression, no acknowledgement of his having heard his sister in law. Elizabeth tried again. "Charles, would you like for me to have Jane brought down the hall to see you?"

Suddenly, a small voice was heard. "No."

Elizabeth was stunned. "You do not wish to see your wife?" She asked.

"No. Keep Jane away from here. She can have the marriage annulled. She can find a real man to marry, someone who can give her what she deserves. Not someone like me, I can give her nothing."

~~~~~~~ ** ~~~~~~~
~~~~~~~

CHAPTER 18

Albert Carrington and Richard Fitzwilliam had spoken with Darcy with regards to the accident. Due to the attempt to kill Darcy, and the reports that had reached London of the carriage being Darcy's and the rumor that there were no survivors, the family agreed it would be better to allow the perpetrators to believe they had succeeded. From there, they would wait to see how people behave. Though they had been certain of Anthony being behind the attack made by Wickham, they wondered on Lady Catherine's behavior as well. And Caroline Goodman could not be discounted either, as she had made her feelings well known. They would have to wait and see how each of these unfriendly people would behave if they thought Darcy and Elizabeth to be dead.

The staff at Pemberley were instructed to behave as if the Master and Mistress were dead, putting a black ribbon wreath on the door and each of the servants wore a black armband. Darcy and Elizabeth kept to the family wing of the house, mainly keeping watch over Bingley and Jane.

Three days after their arrival at Pemberley, Lady Anne had gone downstairs to speak with Mrs Reynolds to arrange something for Georgiana to eat, when there was a commotion at the front entrance door.

She walked towards the door, finding the butler and two footmen attempting to refuse entrance to the house by Lady Catherine and Anthony. "What are the two of you doing here?" Lady Anne nearly shouted at her sister and nephew. "You have no authority to be in my son's home. Leave immediately."

"Ah, but sister, your son is dead and no longer owns this estate. We have come from the solicitors, and have been told that we stand a good chance of inheriting Pemberley, as William had no heirs." Lady Catherine smirked. "Anthony would be able to take over control of this estate, as his own inheritance has been stolen from him."

"My brother squandered his inheritance, Lady Catherine." Richard declared as he came down the stairs. "Your solicitors will have no luck in stealing the estate from the heir. Lord Matlock and I are supporting the true heir to Darcy's estate and fortune."

"Who is this heir?" Anthony fumed. "Darcy had no child, his wife is dead, and there is no one to inherit."

"There is no need for you to worry over the heir, for we are keeping her safe from harm. I have hired more guards to protect the estate, and no one will be able to harm the person." Richard glared at his brother.

"Her?" Lady Catherine frowned as she attempted to determine who was to inherit. "I assume you are saying that Georgiana is to inherit her brother's estate."

"No, my daughter is not the heir. But have no fear, the heir is deserving of the inheritance and is well loved by the servants and staff already." Lady Anne smiled. "Now, sister, I will ask you to honor my son by taking our nephew and leave this estate immediately."

"Not until I speak to the heir. You stated that it is a she, is it someone who will need a husband? Anthony would be a good husband."

Richard began laughing. "A good husband? He is well known amongst the demimonde, having bedded a majority of the ladies. And he would gamble the inheritance away in short time, leaving Pemberley in the same shape as Matlock is now."

"I would watch my words, Richard." Anthony hissed. "You are not as safe as you might think."

"Will you hire someone to do your dirty work, as you always have?" Richard stepped to his brother, standing mere inches from his face. "You cannot take care of matters yourself, so you hire soulless people who will do whatever you wish for money. With Lady Catherine supporting you, you have the funds to hire such low lives."

"I would never support such behavior." Lady Catherine shouted. "How dare you accuse me of such?"

"Someone paid for the carriage to be damaged, causing the accident. Who ever paid for the damage to be done is just as guilty of murder as the person who accepted the payment. Someone hired Wickham to attack Elizabeth, nearly killing Darcy and Elizabeth. That person is just as guilty as Wickham for the attacks."

"Anthony swore that he had nothing to do with the attack or the accident. He would not lie to me." Lady Catherine stated with an air of superiority. "I am well aware of his gambling debts and the fact that he has kept several mistresses and frequented the brothels in Town. I have known this for many years. And I am working with him to reform his good name."

"You are free to do so, but do so elsewhere." Lady Anne exclaimed. "We are in mourning, and do not wish to have either of you here."

~~ ** ~~

Darcy received word from Mr Bennet on the

passing of Mrs Bennet. Elizabeth was grief stricken, her mother was gone, and she could not travel to Longbourn to say her farewells to the lady who had done so much for her all of her life. She spoke with Jane, both of whom realized that it would not be wise for Elizabeth to travel to Longbourn, especially since the Darcys were supposed to be dead themselves. Elizabeth also hated the thought of leaving her dearest sister, who was far from recovered enough to make the journey.

The sisters wrote a letter to their father, expressing their sorrow and love.

Charles was still recovering, he was unable to bring himself to see his wife or speak other than the basic civilities to anyone else. This tore at Jane's heart, wishing she could be of comfort to her beloved husband.

~~ ** ~~

Mr Bennet was in his study when Mrs Hill knocked on the door. "Mr Bennet, you have guests."

"I am in no mood to entertain guests, Mrs Hill. Accept their cards and send them on their way."

"Brother, what a fine way to welcome me home." Came a female voice from the hallway.

Mr Bennet's eyes narrowed as he recognized the voice, yet was unable to believe the person owning the voice would be in his house. "Sarah?" he asked.

"Indeed, Brother, I have come to be at your side." Sarah Bennet Dalton entered the room, followed by her two sons, Phillip and Gregory. "I heard of the tragedy which happened to Lizzy and her husband, and when we arrived, Mrs Hill informed us of Fanny's death. Oh, Thomas, I am so sorry for your losses."

"I am surprised you came here." Mr Bennet stated in a neutral voice.

"I have long come to terms with our father's behavior after our mother died. I decided it was high time to rid myself of the ghosts from my past." Sarah took the seat in front of the desk, while her sons moved chairs to sit on either side of her. "Besides, Gregory is to inherit the estate, so I will need to come to terms with being in this house."

"It is a pleasure to see you, Sister. It has been, what, over ten years since we last saw each other."

Sarah smiled. "I believe that Lydia was only a year old at the time, so it would be closer to four and ten years. That was a pleasant visit, with your family coming to our estate. Phillip and his father have been so busy the last few years in making improvements to the estate, I am pleased to see all the ways they have made life better for all of us."

"Perhaps Phillip can give me suggestions on how we can improve Longbourn." Mr Bennet stood and walked to the sideboard, pouring himself a drink. "Would any of you care for a glass of brandy?"

The young men nodded their heads, and accepted the glasses they were handed. Sarah asked for a small glass of wine, which she was given. Mr Bennet then returned to his seat. "My eldest daughter and her husband are staying at the Darcy estate, attempting to assist Fitzwilliam's mother in estate matters. Jane is ill from the losses of her dearest sister and now her mother, and her husband wishes to make certain she is well before they travel here."

"Poor Jane. To lose her dearest sister and her mother, in such a short time." Gregory stated. "Mamma has told me of how dear Cousin Jane and Cousin Elizabeth have always been."

"Yes, it has been a difficult time. And Mary is taking the loss with great pain. With Lizzy and Jane wed, Mary had become Miss Bennet and was adjusting to her new role in the family. Now she will be acting as my hostess, with her mother gone."

"If you would like, Brother, I would be willing to remain here for some time." Sarah offered. "With my husband long dead, and my boys living their own lives, I have not but time on my hands."

"You know you are always welcome, Sarah. This was your home as a child." Mr Bennet smiled. "Now, if you do not mind, I would like to rest. I have found sleeping to be quite difficult since losing my Lizzy and my wife."

"Of course, Uncle." Phillip replied. "Mother, let us have the housekeeper show us to our rooms. I am sure you will wish to refresh as well."

"Yes, yes, it was a long and dusty trip."

After the Daltons had left his study, Mr Bennet poured himself another glass of port and contemplated the situation.

Mr Bennet had been close to his sister when they were younger. When Sarah was only five and ten, the son of the grounds keeper began to flirt with her. The young man was never improper, but Mr Frederick Bennet did not like anyone looking upon his beloved daughter. One afternoon, the young man placed his hand carefully on Sarah's arm to steady her after she had stumbled. Unfortunately, Frederick Bennet witnessed the event and was furious. He claimed the young man had ruined his daughter, and that they must have been meeting in secret and carrying on an affair. Bennet sacked the grounds keeper, sending the man and his family from Longbourn immediately.

Bennet then arranged a marriage between Sarah and Mr Paul Dalton. Fortunately, Mr Dalton was a good man, and he always treated Sarah with kindness. But while Bennet was alive, he refused to allow his daughter to visit her ancestral home, treating Sarah as if she had been found making love to the young man. When Bennet's wife took ill, Thomas begged his father to allow Sarah to visit, to see her mother one last time. Bennet refused to allow his daughter to come, and Sarah never saw her mother again.

Thomas had kept in touch with his sister and her family, and after Bennet had died, Thomas extended an open invitation to his sister to come to Longbourn whenever she wished to visit. Sarah always found a reason to be busy and unable to visit.

The Daltons had been blessed with their two sons. Their youngest child was a girl, sweet natured and pretty; Miss Ruthie Dalton was the delight of her parents' lives. Unfortunately, an outbreak of influenza tore through their estate and neighborhood. Ruthie and her father were both lost to the illness. Sarah's letters took on a sadness after the deaths, a sadness which never disappeared, though the deaths had been more than ten years previous.

Now, finding his sister arriving unannounced, Mr Bennet was surprised. He knew he should notify his daughters immediately of this development.

My dearest Lizzy and Jane,

I was shocked to have a recent, unannounced visit from my sister and her two sons. This is the first time in over five and twenty years that Sarah has been at Longbourn, and her behavior is quite odd. I have not spoken of Elizabeth and Darcy being alive, nor of Jane and Bingley being injured. I simply informed her of Jane being at Pemberley to aid Lady Anne.

I would not have bothered you with this news, but, as I said, my sister's behavior is unusual. With all that has happened in the past half year, I am finding myself being more judgmental in my dealings with others. There is something odd about the way she has waltzed into the house, a house she has insisted she would never enter ever again, as if she had been here every day of her life. And she wishes to stay here, to be of comfort and assistance to me during this trying time.

I do not understand what could be the reason for my sister to be involved in all that has been happening, especially with her younger son inheriting Longbourn. It has been many years since we have seen Phillip and Gregory, so I cannot believe them to have any reason to harm anyone in our family. But there was just something nagging me with regards to their sudden visit, and felt I should inform you.

You are all in my prayers.

Your loving father, T. Bennet

~~ ** ~~

The letter arrived by express to Pemberley. Elizabeth read it to Jane and Darcy, all of whom were surprised by the news, yet agreed with Mr Bennet's assessment of the situation.

Another letter arrived that day for Charles Bingley, from Mr Geoffrey Goodman.

Mr Bingley,

Forgive me for writing in such a manner. I am concerned and require answers to several questions.

When I first met your sister, she claimed you and your elder sister, Mrs Hurst, were attempting to have her placed in an asylum due to your being embarrassed by her. She claimed that she had tried desperately to meet with your approval, but that your standards were far too stringent and impossible to meet. She also claimed you had attempted to kill her, which forced her to flee for her life and hide from you and Mrs Hurst.

I now find many discrepancies in what my wife has told me in the time we have been married.

Caroline claimed that you would refuse her the dowry your father had established for her, yet, when I requested the dowry, you gave it to me with no difficulties. Then there were her outings. Most days, while we were staying at our townhouse in Town,

Caroline claims to be shopping when she goes out. I have recently caught her in lies. When I finished my business early, I decided to surprise Caroline by meeting her at the modiste she had stated she was to visit for a fitting. The modiste was surprised, as she has never heard of my wife, even though Caroline has claimed to have been to the shop on at least a dozen different occasions. When I asked Caroline how her trip to the modiste had been, she went on to tell me of the gowns she had ordered and how long the fitting had taken. She continued to claim the modiste being the one I had visited, not knowing of my having spoken to the lady and her staff.

Another issue, which I hate to discuss with you in such a manner, is the fact that your sister was not an innocent when I took her to bed the first time. It is my belief that your sister has been with several men, as there are times I believe I have heard her cry out another's name when in the throes of desire. And she has far too much knowledge of intimacies than a maiden should possess, even after a few months of marriage. There have been times that I would have sworn I was with a harlot rather than my bride who was supposedly an innocent when she came to me.

I am also concerned as to what she is doing with her pin money, as she never seems to have any funds available and needs more, yet she never purchased anything. I do not begrudge her the funds, I am not poor and she is welcome to whatever she needs, but I am growing more and more concerned.

The final step was when we received word of your wife's sister and her husband having been killed in an accident on their way to Mr Darcy's estate. I was deeply grieved by the news, knowing they were newly married and beginning their life together. Caroline smiled as she read the article in the paper, a look that was truly frightening. Her smile was evil, there was no other way to describe it. And Caroline made the comment, softly, though I heard her. She said "he should have been smarter than to marry that country chit. If he had, he would still be alive."

So, as you can see, I am confused as to the parting between you and my wife, as well as her past. If you could be kind enough to answer my questions, I would be grateful.

Sincerely,

Geoffrey Goodwin

~~ ** ~~

Everyone had a different opinion as to whom was behind the attempts to kill Darcy and Elizabeth. Lady Anne, Charles and Darcy were leaning towards Caroline Goodman being the culprit. Lord Matlock, Richard, and Lord Albert were still holding belief in Anthony and Lady Catherine being involved. Elizabeth was unsure who was involved, and was becoming jumpy around anyone. And Jane, sweet natured Jane, never wished to think ill of anyone.

Bingley and Jane had begun to heal, though Bingley still had no feeling below his chest. He still refused to allow his wife into his rooms, and his attitude was completely gloomy. He was sure that his sister was responsible for the carriage accident which had left him paralyzed, and his anger grew daily towards her. When he learned from Goodman's letter that his sister had hoodwinked her husband, Bingley's anger grew stronger.

"She deserves to be locked up in an asylum. If I could only prove she was responsible for our accident and hiring Wickham to assault Lizzy…I would do whatever was needed to put an end to Caroline's reign of terror."

"Bingley, your sister had no notion that it was you and Jane in the carriage. She would never have caused you such harm." Darcy tried to calm his brother in law.

"It does not matter, Darce. She is violent and nearly killed all of us. In the process, people were killed. The men Wickham hired, as well as the men on the carriage. All of them are dead because of her desire to make you pay for not marrying her."

"Charles, we are not certain that it is Mrs Goodman who is behind all of this." Elizabeth stated.

"Have you not read the letter from her husband? Constantly needing funds yet never purchases anything. Lying to him as to where she is spending her time. Having lovers…that is something I have suspected for many years. And her behavior when she read of the accident. She wishes to see you and Darcy dead. Does this not answer any doubts that she was involved?"

Darcy frowned. "You have suspected that she has had lovers, before she married Goodman?"

"Yes." Bingley said as he turned his head to look away. "If I am correct, she has had at least a dozen over the years, before her marriage. I suspected the men, but I could never bring myself to accuse her."

"And she thought she was fit to be my wife? If I had found my wife had lost her virtue before our marriage, and of her own volition, I would have divorced her and left her in disgrace."

"Caroline always thought she was discreet. Unfortunately, she was not silent, and I saw a young man leaving her rooms late at night after one of her more...vocal...evenings. He was still dressing himself. He never saw me, and I truly wished I had never been witness to such a scene."

"Does anyone else know of her relations?" Darcy asked.

"I am sure Louisa knows, though I doubt you would ever be able to get an admission from her." Bingley said as he stared out the window from his bed. "I will write to Goodman, inform him of the truth surrounding my sister leaving Netherfield and escaping to Town, the reason behind her tales of woe she told him, and her probable exploits. He will need to use caution in confronting Caroline, as we are both well aware. Caroline can become violent when she feels trapped."

"Write the letter and I will send it express to Mr Goodman. Now, I bring word from your wife. She wishes to see you, Charles. You should really take the time to see her, speak with her."

"I cannot, Darcy. Do you not understand, I am a shell of a man, and will never be able to care for Miss Bennet as I would have before the accident? It is not fair to her. She deserves to have a whole man for a husband, not this helpless cripple who she would be forced to tend as she would a child. And she deserves to have her own children, something I will never be able to give her now."

Darcy shook his head. "You have one of the dearest ladies frightened and in tears as she waits to speak with you. What my sister in law deserves is to be allowed to love the man who has her heart. That person is you, Bingley. Pure and simple. It is time to decide to pull you head out of your arse and be a husband to Jane."

~~~~~~~~ ** ~~~~~~~~
~~~~~~~~

CHAPTER 19

Bingley wrote to Mr Goodman, informing him of the true nature of the departure of his sister from Netherfield, her violent attack against himself and her attempt to attack their sister, Mrs Hurst, and many other details. The letter was quite long, with as many details and a list of witnesses to verify most of what Bingley wrote. He decided to have Darcy's steward address the letter, so Caroline would not become suspicious by his handwriting.

A week after the letter to Goodman was mailed, a letter arrived addressed to Jane.

Mrs Bingley,

I was grieved to hear the news of the death of your brother in law. Such a tragic end for such a handsome and important man, though it was not unexpected with the sort of company he kept after marrying your sister.

I fear for my own brother's well being and am taking steps to protect him from the same sort of tragedy happening to him due to his ill advised marriage to the wrong sort of person. I hold you and you inappropriate family for the loss of Fitzwilliam Darcy, and what he could have been, especially had he chosen correctly and married me instead. My brother should cut his losses and abandon you immediately, and if he does not I will take steps to have him declared incompetent and placed in an asylum. Then I will be in charge of his welfare as he attempted to be in charge of mine.

Take care and begin to pack your belongings. You will be hearing from me shortly.

Mrs Caroline Goodman nee Bingley

Jane turned the letter over to Darcy. Darcy opened the door to Bingley's room, and walked over to where Bingley was seated against the pillows. "Your wife just received a letter from your sister." Darcy held the letter out.

Bingley frowned. "From Louisa? Is she well?"

"From Mrs Goodman. And the letter is evidence of your sister's illness. It is threatening to Jane and blames Elizabeth for my alleged death."

"WHAT!" Bingley roared. "We must send word to Goodman, Caroline must be placed in an asylum, for all of our welfare." After reading the letter, Bingley shook his head. "This is yet another reason for Jane to be rid of me, all I can do is bring her pain and endanger her."

The door was still open, and Jane was standing outside, heartbroken that she was not allowed to enter the room where her husband was. Hearing her husband's words, fury began to rise in the normally docile young lady.

Jane pushed the door open further, and hobbled towards the bed with the crutches that had been brought for her use. "Charles Bingley, you are a fool. You are being selfish and think so little of me as to leave me alone, rather than fight for me. I thought you to be a far greater man, one who would fight for what was his and do all within his power to keep me safe and loved. I belong in an asylum for believing that you loved me. What a stupid, stupid child I am to have ever fallen for your words. You wish to be rid of me, you must never have loved me if you can turn me away so easily. So live your life alone and pitied. I am leaving for Longbourn. My father needs me to be at his side, as it is difficult for him since Mamma's death."

Bingley was shocked at the strength behind this declaration. "I have never lied to you, Jane. I love you, dearly and truly love you. I cannot be selfish, I must release you for your own good. How can I expect you to be forced to be with me in such a condition?"

"If you love me, you would honor your marriage vows. For better or worse, in sickness and in health. You promised to love and cherish me for the rest of your life. Lies, Charles Bingley, all lies." Jane turned to flee the room, though she became dizzy and at the moment she reached the door, she collapsed to the floor.

"JANE!" Bingley cried out as Darcy rushed to his wife's dearest sister. Elizabeth came running down the hall.

"What has happened?" She cried out to her husband. "Is Jane injured?"

"She was shouting at Bingley, and when she turned to leave, she collapsed to the floor." Darcy replied, scooping Jane into his arms and carrying her down to the rooms she was staying in.

All the while, Elizabeth was calling out to the servants for someone to fetch the physician, for Mrs Reynolds to come to Jane's rooms, and all the while, Charles Bingley was shouting for someone to tell him what was wrong with his wife.

Within an hour, the physician was in Jane's rooms, checking on her condition. Darcy and Elizabeth were ushered into Jane's bedchamber to speak with the man. "I believe she was overcome with fatigue and the strain from all that has happened of late. You said that she was upset and lost her temper just before the collapse?" Seeing the nod from Darcy, the physician nodded as well. "With rest and proper nourishment, as well as calm and quiet, I am sure that Mrs Bingley will be recovered soon enough. Now, I must be on my way. Mrs Helen Barr took a fall climbing in the loft in the barn and broke her leg. If you need me, send word."

~~ ** ~~

Elizabeth remained with her sister, reading a book as her sister slept. Every five minutes or so, Bingley's valet was sent to check on Jane's condition for his master. After an hour of constant visits from the valet, Elizabeth had had enough. She left her sister's room and marched down the hall to her brother in law.

"Charles, if you desire knowing of your wife's condition, then find a way to come to her room and see for yourself. She does not deserve the way you have treated her, and if she is so important to you, as she was when you married, you will make the effort to tend to her needs. You have the use of your hands and arms, you have means of offering my dearest sister compassion which can come from holding her hand or embracing her. Instead, you have denied her contact since the accident. You have not cared for her feelings, only your selfish regard of how she should live, without her opinion. Stop sending your valet every few minutes. You have told my husband and others that you do not wish to continue with your marriage, so decide whether you care for Jane or leave her be. It is all or nothing, Charles, either you love her and wish to be a part of her life, or you push her completely away and leave her be. But if you push her away, there will be no sending people to ask after her welfare or asking my husband and myself how Jane is. I will not have it." Elizabeth then left the room, leaving behind a very shocked Charles Bingley in her wake.

~~ ** ~~

"Caroline, we must be careful. We cannot be seen together." The young man said as he tried to pull back from her tempting body. She knew him well, she knew how to make him lose control of all his rational thought. The way she was moving her hands over his body, he was having a difficult time staying strong to his resolve. "We must stop this affair. Your husband nearly caught us the last time."

"Geoffrey is a fool, and I have him wrapped around my little finger. He will believe whatever I tell him. Please, I cannot get enough of you. I must feel your strong body as you take me."

The pout on her lips told him that she would plead and beg to get her way. And, as always, he would give in to her. "You underestimate your husband. I do not wish to be caught by him, the gossips would be in a frenzy and we cannot be connected. It would ruin all the hard work we have already set in place. If we are not careful, all our hard work will be for naught."

"Darcy is dead, as is his harlot. We are going to take Pemberley from Darcy's family, and then ruin the remaining Bennet family. With Darcy and that chit dead, there is no other person who can take possession of such a grand estate." Caroline stated in a voice like a small child who did not wish to do her lessons.

"But, my dear Caroline, I have told you that this is a delicate situation. We must use care in how we handle everything, as we do not wish to be connected with Wickham or the carriage accident. Culiver has been careful, but it would not take much to make him forget his loyalty to us if he were caught."

"Then we should kill him and be done with it all. We no longer require his assistance."

"Caroline, do not be foolish. We are the brains, while Culiver is our brawn. We might need his assistance again. If your brother was to get in our way, could you kill him?"

The frustration was clear in Caroline's expression. "Why he felt the need to be involved with that Bennet family, I will never understand. I wonder why he is still at Pemberley, with his friend dead. Does he think he will be able to weasel his way into taking control of my home?"

"Perhaps he is being comfort to Lady Anne. Have

no fear, we will deal with your brother if he strays into our path." The man's lips came down harshly to Caroline's, his desire and need of her was obvious. Caroline nearly purred as she got what she desired most from her lover.

~~ ** ~~

For three hours, Bingley sent his valet to Jane's rooms to learn how she was, and for three hours, the valet was refused any information of his wife's well-being. Bingley was becoming frantic.

Thinking of what his wife and her sister had said to him that very day, Bingley had to admit that he was behaving like an arse. How could he proclaim to have such deep love for Jane, yet turn her away from his life so easily? Did she mean so little that he could cast her from his life?

Determination grew inside him. Bingley became obsessed with knowing his wife's condition, and with each refusal of Jane's loved ones to keep word from him, his fear of his wife dying took hold of his heart. He finally realized that his love for Jane was stronger than anything else in his life, and the thought of not having her at his side had been tearing his heart to pieces. Bingley knew he had to find a way to his beloved's side, to tell her what an idiot he had been to think he could put her from his heart.

~~ ** ~~

Having fallen asleep at her sister's bedside, Elizabeth woke to the strangest sound in the hallway, nearing Jane's bedchamber door. There was a scratching noise on the door, causing a confused Elizabeth to open it. To her surprise, Bingley was on the floor, having pulled himself along the corridor by inching his body along using his arms, until he reached his wife's bedchamber door.

"Mrs Darcy, might I come to see how my wife is doing?" He asked.

"Of course, Charles. Would you like me to find my husband or a footman to assist you? I am certain Jane would find comfort if she woke with your arms wrapped around her."

Bingley looked at the floor for a moment before raising his eyes to his sister in law. "I would be grateful. I am exhausted after making my way this far, I doubt I could go much further."

Biting her lower lip to keep from smiling, Elizabeth nodded her head and went down the hall to find her own husband. "William, could you come to our brother's aid and assist him to complete his journey?"

Darcy was confused. "Where has he journeyed

to?"

"My sister's bedchamber to check on her health." Elizabeth finally allowed her smile to warm her expression. "I know I was harsh on Charles earlier, but I just could not tolerate his behavior any further. And if it is responsible for his having squirmed like a worm, all the way down the hall to Jane's room, I will applaud myself."

"Remind me never to cross you, my love." Darcy said as he placed a gentle kiss upon her lips. "Come, let us rescue my brother."

The couple made their way to Bingley, and Darcy lifted the man, carrying him to the bed where Jane was still asleep. Once Bingley was on the bed, Darcy and Elizabeth left the room, giving the couple some privacy.

~~ ** ~~

Jane felt warm and comfortable as she woke. It had been weeks since she felt secure, loved, and at home, for it had been weeks since she woke in her husband's embrace. *But how can this be? I am surely dreaming still.* Opening her eyes slightly, she could see there was someone lying beside her on the bed. She turned her head and tears sprang to her eyes. Sleeping beside her, one arm draped over her, was none other than her beloved Charles. Though she was confused as to how he had come to be in her bed, Jane Bingley could not be happier.

Moving slightly, Jane was able to snuggle into her husband and placed her head on his shoulder. Her arms snaked their way around his body, holding him close. After the previous weeks, she was of no mind to release him from her grasp.

"My dearest Jane, are you well?" Charles asked in a sleepy voice. "I have been so concerned."

"I am well, now that you are here with me. How did you come to be here?"

"Between your tongue lashing and the one your sister delivered later, I finally took my head from my arse and realized how dearly I love you and cannot live without you. Can you ever forgive me, my love?"

Nodding her head, Jane smiled. "My sister gave you a piece of her mind?"

"After her verbal flogging, I now feel a deeper respect for our brother in law. I never wish to be on her bad side again."

"Ah, yes, Lizzy is quite proficient when it comes to chastising people, especially if they cause her harm. She has always been my staunchest protector." Jane giggled. "Are you well, Charles? I have been so worried about you."

"I am crippled, my dearest. The physician is not certain of my recovering, though he said there is a large bruise near the spine which has yet to heal. He said that it may be putting pressure on the spine, but I have accepted the worst, that I will be this way permanently. That is why I pushed you away. I cannot bear to be such a burden to you. It will be like taking care of a child, yet I will not be able to be a proper husband to you."

"You are my husband, Charles Bingley. As I said, in good times and bad, in sickness and in health. Our vows were not for good times only. They are not easily broken, as you attempted to do. I wish to be at your side for the rest of my life. No matter what the future brings, no matter what happens, I am you wife forever."

Bingley nodded his head as he kissed her head. His lips left a trail down until they met her lips, and they took comfort from each other until the couple fell back to sleep.

~~ ** ~~

Sarah Dalton walked out with her eldest son on the land of her childhood. She had never forgiven her family for the betrayal that she suffered in her teens. Though she knew her mother could not go against her father's decision to marry Sarah off, her mother never went against Bennet's dictate to never contact her daughter again. Not once, in the two and ten years between being forced to marry and her mother's death, did Sarah hear from her mother.

Thomas Bennet had defied his father in secret, writing to her when he was at university. After their father's death, Thomas openly contacted his sister, even welcoming her to Longbourn before their mother's death. Sarah refused. If her mother could not be bothered to contact her, Sarah had no desire to contact her mother.

After their mother's death, Sarah met with her brother and his family twice in Town. Mr Dalton had purchased a house in London for his wife to enjoy part of the year away from their estate. She had always wished for a daughter, and was disappointed to have never had one of her own. Sarah instantly fell in love with her eldest two nieces, especially Elizabeth, finding her vivacious nature appealing.

Sarah never liked Fanny Bennet, as she could not separate the new Mistress of Longbourn from the former. She was also envious of Fanny's being blessed with daughters. Several times, Sarah had attempted to convince her brother to allow Elizabeth to come live with the Daltons, but Thomas had refused to be parted from his dearest daughter in such a manner. He allowed Jane and Elizabeth to journey to his sister's home once, but Elizabeth was not fond of their estate. If she was not happy with the nature available to her, Elizabeth quickly became melancholy. So Thomas had declined further attempts from his sister for Elizabeth to visit.

Phillip could sense a change in his mother in the past year. She had become obsessed with Longbourn, with her brother's family, and especially with her second eldest niece. Sarah had insisted on Phillip working closely with Gregory, teaching the younger brother the workings of running an estate. The past year, Gregory had traveled a great deal, spending more time away from Phillip, stating he was well versed on being master of an estate.

"Mother, do you think it is wise for us to remain here? I can sense a change in you since we arrived. You are not comfortable here, it is obvious."

"Phillip, have no fear. I am well. A few ghosts are haunting me, but I am putting them in their place."

"Let us travel to Town for a fortnight. You always enjoy attending the theater and visiting the museums. And it has been an age since you last went shopping. I promise to dedicate two full days to taking you shopping." Phillip smiled as he patted his mother's hand.

"I have plenty of garments, Phillip. No, I believe I need to be here for the time being. I must come to terms with my past. For too long, I have held such bitterness towards this estate and my family. It is time to be free of it. Then we can work on the future. We need to find you a wife, and I need grandchildren to spoil. You and your brother need to start working on your own families."

As this was a familiar conversation, Phillip smiled. "Yes, Mother, I know that you require at least six children from me, and at least half of them daughters for you to spoil."

"Of course. I have dreamed of taking a daughter or granddaughter shopping for new gowns." Sarah said, squeezing her son's arm. "Sons are nice enough, but you never allowed me to put ribbons in your hair."

Phillip laughed. "Greg was the prettier one. Lace was more his style."

"Oh, Phillip, I have missed our walks. It seems as if it has been ages since we last spent time like this together." Sarah smiled.

"I have missed being with you as well, Mother. I was thinking, perhaps we should take a trip this year. You have wished to visit Ireland. We could take a month and travel the countryside there."

"Perhaps, Phillip. Time will tell if we will be able to make such a trip. Until then, we shall remain here and do what we can to comfort my brother and his family. And your brother will remain here, preparing for his future."

Phillip nodded and the pair continued to walk towards Oakham Mount. Upon arriving there, Sarah looked around her and smiled. *Oh, yes, preparing for our future.*

~~~~~~~~ ** ~~~~~~~~
~~~~~~~~

CHAPTER 20

Elizabeth was pleased that her sister and brother in law were finally comforting each other. It had been terrible to watch Jane's face when she was denied seeing her husband day after day, hearing how Charles was pushing his wife from him. Jane was in misery, yet she would not allow her sister to comfort her, for her main concern was for her husband's care. This did not surprise Elizabeth, as she had always known her sister's tender heart.

Now that the concern for her sister's marriage was lessened, the pain of knowing the loss the rest of her family was feeling was greater. How Elizabeth wished she could be at her father's side, to read to him, to play chess with him. Any of their past enjoyment, which would bring him comfort at such a time. Tears welled up in Elizabeth's eyes as she walked through the conservatory and saw one of the red roses blooming. Red roses had always been her mother's favorite. Mrs Bennet was not a great lover of being outdoors, but she had a green thumb and spent many hours in the conservatory at Longbourn. Her flowers took prizes at the fair in Meryton the past five years, and her herbs were sought after by the apothecary and others in the neighborhood, for their fine quality.

Mrs Bennet had sent starts of her favorite rose

bush for the Darcys to enjoy at Pemberley. Elizabeth had one prepared for the flower garden below her private study, and another would be kept in the conservatory, allowing flowers year round. The Mistress of Longbourn had also sent some of her herb starts. All of her mother's favorites surrounded Elizabeth, bringing her comfort. *Mamma, I can feel you here, with me. I miss you, Mamma.*

Elizabeth reached over to stroke the leaf of one of the lavender starts. Suddenly, a flash of memory brought a smile to her lips. Elizabeth remembered an assembly, when she was near five and ten, when one of the young men in the neighborhood exclaimed Jane's beauty being far superior to her own. Even Jane's preference of scent, rose, was deemed to be far superior to the second Bennet sister's preference. Mrs Bennet had taken her daughter's hand, and holding a piece of lavender between her fingers and thumb, smiled.

"Lizzy, roses are beautiful and they smell wonderfully. But think of all the good lavender does for people. It is calming, aids in people being able to sleep. It is a pleasant fragrance, which also blends well with other scents, or can stand alone. No, lavender is the scent for you, as it is so much like you. Beautiful on your own, or with others, calming and kind to people, and resourceful. That is my dear girl, my Lizzy.

Though I love Jane, she is more the perfect rose, than the endearing lavender."

"Thank you, Mamma. I had never thought of flowers being like people."

"Everything in life can be the same. There are stones which are strong and hard, and able to aid us. There are some that are delicate and soft. And there are some which are beautiful, with no other real purpose in life. Trees, plants, flowers, they are the same. Remember always, my dear Lizzy, how precious you are. You are one of a kind, and have been a blessing to me and your father, all of your life. Now, scoot along. It is time for you to beat your father at chess."

Though Elizabeth had always believed she was not as liked by her mother, as she had always been her father's favorite, she also knew that she was important and loved by both of her parents.

Lost in her thoughts, she did not hear the man who walked up behind her. Suddenly, there were strong arms reaching around her and pulling her back into his chest. "How are you, my love?"

"I am well, William. Just, so many thoughts coursing through my mind at the moment. I was remembering Mamma, explaining how fragrances and stones were like people. I miss Mamma."

Darcy leaned in to place a kiss behind his wife's ear. "I know, my dearest. I wish we could go to Longbourn, immediately. I wish to be of some use to your father."

"He understands why we have not come. He wishes to see the person responsible for nearly killing his two eldest daughters, caught and made to pay for their crimes. I doubt it will be much longer before the culprits show themselves. So far, Anthony and Lady Catherine have tried to take the estate, and Caroline Goodman has showed her intensions. I have a feeling whichever of these is the scoundrel, they will soon make their next attack. Being dead in the eyes of the world, though it has its pluses with no one coming to bother us, is a pain in the rump."

Elizabeth smiled. "I miss my family. After everything that has happened, they have always been at my side to love me. Mamma's death has been difficult to accept. I feel as if she will still be there when I return to Longbourn."

"I was at the Matlock with Richard when my father died. I was sure that, when I returned home, Father would be sitting in his study, going over plans for the estate. The first year was difficult, as I could not come to terms with referring to the study as mine, or the Master's suite being my rooms. Only after I graduated from the university and remodeled those rooms did I finally take possession of those areas of the house here and Darcy House. There are still some places I expect to see Father come from a room or see him riding his horse across the land. I believe it is a way of keeping our loved ones close to us at all times, even after they have left this world."

"I was thinking of Mamma's plants in the conservatory at Longbourn. She had such a way with plants, though she hated being in nature." Elizabeth chuckled. "Shall we have a tray of refreshments sent to our rooms? I have not eaten much today, and my stomach is somewhat upset with my neglect."

Hearing a slight rumble for his wife's belly, Darcy laughed. "Then it is time to fill that neglected belly. You need to keep your strength up."

~~ ** ~~

The man sitting across the table from Mr Culiver tapped his fingers lightly on the arms of his chair. "So, Culiver, are you prepared to assist me in this final endeavor?"

"Sir, I am not certain I will be able to be convincing."

"It will not take much. I have papers forged which will add credibility to your tale, and there will be no possibility of discovery. I have been assured that there was a distant cousin of Gerard Darcy, his father's second cousin's son. I have learned the man is living in the wilds of Canada, and has never been to England. With Darcy out of the way, it will not be difficult for the estate to be taken from Lady Anne's family. If anyone gets in the way of my achieving my goal, I will see that they are eliminated."

"But I am concerned, as Lady Anne and Lord Matlock are of the peerage, they have influence to have things done for them." Culiver gulped at the thought of what they could possibly do to the likes of him.

"Have no fear of those two. I will take steps to put them in their places, if they are foolish enough to make any problems for me."

"Very well, Sir. I will plan to leave for Lambton in the morning. And where will you be traveling?"

The man leaned forward, clasping his fingers together. "I will be nearby, and prepared to handle Lady Anne and Lord Albert should they interfere."

Culiver waited for several moments before he said farewell to the man. He wondered how he had gotten to such a place in his life. He hoped soon he would finally be able to escape from England. His employer would never leave him be, so escape would be necessary to avoid being dragged into more of the man's business.

~~ ** ~~

Bingley was pleased to wake each morning with his wife in his arms. Elizabeth had been correct, his arms and hands worked fine and they were well used to find comfort in holding his wife. Jane had suffered so much, though she was never one to complain. Few people understood exactly how deeply Jane Bingley, nee Bennet, felt things.

After realizing he could not live without Jane by his side, Bingley decided to devote himself to her care. While he lightly ran his fingers over her arm, he felt a sudden tingling feeling. Could it be? Am I beginning to regain feeling in my body? Or is this wishful thinking, and I am remembering what it felt like to be with my wife?

Jane began to wake. "Good morning, Charles." She yawned and stretched. "Shall we eat before James comes to do your exercises?"

"Yes, that would be fine." Bingley leaned over to kiss his wife. "How are you feeling today? Are you in pain from your leg?"

"My leg is healing well, Charles. I should be free of the splint in another three weeks. It is difficult to believe that it has been a month since the accident. And Mamma has been gone for nearly as long. How I wish I could see Papa."

"He had planned to travel here, with your sisters, but his sister and her sons are still at Longbourn. He believes if he leaves to come here, they will wish to accompany him here. We cannot keep Darcy and Lizzy safe if more people discover they are still alive." Bingley replied. "The letter which was received yesterday spoke of how your father wishes to be here, with us."

"I still cannot understand why our aunt and cousins are at Longbourn. Aunt Sarah has pointedly refused to come before. Why would she suddenly wish to come now?"

"Until we know more, your father does not wish to take a chance with any of our safety. He is just as curious as the rest of us in this matter."

~~ ** ~~

Lady Anne was called to the study at Pemberley. Mrs Reynolds informed her there was a man wishing to speak with her, with regards to the estate. Realizing this was most likely one of the men involved in the attempts on her son's life, Lady Anne signaled the housekeeper.

"Lady Anne, this is Mr Walter Culiver." Mrs Reynolds introduced the former Mistress to the visitor.

"Mr Culiver, might I ask what the nature of your visit is? Our family is in mourning and has much to deal with."

"Lady Covington, I will come straight to the point. I have paperwork documenting that I am your son's heir, and I will be taking possession of Pemberley and the Darcy holdings."

"Forgive me, Mr Culiver, but I do not understand how you could be my son's heir."

Culiver pulled out the forged papers. "My mother was the daughter of your late husband's, Gerard Darcy, second cousin. As there are no other male heirs in the Darcy line, I have traveled here from Canada to take possession of my heritage."

"I believe the only male relation there was in the Darcy line is a descendant of a second cousin to my son's great grandfather. His name was Roland D'Arcy, and he was last known to be in northern France. The relation who went to Canada died, as we have documentation to this matter. Believe me, Mr Culiver, we have had the best men in England and the continent investigate my late husband's lineage. You are a fraud."

"My lady, I would highly recommend you reconsider your words. It is not only me about which you need to worry. There are others, who are far more dangerous, who will stop at nothing to achieve their goal. You have your current husband's estate, you need nothing of Pemberley. It is not worth losing your life to fight these people. You have already lost your son for his foolishness. Give in to the demand for this estate."

"I have no intention to give in to the demand, and even if I did, I have no legal right to give Pemberley to anyone. Pemberley, and the Darcy holdings, belong to my son and his wife. The only heir will be born of their marriage."

"You have lost your mind, Lady Covington. Your son and his wife were killed when their carriage overturned. They are dead, so they cannot be Master and Mistress of this estate."

"I believe my mother is correct." Came a strong baritone voice from behind Culiver.

Turning around, Culiver paled at the sight of Fitzwilliam Darcy standing before him. "Mr Darcy, we were told you were dead."

"And just who are you? We know that you are not any relation to anyone named Darcy, and not in any way in line to inherit this estate. From what you have said, I believe you are involved with the damage to the carriage, which caused the accident."

"I…I…do not understand of what you are speaking. I was notified of your death, and that I was the heir to the family estate. Are you saying someone attempted to kill you?" Culiver was attempting to think fast on his feet. This was not in any of the plans that had been discussed with his employers.

"Mr…Culiver, was it? You are a liar. You know everything, as you were involved with the carriage accident. If I am not mistaken, I would place a bet that you were involved with George Wickham in the attack on my wife, before we married."

"I know no one by that name. I…that is to say…I am confused by all…I am offended by your accusation."

Darcy walked up to the man, standing mere inches from him, leaning toward Culiver, who was much shorter than the Master of Pemberley. "Do. Not. Lie. To. Me. I am certain you know all about these attacks against my family. Now, you will begin to tell me everything, or I will turn you over to the magistrate. With the evidence we have found, it would not be difficult to prove your involvement. You will hang for your part of the conspiracy, unless someone of import speaks up on your behalf."

After several moments Culiver knew he was caught. "I was hired to destroy you, Mr Darcy. There are two people who hired me, a man and a woman. The man is evil, he will kill me when he learns I have failed him. He was going to when Wickham failed, he was certain Wickham would have informed you who I was, and my employers wanted no connection to what happened."

Fury was nearly boiling over in Darcy. This man knew who had hired Wickham to assault Elizabeth. This man had led to all the misery and death that was related with the event. And this man was involved in the carriage accident which killed two good men and nearly killed Jane and Bingley. Fortunately for Culiver, Richard Fitzwilliam had come from behind Darcy and took hold of his cousin's arms.

"You despicable man. You murdering, piece of filth. Because of you, Wickham nearly killed my wife. Because of you, my wife's sister and brother in law were nearly killed. Because of you, two of my servants were killed. Wickham and his friends are dead because you hired them to destroy my wife's life. All of these deaths and injuries are due to you, and yet, you walk into my home, attempting to take possession of all I own. I will see you hang for what you have done."

"If you hang me, I cannot help you find the people who are behind all of this. I am only hired to do this, I was not the one who devised all these plans. You will never find them if you kill me." Culiver shouted frantically.

"He is correct, Darcy." Richard said in his cousin's ear.

"Start talking, or I will take my chances." Darcy growled. "Who are these people, and why do they wish to harm me?"

"The lady is Caroline Goodman...formerly Bingley. She is the one who found me and introduced me to him. She is insane, but he is completely evil. Be careful in your dealings with him, as he will cut your heart out with a spoon, without a thought."

"And what is his name." Darcy asked impatiently.

"Gregory...Gregory Dalton."

~~~~~~~ ** ~~~~~~~
~~~~~~~

CHAPTER 21

Darcy sent an express to Longbourn, informing his father in law of the news. Another express was sent to Geoffrey Goodman. Preparations were made for the battle which was to come.

The ladies were instructed to remain inside the house at all times, and the male servants were all armed. The tenants were all called to the grand house and informed of the need to be watchful and cautious of any strangers they saw, reporting to the guards or the house anyone or anything out of the ordinary.

~~ ** ~~

Standing before the mirror, Caroline ran her hand gently over the fine fabric of her gown. She could not wait until the day she could be rid of her husband, she had only married the man to escape her brother and sister, and for his money. If she had only known she would meet Gregory Dalton a week after her wedding. But then again, Gregory was not looking for a permanent relationship, other than being her lover.

Looking back at the number of men she had been with over the years, she had to admit that Gregory was, by far, the best lover she had enjoyed. But he had made it clear that his heart belonged to his cousin, who had recently died.

As she prepared to leave, she noticed her husband standing in the door frame. "Geoff, what brings you here?"

"Can I not wish to see my beautiful wife? The past few days have been so busy, I have not had as much time to admire you as I would have wished."

Caroline cringed internally at his words. She hated to bed her husband, wishing that he would continue working on his business with his steward rather than allow him time to think of coming to her.

"And what do you have planned for this day, Caroline?" Goodman asked.

"Marjorie Simpleton and Mrs Jepson are meeting me for some shopping this morning. We heard of some new lace which arrived from the continent which is supposed to be all the rage in Town."

"Ah, Mrs Jepson, it has been some time since I last spoke with her. Her son and I went to the university together. If I remember correctly, his wife recently had a babe. Perhaps I could accompany you, as I would dearly love a chance to speak with Mrs Jepson."

"Well, I am certain you have much more important work to do than escort some ladies about their shopping excursion. I will ask her about the babe and report back to you. Perhaps, later in the week, we could have her to dine with us."

"My plans for the day have been cancelled, and spending the time with such company would be delightful. There is a new tea house on Plumbton Street, perhaps we could stop there for refreshments." Goodman knew his wife was not planning to shop, but he wished to see her reaction.

Turning towards the nearby table, Caroline walked towards it to gather her belongings as if to leave. "Dear Geoff, Marjorie expressed a need to speak with Mrs Jepson and me on a personal matter. You know it would be uncomfortable to speak openly if you are with us. We can go together another time."

"Well, Caroline, as I spoke to Marjorie only last night, and she told me she was leaving Town for her aunt's house in Brighton, I must call you a liar."

A gasp could be heard from Caroline. "You dare to call me a liar? You dare to check up on me? I have never been so insulted in my life. I thought you were different than my brother and sister, but you are worse than they are. All of your promises to protect me, to care for me, all were words."

"Ah, your brother and sister. Caroline, I know the true reason you left your family and latched on to me so quickly. Your attack on your brother, the attempted attack against your sister. I know of your attempt to seduce Mr Darcy into a compromise. And I am well aware that I was not your first lover, nor have I been your last."

Lifting her hand, Caroline made to smack her husband's face. Goodman caught her hand before it struck. "You have played me for a fool, but no more. I am meeting with my solicitor today. I will have you locked away, in an asylum, by the end of the day."

"You will not. I am leaving here this very moment." Caroline grabbed hold of her reticule and dipped her hand inside, drawing out a pistol. "Either back away, or you will force me to kill you."

"Good God, Caroline, what are you doing? You truly are insane." Goodman was shocked at the extremes his wife had taken. "Put down the gun at once."

"Back away from the door and let me leave, or I promise I will shoot." Suddenly, Caroline could hear footsteps on the stairs. As her eyes diverted towards the hall beyond her husband, Goodman grabbed hold of the gun barrel, struggling with her to point it in a safe direction. In her fury, Caroline clawed at her husband's face, drawing blood around his eye. Trying to regain control of the pistol, the barrel ended up pointed towards her as she squeezed the trigger. The bullet struck her in the chest. Caroline's eyes grew larger, before she slumped to the floor, dead.

Goodman collapsed beside his wife's body, weeping uncontrollably.

~~ ** ~~

He was sitting behind his desk in the study of his house in Town, when Gregory Dalton received a letter from his mother. Only Sarah and Mrs Goodman knew of his address, his own brother had no clue of the wealth Gregory had accumulated in the past few years.

The past began to flow before Gregory's eyes. Ever since he could remember, his mother had told him of his presumed betrothal to his second eldest cousin, Elizabeth Bennet. Gregory knew that Elizabeth would understand the trials of being second born, always being pushed back and undervalued in comparison. Though his father was decent enough, Mr Dalton had instilled in his sons the belief in society's rules of first born being the heir and the second born being the spare. As he grew older, Gregory grew bitter at his brother's treatment over his own.

But all his life, Gregory had been promised something his brother could not have, Elizabeth Bennet. Sarah Dalton had groomed her son to marry her niece, the girl she wished to have as a daughter. If she could not convince her brother to give Elizabeth to her, she would still win Elizabeth through marriage to Gregory. As she spoke of the future, Sarah painted a beautiful portrait of Gregory and Elizabeth being happily married to each other, with many children blessing the union. Gregory knew how desperately his mother wished for grandchildren, especially granddaughters she could dress in pretty dresses with ribbons and lace.

Hard work had paid off, as Gregory was able to save two thousand pounds by the time he was twenty. He had also inherited twenty thousand from his father's mother. Investing a majority of the funds, by the time Gregory was five and twenty, he had built a tidy nest egg. It was then, as he had purchased his house in Town near the more fashionable area, that Gregory decided to hire two people to keep a watchful eye on his intended, making sure she was well.

When word reached his ears of her courtship with Fitzwilliam Darcy of Pemberley, Gregory was furious. How could Elizabeth betray him so? That was when Culiver was hired to see Darcy's reputation ruined. When he heard of Wickham's attack on Elizabeth, and how she nearly died after her near loss of virtue, Gregory went wild with anger. If Wickham had not been apprehended, Gregory would have hunted him down and torn him apart with his bare hands. Then to learn that his beloved Elizabeth was staying in Darcy House in Town, receiving treatment from a surgeon, the besotted cousin nearly went insane. How could he even rush to her side, declare his love, insist she marry him immediately, when she was in the townhouse of the rich gentleman from Derbyshire? It took every ounce of self-control Gregory had to keep from storming the door to Darcy House and removing his betrothed from his enemy's home.

After all his Lizzy had been through, her mind must have been addled in the attack, for Gregory was soon to learn that she married Fitzwilliam Darcy in a private ceremony at his townhouse. *Perhaps she felt she owed him for all he had done for her? Or maybe she could not remember what she owed me and our family?* Gregory continued to mull over these questions when he thought of the betrayal he had been served.

When he happened to catch a glance of the Darcys one evening at the theater, the look of happiness which his Lizzy wore made Gregory violently angry. The feel of utter betrayal was more than he could tolerate. That was when he hired Culiver to see the carriage was damaged, in hopes that there would be a terrible carriage accident which would take one or both of the Darcys' lives.

The pain he felt when he learned his beloved Lizzy

had died was overwhelming to Gregory. His heart turned to stone. When his mother learned of Mrs Bennet's death, she had decided to return to the home of her youth, to silently gloat over her brother's loss of his dearest daughter. She felt that he deserved to lose Elizabeth, for if he had allowed Sarah to have her years before, Elizabeth would still be alive. But visiting the places he knew had brought Lizzy joy soon forced Gregory to retreat to Town to nurse his wounds and prepare for his final attack against the Darcy family, to take all that had belonged to Fitzwilliam Darcy as his own. It would soon be over, and the only thing Gregory regretted was that he could not reclaim Lizzy from Darcy's hold over her.

Smiling, Gregory opened the letter to see what his mother had to tell him from Longbourn.

My beloved Gregory,

I cannot wait to see you again. You have only been away for a week, yet it seems like an eternity. It will be a blessing when you have finished your business and are able to take possession of your new estate. To think, I will be Mistress of Pemberley, taking your upstart cousin's place. Serves her right, throwing away your love for the wealth and glory of being Mrs Darcy of Pemberley. She did not deserve such a wonderful man as you.

Please send word as soon as you are ready to move to Pemberley. I have heard the estate is remarkable, and I cannot wait to see it for myself.

Once we are settled, you must begin your search for a wife. I so desire grandchildren, and you will require an heir to whom to leave your estate. You are grieving the loss of your beloved Lizzy, I know, but it cannot overrule your duty to provide children. You must take a wife, even if she is nothing like our dear girl.

Until we are together again,

Your loving mother, S. Dalton

Gregory was pleased, his mother was anxious to see their future home. At first, Sarah had been apprehensive with regards to living at Pemberley, but she decided that taking the property of the man who had taken Gregory's wife was just and fitting.

A knock was heard on the study door. "Enter" he called out. His butler opened the door and stepped to the front of the desk.

"An express just arrived, Sir."

"Thank you. Is the rider awaiting a response?"

"He is." The butler stated.

"Send him to the kitchen for something to eat. I will have a reply momentarily."

The butler left the room as Gregory began to read. It was as he expected, Lady Anne and Lord Matlock were fighting the information Culiver had taken with him. Gregory knew he would have to remove them from his path to being Master of Pemberley. He quickly wrote a response to Culiver before ringing for the butler to return.

"Have my bags packed to travel within the hour. Here is the message for the rider to return. And send for Liam to travel with me."

"Very good, Sir."

~~ ** ~~

Reading the express from his eldest daughters and their husbands, Thomas Bennet was not completely shocked to learn of his nephew's involvement. He had been curious about his sister's behavior, one moment kind and loving, and the next moment she was cold and distant. Mr Bennet was certain that his eldest nephew was not involved in what had happened, Phillip had seemed just as confused with his mother's behavior as Mr Bennet was.

First order of business, in Mr Bennet's opinion, was to protect his younger children. He penned a letter to his sister in law, Mrs Philips, who lived in Meryton, then called for Mary to come to his study.

"Papa, Mrs Hill said you wished to see me."

"Yes, child, come in and shut the door." Once this was done, Mr Bennet motioned for his daughter to take a seat. "I have asked your aunt, Mrs Philips, to allow you and your younger sisters to come stay with her in Meryton. It is not clear as yet, but I may need to travel to Pemberley soon, to assist Jane and Bingley."

"Are they recovering from the accident?" Mary asked. Of the younger daughters, only Mary, being the middle and most level headed of the trio, knew the truth of the alleged fatal carriage accident.

"They are, though there are some things happening at Pemberley, and I may need to make the journey."

Mary nodded her head. "If you do, please give my sisters a kiss for me and tell them I miss them terribly."

"You are a good girl, Mary. I will pass your good thoughts along to your sisters and their young men. I am certain they will appreciate your kindness."

Once Mary had left his study, Mr Bennet called for Mr and Mrs Hill to join him. They quickly settled into the chairs before their master's desk.

"Unfortunately, I need to ask your opinion of my relations. My sister and her sons are a mystery to me and it is vital I determine as much of the truth to their being here as possible. In your dealings with them, what can you tell me?"

Mr Hill looked at his wife, then back to Mr Bennet. "My wife and I were just speaking of this subject last night. Mr Bennet, we have been with you for more than twenty years. It bereaves me to speak ill of anyone in your family, but there is something wrong with your sister and her younger son."

"How so? What has caused you to think this way?"

Mrs Hill joined the conversation. "Mr Bennet, last night, after dinner, I overheard Mrs Dalton speaking. At first, I could have sworn there were two people in the room, carrying on the conversation between them. I caught a glance into the room, only to be surprised in learning there was only Mrs Dalton. She was frantic one moment, speaking of being betrayed by Miss Lizzy, then she turned pleased, as if she were glad of the carriage accident. From the sounds of her discussion, it was as if Mrs Dalton believed Miss Lizzy were engaged to her younger son, your heir. I then heard Mrs Dalton say that it was your fault your favorite daughter died, for if you had only let Miss Lizzy live with her when she asked, our dear girl would still be alive." Mrs Hill took a handkerchief from her pocket and dabbed her eyes.

"I am sending the younger girls to Meryton to my

wife's sister, for I fear for their safety while my sister is here. What do you think of my elder nephew?"

"From what I have seen of Mr Dalton, he is a kind and caring young man, and he seems genuinely confused by his mother's behavior. The younger man is frightening, very cold and calculating. I believe he is not to be trusted, but Mr Dalton I find to be worthy of trust."

Mr Bennet nodded his head. "I thank you for your honesty. Now I must relay to you some news which has to be kept in the utmost secrecy. Mr and Mrs Darcy were not in the carriage which overturned. My dear Jane and her husband were in the carriage, though they survived the accident. We have kept this news secret to see what the person responsible would do next. I received word this morning that my youngest nephew is now attempting to steal Pemberley from Mr Darcy's family. We are sure Gregory will make some sort of attempt against Lady Anne and Lord Matlock."

Mrs Hill gasped as her husband let loose a curse. Mr Hill was able to regain control of his emotions. "Mr Bennet, whatever you require of us, you know you only need ask. You are like family to my wife and I. We will do whatever we can to protect you."

"I know, Hill, and I am grateful for your loyalty

throughout my life. I could not ask for better friends than the two of you. If you would, have a bag packed and put to the side, for I may have to travel quickly and not have time to spare."

With a nod, Mrs Hill prepared to leave the room. Mr Bennet smiled at the devotion his staff showed him and his family. He would make sure they were properly rewarded when this was over.

~~~~~~~~ ** ~~~~~~~~
~~~~~~~~

CHAPTER 22

The plan was to have Culiver meet Gregory in Lambton at the inn. Richard and one of the young stable hands, Ross, would be with Culiver. It was believed Caroline Goodman would not travel with Gregory, so they would not risk her being able to identify Richard as Darcy's cousin.

The men would suggest to Gregory that the first line of attack should be against Lord Matlock. They would claim the man came by carriage every Friday to Lambton to do some shopping. He was always alone when he made the trip, and the carriage could easily be overtaken before leaving the border of Pemberley. What Gregory would not know was that Darcy would be inside the carriage, armed to the teeth, and ready to take Gregory down, once and for all.

Gregory and Liam arrived at the inn, and met with the other men. Richard had disguised himself well, as to not be recognized by the residents of Lambton, and he kept to the back of the dining room as the men spoke.

"There is a line of woods to the east side of the road from the entrance to Pemberley's estate to the main house. On the west side of the road, near the border, is an unused cottage. Richie has worked at Pemberley, and he knows the land well. Ross is his brother, and he knows it nearly as well. Their father used to be the gamekeeper, until he died. The boys were too young to take over the work for their father, so they were cast out of the estate. I promised them I would speak with you of finding them work when you took over as Master." Culiver said to his employer.

"If you men perform well at this task, I am certain there will be positions for the likes of you at my estate." Gregory smiled. "So Lord Matlock is predictable on his trip to Lambton each week?"

"He makes the mercantile by eleven every Friday." Richie said. "After the mercantile, he goes to the bookshop, then to the apothecary. Then he has tea at the tea shop and returns to Pemberley. I would say he is predictable."

"You have been observing him for some time?" Gregory asked.

Ross nodded his head. "My brother and I had thought of robbing him, but we decided to throw in with Culiver when we heard his plan. Less chance of being caught if there was more of us."

"Safety in numbers, you are quite right at that. So you would suggest taking the carriage inside Pemberley grounds rather than outside?"

"Yes." Richie said. "Easier to hide in the trees if

need be afterwards. Past the border, there is nowhere to hide as good."

"Very well. Let us prepare, as tomorrow is Friday. Get a good night's sleep and we will meet just after sunrise."

Once the other men had left them, Gregory stopped Culiver for a moment. "Do you know where the Darcys' graves are? I would like to pay my respects."

~~ ** ~~

Friday morning dawned bright, and the men met as planned. After they enjoyed their repast, they set out for their locations to hide themselves and wait for the carriage.

They had split into two groups. Richard and Culiver went to the west side of the road, behind the shack. Ross went with Liam and Gregory to the east side, in the woods.

Just as planned, the carriage came rolling towards them and the attack began. Only the attack was not as planned, as the group from the east was not to be seen. Darcy jumped from the carriage and joined his cousin as they searched the woods for the men. After a few minutes, they located Ross, unconscious and bound, lying on the ground. Gregory was nowhere to be seen.

~~ ** ~~

With Bingley and Lord Matlock disabled, and Darcy and Richard executing their plan to capture Gregory, Lord Albert was left to watch over their loved ones at the house. The family was to keep to the second floor, in the west wing, where the drawing room and music rooms were near the library. Elizabeth decided to keep herself busy in the sitting room which was attached to the Master and Mistress suites, attempting to work on the ledgers for the house as well as go over the menus for the following week.

The Master and Mistress suites were located in the east wing of the house, with the other family suites. Charles and Jane Bingley were in their rooms, as Jane was fatigued and Charles was to have his exercises done by his valet. Lady Anne and Georgiana were in the music room, as Georgiana practiced her music. Lord Matlock and Lord Albert were in the library, attempting to read.

Hannah had just left her Mistress, going to the kitchen to have some tea with mint sent to Elizabeth, as the lady was having an upset stomach. She left the door from the servants' hall into the sitting room open as she left, carrying some bedding to be laundered.

Elizabeth looked up when she heard someone enter the room, thinking it would be Hannah. Instead, she found two men holding a knife to the throat of one of the scullery maids, a young girl named Lucy. One of the men was unknown to her, but the other had been a part of her life since she was young.

"Gregory, what are you doing here? What do you think you are doing, holding Lucy in such a manner?"

"Ah, my dear Lizzy, as feisty as ever. Did you honestly believe I would not come for you? Did you honestly think I would release you from our future together?"

Confused, Elizabeth tried to understand what had caused her cousin to behave in such a manner. "Of what are you speaking, releasing me from our future? Do you believe there was an attachment between us?"

"Of course there was. You knew of it, as I did. It was the wish of our mothers, from our births. My mother stated she waited for the second born, so we would both be equal. Mother always said we were formed for each other."

"You are mistaken, Gregory. There was never an understanding between us, my father impressed upon his desire for my sisters and I to marry only for the deepest love. I fell in love with William."

"Nonsense. You were betrothed to me, you knew it. Mother tried to have your father allow you to live with us, but he was selfish, forcing us to wait until you were grown. Then he turned out to be a liar, giving you to another man. I should have killed him for his betrayal. He knew I loved you, how could he give you to another?"

"Papa never promised me to anyone, until William asked for permission to marry me. There was no attachment or arrangement between the two of us, Gregory. Your mother spoke incorrectly. It was her desire, not anyone else's."

"How dare you speak of my mother in such a manner? I will not tolerate disrespect towards Mother when we are married." Gregory stepped closer to Elizabeth, handing Lucy to Liam. When he was near enough, Gregory reached out his hand and smacked Elizabeth's face. "You must learn your place, and Mother is the rightful Mistress of my home until she dies. You will be my wife, but you will take your place behind Mother, doing as she commands."

"Please, Gregory, I am married to William. I am happy with him. Can you not see I am happy?"

"You are to be happy with me, not with him. I will not allow you to betray me any longer. Come with me now, or I will kill this girl."

"No, Gregory, do not harm her. I will come." Elizabeth tried to calm her cousin. "You should release Lucy, I will come, I promise."

"Your promises mean nothing to me, cousin. The girl will be released when we are safely away from the house."

A knock was heard on the door from the hall, just before the door opened. Lord Albert poked his head inside to speak to Elizabeth, but, upon seeing men in the room, he attempted to come to Elizabeth's aid. As he reached her side, Liam threw his knife, striking Lord Albert in the arm. Elizabeth screamed and attempted to go to Lord Albert's side when Gregory grabbed hold of her, dragging her out of the room, through the servants' hall.

Once they had escaped the house, with their captives in tow, Gregory and Liam headed towards the stables. Gregory gave Liam orders to saddle three horses, they would leave the ones they had brought behind for fresh ones.

"Gregory, you know I fear horses. I cannot ride on one." Elizabeth cried out, trying desperately to come up with a plan.

"I told you when you were a child that you were

foolish. Just because you saw that man fall from a horse and die from his injuries, is no reason to fear horses. You will do as I say and ride on one of the horses."

Out of the corner of her eye, Elizabeth saw someone moving near the door of the stables. A sudden thought crossed her mind. Her husband had introduced her to some of the horses which Pemberley had, telling her about each of them. Most of the horses had been raised by Darcy, and he knew most everything about each one.

One of the first stalls held Apollo. He was a fine stallion, strong and beautiful, he had one major flaw in his character. The horse did not like loud, shrill sounds. When he heard them, Apollo would go wild.

Seeing Liam enter the stall to saddle Apollo, Elizabeth saw her opportunity. She was certain there were others hiding out of sight, waiting for the best moment to swarm in to rescue her, so, when she saw Gregory standing in the door of the stall with his back towards the horse, Elizabeth gave a long, loud whistle. As predicted, Apollo began bucking and kicking at everything near, including kicking backwards into Gregory, knocking him forward. Elizabeth grabbed hold of Lucy's hand, pulling her into a nearby stall, hiding behind the bale of straw. They could hear the commotion going on around them.

Liam was being knocked around the stall, striking his cheek against one of the nails which held a rope. He cried out for help, trying desperately to calm the horse. Darcy, Richard, and three other men rushed into the stables, Darcy immediately calling out for his wife.

"I am here, William." Elizabeth called out from her hiding spot. As soon as her husband saw her, he gathered her to his chest and would not let go. "Is it over?" She asked as she sobbed against his shirt front.

"It is." He replied softly. As they stepped from the stall, she could see Gregory, lying on the ground. When he fell forward, he landed on a pitchfork which Lucy had knocked over as she was dragged into the stables. The prongs of the pitchfork had pierced Gregory's chest, sticking out the back of his torso. His eyes were open, yet vacant. The man who had brought so much pain and agony to their lives for the past months was dead.

"Lord Albert, is he…"

"He will be fine. It was a minor cut to his arm. Albert was the one who found me and Richard, directing us to where you had been taken. My dearest love, I nearly lost you again."

"I am safe, my love. And now it is over."

"We must send word to your father immediately. Your aunt must be taken into custody before she harms your father or your other sisters."

"What of Mrs Goodman?"

"An express arrived just before Albert came to speak to you. Caroline Goodman is dead. She attacked her husband when she was confronted with her lies, pulling a gun on him. In the struggle, the gun discharged, striking her in the chest. Bingley is saddened, though he is worried more for your safety."

"We must go to the house at once. I wish to see Lord Albert for myself, as the vision of the knife striking him is haunting me."

Darcy wrapped his arm about his wife's shoulders and led her to the house. As soon as their family members saw them, they hurried towards the couple. Lady Anne and Georgiana led the Darcys into the Bingleys' room, where Bingley was demanding someone carry him so that he could aid in finding Elizabeth. Jane was attempting to calm her husband, at the same time she tried to still her runaway heart which was filled with fear for her sister's welfare. When the Bingleys saw Elizabeth being led into their suite, Jane rushed to her sister's arms.

"Lizzy, I have been so worried for you. Are you well? Were you injured?"

"I am fine, Jane. A few bruises, nothing more. It is over. Our cousin is dead."

"Lizzy, it still seems so strange to me. Why would Gregory do all of this? He was set to inherit Longbourn, why would he wish to harm you and William? Why would he try to take Pemberley?"

"It is a long story, Jane. Perhaps we should wait until your sister has had a chance to freshen up and rest." Bingley said, trying to calm himself as much as his wife.

Jane nodded, wiping tears from her eyes. "Of course, how foolish of me. Lizzy, you must wish to wash up and put on a fresh gown. Would you like some assistance?"

Darcy intervened. "Forgive me, Jane, but I would like some time alone with my wife. Albert, if you or my mother would be so kind, could you write a message to Mr Bennet, informing him of the events here. We should travel to Longbourn as soon as possible, I fear for the other Bennet family members, with Mrs Dalton and her eldest son still visiting Longbourn. Send the message express, and please inform him Lizzy is safe and we will be on our way soon."

Lady Anne nodded her head. "I will take care of the message, as I wish Albert to rest. He is putting up a brave front, but he is in pain."

"I will have horses prepared for us to travel in two hours." Richard stated to his cousin. "We should take some men with us."

"See to it, Richard." Darcy said as he stepped past his cousin. "And thank you."

"I am pleased with the outcome, cousin."

~~ ** ~~

Mr Bennet asked his eldest nephew to join him in his study. "Phillip, I need to ask you some important questions."

"Of course, Uncle. Is something wrong?"

"Is your mother well? She seems to be having emotional swings, one moment pleasant, then she becomes nearly bitter and hateful. Has this been something that has developed since arriving here?"

Phillip thought for a few moments before standing and walking towards the window. Staring out, Phillip began to speak. "My mother has had a difficult time the past twenty years. I am not sure you were ever told much of the time when my sister was alive."

Phillip turned his head, seeing his uncle shaking his head, continued. "Mother was thrilled when she gave birth to Ruthie. She was such a sweet little girl, always smiling and full of life. And her beautiful brown hair hung in ringlets. When Ruthie learned to walk, the curls bounced with each step and you could see the sparkle of pure joy in Mother's eyes. When the influenza epidemic struck, Ruthie struggled for three days with an extremely high fever. You could see the life seeping from her small body. She died, just two days from her second birthday. Mother was inconsolable, and then she sank into a deep melancholy. After you and your wife had your second daughter, Mother became obsessed. With each additional daughter born, Mother grew more and more desperate to have a daughter, and she felt you should have been willing to give up one of your five. Cousin Elizabeth was so close in looks and spirit to my dear little sister, and from the moment Mother first saw your daughter, she knew that Elizabeth was her choice of daughters."

"She tried to convince me to allow her to raise Elizabeth, even when Lizzy was only ten years old. Sarah was furious with me, but she decided she did not wish to lose contact with us." Mr Bennet stated. "It was Lizzy she did not wish to lose contact with, not the rest of us, am I correct?"

Phillip nodded his head. "Mother and Gregory spent much of their time together. Even when

Gregory went off to school, Mother took a house nearby the school to be close to Gregory. I will be honest with you, Uncle Bennet, my brother frightens me. He is known to be extremely hostile, he was even accused of beating a classmate near death. So I have tried to be cautious of angering my brother."

"Do you think he would be involved in harming my daughter?"

"If you had asked me a year ago, I would have said Gregory would never have harmed Cousin Elizabeth. But I have to admit, after he and Mother discussed Elizabeth's marriage to Mr Darcy, I have seen a distinct change in both of them. Did someone cause the carriage accident? Was Cousin Elizabeth and her husband murdered?"

"The carriage was sabotaged. It was damaged purposely to cause the accident."

Phillip was distraught. "Good God, Gregory, why would you do such a thing? Uncle, forgive me, I should have known he was dangerous to your daughter and her husband. I should have been able to stop Gregory from causing their deaths. And Mother, I am certain she was involved in this. She was furious that Elizabeth married Mr Darcy. She believed Elizabeth and Gregory were meant to be together."

"Then we need to take steps to stop her from

further harming my family." Mr Bennet stated.

~~~~~~~ ** ~~~~~~~
~~~~~~~

CHAPTER 23

Gregory's body was loaded on a wagon and taken to Lambton to the undertaker. The magistrate had arrived at the house just after Liam had been secured to a chair in one of the smaller sitting rooms on the main floor of the house. Culiver was also in custody, though he was continuing to be cooperative. Between the testimony of Culiver, Liam, Darcy, and Richard, most of the information was collected. The magistrate, Mr Fullerton, then spoke with the young maid, Lucy. While Lucy was being questioned, Elizabeth prepared for being next for Mr Fullerton to speak. She was shocked when Mr Fullerton finished with Lucy and made his way from Pemberley to his home, with Liam and Culiver being transported to Lambton to the jail, to be guarded by the sheriff and two extra men.

As soon as the magistrate declared the Darcys and their party clear of charges, preparations were finalized for them to travel to Longbourn. They were determined to get to Mr Bennet and the three younger Bennet sisters as soon as possible. Richard and Darcy planned to travel ahead of the others, fearing that the other members of the family were in danger. They were unsure if Gregory's brother and mother were involved in the attempts and, if cornered, would strike out.

"Please, William, be careful. I do not want anything to happen to you." Elizabeth cried, afraid of losing her husband. "I will be joining you as soon as possible."

"My staff has been informed to take the journey carefully, and allowing you frequent breaks. I do not wish you to be overwhelmed and exhausted." Darcy insisted.

"I am well, my love. Have no fear."

"There will be two men on the carriage besides the driver, and they will be armed. There will also be three men on horseback who are armed as well, they will be riding alongside the carriage. Hannah and Mrs Reynolds will accompany you in the carriage."

"We will be safe, William. Tell my father I love him and will see him soon." Elizabeth kissed her husband on the cheek. "Tell my sisters I love them as well."

"Use caution, my love. I will not be able to sleep until you are in my arms again."

Elizabeth nodded, stepping back from Darcy to allow him to leave. She stood strong as she watched him and his cousin ride off, then turned into the strong embrace of her mother in law, sobbing.

"We will be on the road in less than an hour, Mrs Darcy." Mrs Reynolds stated. "The master will see your loved ones are safe."

"Thank you, Mrs Reynolds. Is Hannah finished packing my belongings?"

"The trunk is being loaded at the moment. If you wish to bid farewell to your sister and the others, by the time you return, we will be ready to leave."

Wiping the tears from her cheeks, Elizabeth turned and entered the house, making her way up the stairs to see her family. Jane was crying as she embraced her sister. "Give Papa a kiss for me. And our sisters as well."

"I will, Jane. Take care of Charles."

"She will take care of me, and I will see to her as well." Bingley said from his bed. "Have no fear for us, Lizzy. Be careful and we will see you soon."

After thanking Lord Albert for his attempt to save her, and making certain he would be well, Elizabeth said her farewells to Georgiana and Lord Matlock. Then she said goodbye to Lady Anne and entered the carriage to be on her way.

~~ ** ~~

Mr Bennet inquired as to his sister's whereabouts

from his staff. No one seemed to know where Sarah Dalton was to be found. Phillip became concerned as well, and everyone had began to search the grounds for Sarah. When the sky turned dark at the end of the day, Sarah still had not been found. The search was put on hold until the morning, as there was no light, and the men had exhausted themselves.

The sun rose, and all of Longbourn and their neighbors began to search again. Meryton residents also searched throughout the village. There were no signs of the missing lady, and everyone was at a loss as to where she could be.

Darcy and Richard arrived late the second day of their journey, only to learn Sarah was still on the loose. Though reluctant at first, the men began to tell the tale of what happened at Pemberley, while Phillip was in the study with his uncle. “Have no fear, Mr Darcy. I know my brother is ill, as is my mother.”

“Unfortunately, Mr Dalton, your brother was killed at Pemberley.” Richard explained. “He was attempting to escape with two hostages, including Elizabeth Darcy, nee Bennet.”

“I am not surprised, Colonel Fitzwilliam. My brother would never have stood back and left Elizabeth alone. No matter what, he would have continued to come for her.” Phillip took a sip of the brandy his uncle handed him. "I am pleased to know my cousin and you are alive, Mr Darcy. Uncle Bennet and I have discussed my mother's deterioration since my sister died as a small child. It is my belief Mother has transferred her feelings for my sister to Elizabeth, who was close in appearance to Ruthie when she was young. That is why I believe she has insisted on her desire to have Cousin Elizabeth with us. My brother has always been difficult to understand, as he has never had true emotions as most people would. Mother transferred her devotion from Ruthie to doting on Gregory, giving in to his every whim and never correcting him."

"When will Elizabeth arrive?" Mr Bennet asked. "Should we worry for her safety?"

"I have five armed men traveling with her, as well as two servants riding in the carriage with her." Darcy stated. "I am certain she will be safe. Perhaps we should worry more for the safety of your other daughters. Richard, should we send for men from Town to guard the Bennets?"

"I suggest setting up guards from local men for today. I will send an express to Town to a former lieutenant I served with. He has a service for protection for wealthy clients, and he can send me some tomorrow. Should we have the young ladies return to Longbourn or guard them at Mrs Phillips' home?"

"It is my belief that protecting them here would be simpler, though my sister knows the estate nearly as well as I do. The past fortnight, she has walked about most of the paths and been left alone in many of the rooms inside." Mr Bennet said.

"Would Mr and Mrs Philips be willing to allow us to set up guards around their home?" Richard asked.

Mr Bennet nodded. "Mrs Philips holds the girls as dear reminders of her elder sister. She will wish to protect them as much as the rest of us."

"I fear for you as well, Uncle. Mother has become more vocal on her belief you should have defended her against your father. I know she has told you she does not hold you responsible, but I am certain she does. She held disdain for Aunt Bennet, her having birthed five strong and healthy daughters. And Aunt Bennet became Mistress of Longbourn, replacing Grandmother."

"Why did my sister not tell me how she truly felt? I have tried so desperately to bring her comfort and keep her connected to our family. I wish my father's mind had been right, none of this would have happened. What my sister never knew was the threats our father made against our mother as well. He had suffered bouts of apoplexy which addled his mind, and he became more violent the more attacks he had. I feared for Mother's welfare, as well as my wife's. Perhaps I was wrong, but at the time, I felt it safer for Sarah to be away from here. Your father was a good man, and he took care of her. Her life was in danger in our home until Father died."

Richard asked for pen and paper and began a letter to his friend, while Mr Bennet asked for Mr Hill and two of the stable hands to join the men in the library. Mr Hill and the hands went with Phillip and Darcy to Meryton to speak with Mr and Mrs Philips and the Bennet sisters. Richard and two tenants would watch over Mr Bennet until Phillip and Darcy returned. Then everyone would take shifts guarding the Master of Longbourn.

~~ ** ~~

Elizabeth had pushed her staff to travel longer and push themselves, her desire to arrive at Longbourn as soon as possible was great. The horses and men were becoming exhausted, when they were nearly two hours away from Longbourn.

They stopped to have the horses exchanged, and the ladies entered the inn to refresh while they waited. The innkeeper's wife offered them some hot stew and fresh bread to strengthen the members of the group, after such a long and weary travel in cold weather.

"Mrs Reynolds, perhaps you and Hannah would wish to rest while we wait for the horses to be exchanged." Elizabeth stated. She knew they were exhausted, though they would never have stated such to their Mistress.

"I am fine, Mrs Lizzy." Hannah stated. "You will most likely wish to take a short walk before we leave."

Elizabeth laughed. "You know me too well, Hannah. I will make sure the men know where I am, have no fear."

After informing the carriage driver, Mr Booth, she was taking a short walk to stretch her legs, and with one of the men following at a safe distance, Elizabeth went for her walk. She had much on her mind, especially since they would be arriving at Longbourn soon.

Since the last time she saw her childhood home and her father, there had been many changes. Mrs Bennet's death, Jane and Bingley recovering from their injuries, Gregory attacking Pemberley and attempting to kidnap her. Her fear for her father and sisters was overwhelming, and only seeing them with her own eyes would calm her anxiety.

The walk was only a few minutes, walking only to

the pen surrounding the stable, then returning to the inn. Excusing herself from the others, Elizabeth made her way to the necessary room to refresh herself.

When she did not return for more than five minutes, Hannah began to worry. She went to the necessary room, knocking on the door. "Mrs Lizzy, are you well?" There was no response from inside the room. Hannah knocked again. "Mrs Lizzy, is there a problem?" Finally, Hannah opened the unlocked door, finding the room empty.

The innkeeper's wife came from the kitchen, and, seeing Hannah, spoke. "The lady went out the back door with another lady who had just arrived. They appeared to know each other."

Hannah was concerned and went to find the men. Finding Mr Booth, she asked if her Mistress was in the carriage.

"No, ma'am, I have not seen the Mistress since she went inside. Is there a problem?"

The other men came closer. Hannah was fearful that Elizabeth was in trouble. "Mrs Darcy was seen leaving through the back door of the inn, with another lady. None of you saw her leave?"

All of the men shook their heads, then they all moved to search for Elizabeth. No sign of her was found, nor was there sign of another lady. The innkeeper came from the stable and informed them a lady, who appeared to be in her forties, had arrived alone in a curricle, though she had left shortly after. He was unsure in which direction she had traveled, though it was obvious she had not traveled past the carriage and men.

The three men on horseback, Joe, Winston, and Jolly, mounted their steeds and rode in different directions. While they were gone, Mr Booth sent one of the carriage footmen on horseback to Longbourn. Mr Booth was certain his employer would come immediately, and he could only pray that Mrs Darcy would be found before the Master arrived.

~~ ** ~~

"Aunt Sarah, we must return to the inn." Elizabeth tried desperately to convince her aunt. She had been shocked to find Sarah Dalton at the inn, and even more so when Sarah pulled a pistol from her reticule and pointed it at her.

"Why do you insist on calling me Aunt?" Sarah said, a frown was apparent on her brow. "I am your mother, Ruthie. Now, why did you run away from home? Your brothers have been so worried for you."

"My name is Elizabeth, Aunt Sarah. I am your brother's daughter."

"Ruthie that is enough of such foolishness. You know that my brother's daughter is Jane, and you have never looked anything like her. We will be home soon enough, and then I will send a message to Gregory to come to the house. He has been searching for you so diligently. We have feared you were abducted or you had died. You disappeared so long ago, I had just about given up hope of finding you."

Elizabeth knew from the look in her aunt's eyes that Sarah Dalton had lost her mind. She had seen the same look in Gregory's eyes, and she realized she would be in more danger in arguing with Sarah. Knowing that her staff would quickly come searching for her, Elizabeth decided it was best to play along with her aunt.

"Forgive me, Mother, I was lost. I am pleased to be with you again." She said to Sarah. "Are you well?"

"Now that you are home, I am wonderful, my dear girl."

"Where are we going, Mother? Is it far?" Elizabeth asked.

"Not far. The dower house is comfortable. Phillip should marry soon, so I wished to be out of the main house. And Gregory will be living with us as well."

"Is the dower house large enough for all of us?"

"I am sure that it will be. I doubt Gregory will be with us for long, as he is a favorite with all the ladies. It will not be long before he finds the perfect young lady to marry. Then it will be just the two of us." Sarah smiled at Elizabeth. "In the spring, we can plant flowers outside the house, as there is a garden nearby. And you can help me tend to the herbs and vegetables. It will be so enjoyable. I will ask Gregory to put up a swing from the tree, like you enjoyed as a little girl."

"I love to swing. Soaring through the air has always made me smile." Elizabeth tried desperately to find some way to keep her aunt happy. "You love the smell of gardenias. We should plant gardenias under your bedroom windows."

Sarah smiled again. "You remember my favorite flower. Ruthie, I have missed you so much."

"I have missed you as well." Elizabeth stated. Looking around, she noticed a small cottage come into view. There was no sign of life in the area, so she assumed the cottage was vacant.

"Ah, here we are." Sarah said. "Welcome home, Ruthie."

~~ ** ~~

Darcy had just sat down to eat when his footman

was shown into the dining room. "Mr Darcy, your wife… she has been taken."

"Tell me what happened!" Darcy jumped up from his seat. Hearing the uproar, Richard and Phillip came from the second floor where they had been resting, and Mr Bennet came hurrying from his study.

The footman, who was Mr Booth's grandson, Benny, laid out the details. "We kept a close watch over the Missus, but we thought she would be safe going to the necessary room. Joe had checked the room to make sure it was empty, and then we went to check the horses. Mrs Reynolds was resting, and Hannah was finishing her cup of tea in the dining room. Mr Booth knew the innkeeper and his wife, so we foolishly left the Missus in the necessary room with no guard. It was a lady who took her. They went out the back door, down a path we could not see from the front. Joe and the others went to check the trails for the curricle with which the innkeeper saw the lady. Mr Booth wished me to come find you."

Richard had already sent Mr Hill to have horses made ready for the men. "We will leave as soon as the horses are brought up."

"Benny, was there any sign of a fight or struggle? Was there a possibility my wife was injured?"

"Nothing any of us could see. Please do not fret,

Mr Darcy. I am sure that the Missus is well and we will have her safely returned to you in no time at all."

Mr Bennet insisted on joining the men on their search. He thought he and Phillip would be more likely able to reach Sarah's mind and aid in recovering Elizabeth safely.

Within a quarter of an hour, the horses were saddled and ready to ride, and the men were off to the inn to meet the Pemberley staff.

~~~~~~~~ ** ~~~~~~~~
~~~~~~~~

CHAPTER 24

Winston followed a trail which he thought was made by a curricle. He had found it from one of the main roads in the inn's vicinity, and it turned off to a smaller path. It was not long before he could see smoke coming from a chimney, rising above the trees. As he came around a bend in the path, he could see from where the smoke was coming. There was a modest looking cottage, not in the best condition, but comfortable and clean. In front of the cottage was a horse tied to a hitching post, and a curricle which had been unfastened and pushed to the side. He could see two ladies step from the curricle, one of which appeared to be Mrs Darcy. Winston stayed hidden from the ladies, watching carefully. When he saw the older lady motion with a pistol for the younger to step inside the house, Winston knew he needed the other men. He crept closer to peer inside the house to assure himself of any other people in the cottage before he left for help.

Looking inside the window, Winston verified the younger lady was indeed Mrs Darcy, though he could hear the older lady referring to her as Ruthie.

Winston carefully moved back to his horse, tied in the trees near the path. He was soon on his way back to the inn, and the men who could assist in recovering

Mrs Darcy.

~~ ** ~~

"Ruthie, you must eat something or you will take ill." Sarah said as she took a bite of bread. She had a basket of goods she had brought from the inn with them.

"I ate at the inn, so have no fear. I am sleepy though."

"As I have missed you so very much, I thought to share a room with you, as we did when you were a little girl. I have missed being able to watch you sleep. You were always so sweet when you slept, usually curled up with your doll. Do you remember Betsy? Your father had the doll made with the same color curls and brown eyes. I still have her at the main house, when our belongings are brought here you will have her to place on your bookcase."

"I must warn you, I move about a lot when sleeping. You will have to forgive me if I accidently kick you on the bed." Elizabeth tried to find any reason to encourage Sarah to sleep somewhere else.

"It will be well worth a few bruises to have you at my side." Sarah said as she squeezed Elizabeth's hand. "If you will assist me in bringing some more firewood, then we can go to bed."

Elizabeth nodded her head, and stood up, prepared to step outside. Sarah became agitated. "Ruthie, I insist you do not go outside without me at your side. I cannot stand the thought of something happening to you."

"I must be out of your sight at times. You will have to trust that nothing will happen to me."

"Please, understand, my life was torn apart when you were missing. Gregory did what he could to make me feel better, but it was not the same. You mean so much to me, Ruthie, as I have always wished to have a daughter. I will do whatever I have to so as never to lose you again. Do you understand me? If necessary, I will secure you to the bed or a chair, though I do not wish to treat you so. It is for your own good, my dear girl. You are safer when you are with me."

"Aunt Sarah, you have to remember who I am. I am Elizabeth, not Ruthie. I am your niece, Lizzy." Elizabeth attempted to open her aunt's memory.

Sarah frowned. For a moment, she looked as if she were contemplating Elizabeth's words. Then she returned to smiling and patting Elizabeth's hand. "Ruthie, you must stop this foolishness. You are my daughter and you have finally been returned to me."

Elizabeth shook her head in despair.

~~ ** ~~

Darcy, Richard, Mr Bennet and Phillip arrived at the inn just after Winston's return from the cottage. "Mr Darcy, I have seen your wife, and she is unharmed. I am afraid the lady who has taken her is unwell, she has it in her mind that Mrs Darcy is someone named Ruthie."

Phillip and Mr Bennet instantly understood the situation. "My mother believes that my cousin is instead my sister come back to life. Ruthie died as a small child and my mother never recovered from the loss. My sister had dark curls and was filled with joy, as Cousin Elizabeth has always been."

"Sarah has longed to have Elizabeth as a daughter. She begged me to allow Lizzy to live with her, but I refused. I could not think of not having my dearest girl with us, as well as the fact that Lizzy was not comfortable in her visits with my sister. Even as a child, Lizzy knew Sarah's attachment to her was different than it should be."

Richard saw this as an opportunity to rescue Elizabeth without much risk. Winston relayed all that he had heard as he was watching through the window. The fact that Sarah Dalton believed they were at the dower house of her son's estate was perfect for the deluded woman to accept her eldest child coming to the cottage to visit her.

The plan was made and repeated over and over, until all were completely sure of what would be said and done. Then the men mounted their horses and rode for the simple cottage.

~~ ** ~~

Sarah woke from her sleep to someone knocking on the cottage door. Instantly, her hand went to her pistol, which was in the pocket of her gown. Sitting up on the bed, she turned her head towards the young lady beside her. Elizabeth was sleeping soundly, aided by the laudanum Sarah had added to her tea. In her mind, she saw the potential of her daughter slipping through her grasp and disappearing once again, if she did not take precautions to keep the young lady safely with her. Brushing a stray curl back from Elizabeth's cheek, Sarah leaned over to place a gentle kiss on her hair.

"I love you, Ruthie. I will keep you safe from any harm."

Walking carefully towards the parlor of the cottage, she heard the knocking on the door again. "Go away. I am armed and I know how to shoot." She called out.

"Mother, it is Phillip. I heard the wonderful news.

I could not wait until morning to see my sister."

Joy spread through Sarah at the thought of reuniting her children. "Phillip, oh, my boy. Hold on, I am coming." She hurried across the room to unlock the door. When the door opened, Phillip entered and found his mother embracing him.

"Is Ruthie well? Where is she?"

"She is sleeping in the bedchamber. It is late, did you just return from your trip?"

"Yes, I was...at Mr Davies to purchase the new horses you liked so much. I wish I had been here when you arrived, I am so excited to see my sister."

Sarah smiled as she led her son into the parlor. *All will be well now, the boys will make sure their sister never leaves me again.* "Phillip, she is just as beautiful as she always was. Her hair, such beautiful dark curls. She had it pinned back, but it is as when she was little, unruly and escaping the pins. And her eyes, oh, Phillip, just looking in her eyes warmed my heart. The love and joy seems to just flow from her dark eyes."

"Mother, Ruthie had bright blue eyes, like Gregory." Phillip knew that he had to ease his mother towards the truth.

"No, you are wrong, Phillip. Ruthie has my mother's dark brown eyes. Gregory has bright blue eyes, so much like your father's." Confusion began to plague her mind. "You are trying to confuse me, Phillip. It is late, and Ruthie is sleeping. Come back in the morning and you can see her when she is awake."

"Certainly it is not too late to see my dear cousin tonight, Mother. I will not keep her long, and then she may sleep more." Phillip purposely chose his words to confuse her.

"Are you becoming daft, Phillip? Ruthie is your sister. You referred to her as your cousin. I believe you are exhausted and confused. As I said, it would be best if you came back in the morning, when everyone was refreshed and well rested."

"No, Mother, I wish to see Elizabeth tonight. Please, would you not show me to the bedchamber?"

Sarah held her pistol tightly in her grasp. "Phillip, I insist you leave immediately. You are not well, and I will not risk your sister's health. Ruthie needs her rest."

"I am not leaving this cottage until I know Elizabeth is safe. Mother, please, remember the truth. Remember Ruthie took ill, the same time as Father. She was so little, and the fever ravaged her tiny body. Ruthie died, Mother. She is buried at the estate, next to Father. I know you are heartbroken, Ruthie meant so much to you. Please, Mother, remember my baby sister. The young lady in the bedchamber is my cousin, Elizabeth. It is Cousin Lizzy sleeping in there, not Ruthie."

"NO! It is Ruthie. My daughter returned to me. God would not bless me with such a treasure and then steal her away. He wished me to have her love, which is why he sent her back to me."

"It is Elizabeth, Mother. Uncle Bennet is here, he wishes to come in to see you. Elizabeth is his daughter, you remember how she made you smile when she was a little girl? Allow Uncle to speak with you, Mother. He is not angry with you. He only wishes to make sure that Elizabeth is well and safe."

"His wife has so many daughters, why could I not have one daughter? I wanted a daughter so much, I was thrilled when I had Ruthie. Why did Thomas have so many daughters, and my only daughter was taken from me? It is not right. Thomas can afford to let me have one daughter. Why would he refuse to allow Elizabeth to live with us? All I ever wanted was a daughter to love."

Phillip opened the door, allowing his uncle to enter the room.

"Sarah, dear sister, I am so very sorry for your

pain. I loved Ruthie, as I saw so much of you in her. Please, Sister, will you tell me if my Lizzy is well?"

"I would never hurt her, Thomas. Believe me, she is dear to me. So like my Ruthie. I feel like my heart was ripped from my chest and my arms felt leaden with no little girl to hold in them."

"You have suffered in a way no parent ever should." Mr Bennet moved forward to embrace his sister. "My dear sister, I love you so much. Forgive me for not being more comfort to you all of these years."

Sobbing, Sarah lowered the pistol and stepped into her brother's embrace. Phillip removed the weapon from his mother's hand as Darcy and Richard entered the door. Darcy darted in the direction of the bedchamber, which Phillip pointed out to him.

Seeing Elizabeth sleeping on the bed, Darcy hurried to her side, ensuring she was indeed alive. "Lizzy, my love, wake up." He kissed her cheek.

She started to turn on the bed, taking hold of his hand and bringing it to her chest while wrapped in her arms. This had become her routine when sleeping since their marriage, wrapping her arms around one of his and holding it close to her, as a child might hold a doll while sleeping. "Dearest, we need to take you to Longbourn. You can sleep in your bed at Longbourn."

"No, sleep now." She mumbled as she held his hand and arm tighter to her.

"I will carry you, my love. Let us take you to your father's home." Darcy scooped her into his arms and draped a coverlet over her body. He carried her out of the bedchamber and into the parlor. Mr Bennet looked up at his son in law with concern. "She is well, just very sleepy."

"Mother gave her laudanum." Phillip said.

"She will sleep it off. There does not seem to be any injuries." Richard said as he came towards his cousin.

"She mumbled in her sleep and did not wish to wake." Darcy smiled as he spoke.

Mr Bennet nodded his head, his arms still wrapped around his sister as he shielded her from seeing Elizabeth. Once Darcy had lifted himself and his wife onto his horse and began to ride with his men towards the road, Mr Bennet led his sister to the curricle which had been made ready. Phillip rode his horse beside the curricle, speaking to his mother, reassuring her of his love for her.

~~ ** ~~

When the men rode up to the front of Longbourn's

main house, the door opened as Mr and Mrs Hill came out quickly. The sun had already begun to rise, though Elizabeth was not willing to follow its example. Darcy held her close to his chest as he dismounted his horse, following Mrs Hill into the house and up the stairs to the room she had prepared for Elizabeth.

"Should we send for Mr Jones?" she asked.

"Mrs Dalton gave her some laudanum, and it must have been a large dose, as my wife refuses to wake. She seems fine otherwise, only behaving as a child who is reluctant to give up the comfort."

"So much has happened in the last weeks, I cannot blame our dear girl for wishing comfort as long as she can have it. Is Mr Bennet on his way back? Is he well?"

"He is most likely riding with his sister. I left before he did, so I am not certain. But he is well. They might stop at the inn to use my carriage, as it was still there when we came past. Mrs Reynolds and my wife's maid will be able to assist Mr Bennet with his sister until they bring her here. Mrs Dalton is unstable, so perhaps you should send for Mr Jones, so he will be prepared when they arrive."

Mrs Hill nodded her head as she left the room. Before shutting the door to the bedchamber, she glanced at the young man who loved Elizabeth so dearly. His tenderness and devotion were heartwarming. "God bless you, Mr Darcy." She whispered as she pulled the door closed.

~~ ** ~~

An express arrived at Pemberley, addressed to Lady Anne, from Richard. He explained what had happened with Sarah Dalton, and her abduction of Elizabeth, her delusion in believing Elizabeth to be her dead daughter Ruthie. Relieved, Lady Anne read the letter aloud to everyone else.

Jane was thrilled that the terror that their lives had survived was now at an end. Charles had received word from his sister. Louisa and Hurst had arrived in London and spoken with Goodman. A small, private service had been held for Caroline, and as little spoken of how she died. All anyone knew was that she had had an accident and died. As soon as the service was held, Goodman had his carriage prepared and left Town for his estate. Louisa and Hurst left for Scarborough to visit her aunt.

With Jane's leg still splinted and Charles' disability, they were unable to travel anywhere comfortably. Richard's letter stated Darcy desired to return to Pemberley as soon as Sarah's future was determined. Mr Bennet and his daughters were planning to make the trip as well. After all that had happened, Mr Bennet wished to have all his daughters together and be away from Longbourn.

Another letter arrived, this one from Lady Catherine. She was furious with the deception which had been perpetrated against her and Anthony with regards to the death of the Darcys. The letter belittled all of their family members for lying to them, allowing them to mourn for Darcy. Lord Matlock shook his head, giving up on his elder sister's nonsense.

A letter had arrived for Richard from his people who were watching Anthony and his home. Lord Matlock decided to read the letter, in case there was something urgent to deal with.

This letter revealed an argument which had occurred between Anthony and Lady Catherine, after they had learned of Darcy and Elizabeth being alive. Evidently, Lady Catherine was furious and demanded traveling to Pemberley for an apology from her sister and nephew. Anthony, who had been sober since his cousin's alleged death, had decided he could understand the lies, as he had finally come to realize his foolish behavior would make everyone think he was responsible for the attempts against the Darcys. Anthony had also met a young lady who worked at the mercantile in the nearby village. For the first time in his life, the man had respect for the young lady and wished to be more to win her heart. It was a complete reversal in his behavior and thinking, but everyone knows the difference true love can make in a person's life.

~~ ** ~~

Phillip took his mother to London, at the suggestion of Mr Jones. Sarah was placed in the care of a competent physician who dealt with illnesses of the mind. The physician had a sanitarium on the outskirts of Town, allowing his patients fresh air and green grass rather than a dirty city environment to recover in. As she would most likely spend the rest of her life in the sanitarium, Phillip wished it to be as pleasant as possible. He then decided to take Darcy up on the offer to join the rest of the family in visiting Pemberley.

~~~~~~~~ ** ~~~~~~~~
~~~~~~~~

CHAPTER 25

The following months saw life repairing for the Bennet family and their extended family. Mr Bennet was surprised as love was blossoming, as spring approached, at Pemberley. Richard had remained at Pemberley, discussing plans for the upcoming planting at Matlock. When he was not locked away in Darcy's study, Richard began to notice another of the Bennet sisters was becoming more and more enchanting to him.

Miss Mary Bennet had been thought by many to be the plainest of all the Bennet sisters. She had also been most likely to be found reading a sermon rather than the usual activities of a young lady. The events of the past year had made a radical change in Miss Mary though. She began to look at the world far differently. Mary even allowed Kitty and Lydia to fix her hair and give her suggestions on what clothing she should wear to compliment her coloring. Lord Matlock was pleased to witness the young couple as they became closer.

Another budding romance involved Kitty Bennet, now developing into a beautiful and sweet natured young lady, more a combination of her eldest two sisters in beauty and personality. The young man who found himself feeling the stirring of his heart was

Phillip Dalton. Mr Bennet had come to the conclusion his eldest nephew was a kind and good man, and he knew the match was a good one. Phillip had decided to sell his father's estate, as it had only been in the family for two generations and he never had developed much liking for it. Mr Bennet offered his nephew to be his heir, which had met with approval of all of his relations. Phillip was reluctant at first, after all that had happened, but he eventually gave in to encouragement from the rest of the family. When he did, he asked Mr Bennet for the honor of officially courting Kitty. The honor was given to the young man who had become so important to the entire Bennet family for what he had done during their crisis and afterwards.

As spring came, Phillip returned to Longbourn to see to the planting and improvements which were required on the estate. Mr Bennet would return to his home within a month of Phillip, taking Kitty and Lydia home with him.

Shortly after Phillip left for Longbourn, Jane and Charles announced the news that Charles had begun to have feeling in his lower torso and below. He had begun to feel sensations about the time of Gregory's attack at Pemberley, but he kept the information secret until he knew for certain that he was not imagining the feeling. One day, as his valet was exercising Charles' left leg when the toes began to twitch. From that day on, Bingley worked diligently to strengthen his body.

By April, Bingley took his first steps in months. The family was overjoyed with the news. The Bingleys then began to search for an estate nearer to Pemberley, as Bingley had given up the lease of Netherfield. With Darcy's steward assisting in the search, the Bingleys were able to find the perfect estate to purchase.

Willow Woods was a pleasant estate only twenty miles from Pemberley. It was near the size of Netherfield, though the house needed updating. This caused the previous owner to lower the price, and allowed the Bingleys to make the changes they wished for the estate.

Lord Matlock and Richard returned to Matlock to see to their estate being managed properly.

A letter arrived from Anthony announcing his engagement to Miss Rose Thompkins. He was also planning to go into business with her father, running the mercantile as the elder man had been ill. Anthony wished to sell his home so he could purchase a house in the village for his wife and him, to be near the mercantile. He also invited his father and brother to the wedding which was planned for the end of May.

The Bingleys prepared to move to their new home, and the Darcys decided to accompany them for a visit. Jane wished her sister's opinion on changes she wished to make. Lady Anne joined them as well, leaving her husband and daughter to journey to their estate.

By late afternoon of the journey, Elizabeth was beginning to be nauseous. When they arrived at Willow Woods, Elizabeth was miserable, and quickly made her way to the nearest necessary room.

Hearing his wife in the room, relieving her stomach contents into a bucket, Darcy was concerned. He insisted a physician be called for, and paced until the man arrived. By then, the guest rooms were ready and Darcy carried his wife to her bed. Stepping to the sitting room which connected the two bedchambers of the suite, Darcy continued to pace.

Nearly half of an hour later, the physician exited the bedchambers. "Your wife should be well enough by morning, though I suggest frequent resting as needed, and she eats foods which are bland. Toast, bread, and some tea with mint will also be soothing. But you should be prepared for the nausea to be common over the following months."

Fear was obvious on Darcy's face. His mother was sitting in the chair near him, and realizing what the physician was most likely suggesting, Lady Anne stood and moved to her son's side.

"William, you must calm yourself. If I am not mistaken as to what is being said, Lizzy is going through a normal change that is common to married ladies, especially ones who have such a loving marriage as the two of you have. You have been married for nearly four months now."

Several moments passed as Darcy attempted to decipher what his mother was saying. Finally, it became obvious to the Master of Pemberley. "Is my wife well? Is she pleased?"

The physician nodded his head. Smiling at the young man, he spoke. "Mrs Darcy appeared to be thrilled with the news, though she is tired and in need of some rest. I cannot stress to you the need for her to not be treated like a china doll. She is a healthy young lady, from what she has told me. Exercise in moderation is good for the mother and babe. Make sure she gets plenty of rest and takes as much nourishment as possible."

"You have my utmost thanks, Sir." Darcy said as he hurried to open the door. He could not wait to see his wife, all he could think was to gather her in his arms and tell her how much he loved her.

Seeing Elizabeth's eyes closed as he approached

the bed, Darcy carefully sat on the side. Picking up her hand, he brought it to his lips. Elizabeth's eyes opened and a radiant smile graced her lips. "Did Mr Lofton tell you?"

"We are to have a babe? Is it true?" Darcy asked, afraid he had been dreaming all he had been told.

"You are to be a father, my love. Are you pleased?"

"No, Lizzy, I am not pleased." He said as he kissed her lips. Seeing her fear, Darcy smiled. "I am not pleased, I am overjoyed at the news. I am so proud and thrilled that I wish to climb to the roof of this building and cry out the news to everyone. I could crow like the rooster with so much joy. I love you, Elizabeth Darcy. You have given me the most precious gift."

~~ ** ~~

The Darcy family had a long and enjoyable life. Their first born, Thomas Gerard Darcy, was the first of six children. Each brought their parents love, laughter, pain and comfort.

The Bennet family grew with each passing year, as the sisters married and started their own families. Mr Bennet left Longbourn in the hands of Phillip and Kitty, after their marriage, and spent time visiting his other daughters. Lydia spent most of her time living with the Darcys, though she also visited the Carringtons, spending time with Lady Anne and Georgiana. Lydia had changed over the years, becoming more like her elder sisters, and when she turned twenty and she was introduced to a young man at a ball during the Season in Town, she knew she had made all the changes in her life for a reason. Her heart was engaged, and, within six months, she joined her sisters in marital bliss.

Anthony and his wife had three children, his eldest son became the heir to Rosings when Lady Catherine died the year after his wedding. She had never changed her will, leaving the estate to Anthony's first born son. It was because of her desire to have Anthony's son be her heir that Lady Catherine had attempted to marry him to Georgiana Carrington. After her own daughter had died, Lady Catherine had desired for Georgiana to be the next Mistress of Rosings, and the only way she could fulfill her dream was if her niece married Anthony.

Richard and Mary were wed, and their eight children built Matlock back to its former glory. Lord Matlock was thrilled to have his grandchildren surrounding him throughout the final years of his life.

After the birth of their last daughter, Elizabeth stood at the doorway of the nursery, watching her husband holding the babe up at the window. "See all there is outside? See the beautiful scenery and natural wonders? This is our home. You will be able to run and play outside, though I must warn you that you should behave more like me than your mother. No climbing trees in your dress. Do not follow the example of your sisters, for they have not listened to my advice. Ah, my dear girl, I am the most fortunate father in the entire world. I have the most amazing life." He kissed his daughter on the cheek, before turning around and finding his wife walking towards him.

"We have truly been blessed, William." Elizabeth laughed at the silly behavior of her beloved husband as she wrapped her arms around his waist. "And to think, all of this joy is due to your coming to meet me at Oakham Mount."

THE END

28207801R00210

Made in the USA
Lexington, KY
10 December 2013